DREAMING DOWN THE BONES

REST IN POWER NECROMANCY, BOOK 2

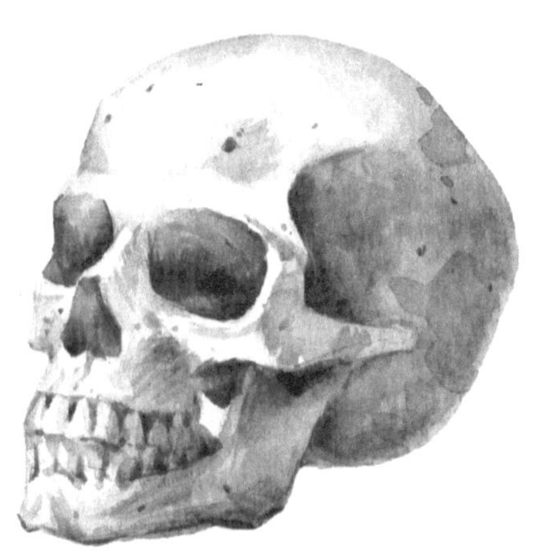

AMBER FISHER

For my mother and foremothers: Shirley, Virginia, Lois, Countess, Estalyn, Julia, Mildred, Ida.

For my father and forefathers: Bruce, Carlton, William, John, Hiram, Herbert, Percy.

I speak your names.

CHAPTER ONE

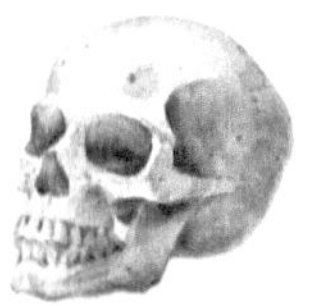

I SAT DOWN in front of my computer, my heart beating a mile a minute. I glanced at myself in the mirror on my vanity, noting the curl of my hair and color in my cheeks. I looked terrified. I tried on a smile, but my lips trembled. I blew my cheeks out in a huge sigh, running my fingers through the roots of my hair, fluffing it out. It made little sense to be nervous. *You act like you ain't never had a phone call before!* I scolded myself. But that felt disingenuous. This wasn't a simple phone call. It was more like the most important interview of my life.

I glanced at my phone for the time. T-minus two minutes. I opened my laptop and pulled up my video conferencing app. I had to type in my password three times because my hands were shaking so badly. *Get it together, Kezia*, I thought. *It's just a phone call. You can do this. You should have been done it.*

After what felt like an eternity, I heard the trill of an incoming connection request. My heart leapt into my throat as I clicked the connect button, accepting the call. The video on the other line was blurry; a camera was in motion. It took a minute for a face to swim into view, the whole time my heart drumming like a marching band in my chest.

Finally, the features of the face converged, and my ex-husband, Marcus, was smiling into the camera as he walked down a brightly lit hallway. "Hi, dove," he said. "How you doing?"

I sucked in a breath and tried to smile. My lips were still trembling. "Good," I said. "You?"

Marcus's smile widened as he looked away from the camera to someone outside of my field of view. Again, my heart sped up. "I'm good. Just trying to get this little monster come say hi." He lifted his chin, motioning for someone to come near. He dropped onto a couch and placed the camera — probably a laptop — down before him. From this angle, the sunlight fell across his face, highlighting the richness of his brown skin. "Come on now," he said. "Quit playing like you shy. You ain't shy."

A shadow appeared first, then a little girl. Immediately, tears sprang to my eyes as she climbed into Marcus's lap, her eyes downcast, her cheeks flushed.

She buried her face in her father's chest, giggling and refusing to look at the camera. She stuck her fingers in her mouth, which her father promptly pulled away, making a face. "Lola, ko ba ṣe pe," he said, his expression stern.

I forced my heart to behave. He must be teaching her Yoruba. It had never occurred to me that he would do so, which was silly. Of course he would teach his daughter the language of his parents, his country, his people. At once, I was filled with pride that my daughter would have access to something I didn't, but also struck with the realization that the chasm between us grew larger every day.

While she squirmed in her father's arms, I examined her. She was smaller than I expected; fragile, even. Her skin was darker than my cinnamon complexion, but lighter than her father's. Her hair, too, was a combination of ours: dark and dense like her father's, but with my wiry ringlets. When she stole a look at the camera, I saw that she had the same almond eyes as her father, but my pug nose and round cheeks. I bit back fresh tears. I wasn't even sad; it was just so much to take in at once. I was overwhelmed at how perfectly her genes mirrored her parentage — a ridiculous thought for a cellular biologist. But what could I say? Humans rarely followed logic.

"Baby girl, say hi to your mom. That's your mom. Remember? She sent you that video a couple weeks ago."

Lola giggled again, chancing another look at the camera. Taking this as my cue, I sat up straighter, smiling hugely and waving. "Hi, baby. I see you. You look so beautiful in that dress. Who gave that to you?"

Lola's grin widened. "Grandma," she said.

"It looks great on you. Is that your favorite dress?"

Lola shook her head. "My favorite dress I can only wear to church," she said with a matter-of-fact pout that made me giggle. "This dress is for playing in."

"What are you playing?" I asked.

But Lola just buried her face in her father's chest again, giggling and shaking. "She looks weird," she whined. "I don't want to look at her anymore."

Marcus poked her in the side with a finger, tickling her. She squealed with laughter, throwing her head back, her ringlets bouncing around her face. I wanted nothing more than to reach out and grab her, squeezing her so tight her bones creaked in protest, drinking up all of that delicious laughter. I pressed my palms against my cheeks, my smile so big my face ached.

She was so beautiful. I loved her so much.

And I would do anything to hold her again.

"She's pretending to be shy," Marcus said as he shifted the girl in his lap, trying to force her to face the camera. But no matter how he twisted, she angled herself away from me, laughing as she did so. "How's Big Ginny? She hasn't had another incident or anything?"

He was right to be concerned, and I was grateful for it. A few weeks earlier, while Marcus and I had been investigating the disturbances at the Temple of the Inner Flame preserve, Big Ginny had suffered a dissociative fugue. Neighbors found her wandering around outside with no clothes on. That would be bad enough, but fugues like the one she'd suffered sometimes pointed to something more ominous — necromantic exposure sickness.

NES, also called the blues, was a condition caused by spending too much time in a necromancer's presence. Not everyone was susceptible — in fact, most people weren't. But in those susceptible, it caused depression, withering, and eventually death. Since she raised me and never got sick, it was a safe assumption that Big Ginny was immune to the necromantic affliction. Still, it was a harrowing experience, and we were being careful.

After all, my affliction *had* killed people: my fourth-grade teacher. Perhaps others.

It was also how I nearly lost my daughter.

In some ways, *did* lose her.

I pushed that thought aside as I looked to the monitor, into her laughing face turned coyly away from me. No, I hadn't lost her. Not forever. Not yet. She was the reason I was fighting. She was the reason I had searched for the past five years for a way to cure my affliction.

I cleared my throat, focusing on the present conversation. "No, she seems okay, but we're not taking any chances."

On the other end, Lola whined. "Daddy, can I *go* now?"

"Ah, princess," he cooed. "Don't you want to stay and talk to Mama? Hmm?"

She scowled at the camera. "No. She looks weird. I want to go play with Grandma."

Marcus glanced my way nervously, afraid of hurting my feelings. "Lola, Mama wants to talk to you. Mama —"

"It's okay," I said. "It's fine, seriously. She...doesn't really know me." *I'm not gonna cry.* "I love you, Lola!" *More than you know.*

Marcus heaved a sigh and kissed her cheek as he eased Lola off his lap and allowed her to go play. She looked at the camera one more time, eyes narrowed, before darting off into the distance. I could still hear her voice offscreen, screeching and laughing as only a child can. I listened for her voice as long as I could, but eventually she must have moved too far; she was gone.

"I tried to prepare her for this conversation," he said apologetically, "but you know how kids are."

I nodded, wiping away the tears that tried to escape down my cheeks. "I wonder why she said I look weird."

Marcus shrugged with a sigh. "No tellin'. Kids are wild. Are you okay?"

I nodded, forcing myself to smile even though my heart wasn't in it. I was sure the expression didn't even reach my eyes. "Yeah, sure, I'm okay. I mean, I will be. I wasn't sure how I was going to feel seeing her after all this time," I admitted. "She looks so much like you."

Marcus chuckled and shook his head. "She looks like both of us. She acts more like you, though. All sass and absolutely no sense of shame."

That elicited a genuine laugh on my part. "Sound like she takes after your mother then."

"You bet stop," Marcus said with a laugh. "She in the other room and you know how gossip travels."

"It's the devil's radio," I agreed. "How about you? How are you feeling? Everything going okay with...you know?"

My question must have hit a tender spot because Marcus shifted suddenly and drew in a sharp breath as he glanced away from the camera. "I *feel* fine," he said. "It's what I don't feel that I'm worried about."

I held my breath. "What do you mean?"

"I should feel *angry*," he said, wringing his hands. "I *want* to feel angry. Because the anger is what will ultimately propel me to seek a cure. But I don't feel angry. I feel..." He dithered, searching for the right word. "...complacent."

I nodded, unsure how to respond. Just four weeks ago, my ex-husband and I had killed a dangerous jinni, but the price of that kill had been high. Using my necromancy, I'd torn the jinni's life source from his body but accidentally knocked it into Marcus, displacing his human life energy with the jinni's. Now, my ex-husband had an expected lifespan of *centuries*.

For a Christian man who looked forward to meeting his Creator, that had been one hell of a blow. Not to mention the loneliness of living long after your family had passed on. It was an unthinkable fate.

"You should speak to someone," I said. "Don't let yourself grow complacent. We still need to fix this. Neither one of us wants you to live another several hundred years. I wonder if —"

"I actually prefer not to speak of this now," he interrupted, his gaze on something in the distance I couldn't see. "But I'll take your recommendation under advisement."

I leaned back and nodded, unfairly hurt. It was his right to talk or not talk about his predicament. But I missed being his confidante. Which was also unfair since I had been the one to leave him. Relationships were complicated. Especially for necromancers. "All right. Well, listen. I have some news. I'm going out of town for a while. Shouldn't make any difference to you, of course, but I thought I'd let you know. Evangeline Morris invited me to come stay at her house in Atlanta for a while. As you know, she's one of the few known necromancers to have cured her affliction. I guess she heard about what we did to the jinni, and now she wants to talk to me. She said we could be mutually beneficial to each other. So I'm heading down there today."

Marcus's expression followed a path from consternation to surprise to joy as a huge smile broke out across his face. "Kezia! You should have led with that, dove! That's wonderful news. Do you know how long you'll be gone? When will you be back?"

"No telling. I'm hoping it won't be longer than a month, but I'll stay as long as I need to cure myself. I'm also trying not to get my hopes up, but it's kind of hard not to."

Marcus nodded. "Yeah, I can imagine. No, let's think positive. This is going to work out beautifully. What about Big Ginny? Where's she staying?"

"Lamont's gonna stay here with her. She won't go to his house. We all had a big fight about it, and Lamont's wife wasn't real happy with the decision, but in the end we all decided it was just easier if we accommodated Big Ginny. Besides, it's not forever. Just until I get back."

Marcus made sounds of agreement on the other end. "And your job at the hospice? Will they hold it for you?"

I smiled, pleased that Marcus still cared. Although we had been divorced for years, the love between us hadn't lessened. On good days, that was a blessing that lifted my spirits and got me out of bed. On bad days, it left me guilt-ridden and wallowing in self-hatred. Today, I was somewhere in between.

"I'm taking a leave of absence. My manager told me to come back when I'm ready. I think they actually like me over there. Having a necromancer around is great for the patients because I've been where they're headed. I help them transition into death. I work with the death energy and the families to keep everybody calm and it just...works."

"That's beautiful, dove. I'm so happy you've found your calling." He touched his fingers to his lips, then the screen, sending butterflies cartwheeling in my stomach. I hated how much I missed his touch. It hurt how much I still wanted him. "Listen, I need to get going. But call me when you get there. Or when you get settled in. Just let me know that everything's okay."

I laughed then. "You just want me to give you the scoop on Evangeline Morris. I had no idea you were such a stargazer."

Marcus chuckled, but didn't deny it. "Get her autograph for me if you can," he joked. "Okay, dove. I have to get going. Please be safe."

I nodded, new tears forming in my eyes. "I will. Give Lola my love, and tell her I'll talk to her soon."

As we ended the call, I felt a tightness in my chest. The call had gone well! I should be happy! I'd seen my daughter for the first time in so many years. I heard her voice. We had a conversation. A short one, but a real one. And even Marcus didn't seem to blame me for accidentally replacing his life force with the jinni's. All things considered, it was a good call.

Still, I felt raw inside.

I closed the laptop and left my bedroom to find Big Ginny in the living room watching her stories on the television. When she saw me, she paused her show, turning wide, hopeful eyes in my direction.

"So? How'd it go? She look okay?"

I nodded. "Yeah. She's good. She looks *great*. She apparently — she speaks Yoruba," I said, my throat clicking. "She's beautiful. We didn't get to talk very much — she was being shy. But still, it was so nice to see her and to hear her voice."

My grandmother nodded, unpaused the television, watched for a few seconds, then paused it again. "Oh, hey, you busy?"

I shrugged. "Not especially. Why?"

Big Ginny struggled to her feet, padded over to me, then pressed a square of paper into my hand.

"What's this?" I asked.

"Shopping list," she said. "Need you to get me some things from Opal before you leave."

I gaped. "Really? You're sending me on an errand? Now?"

Big Ginny huffed. "Just because you takin' a vacation don't mean I am. I still got bills."

I sucked my teeth. I knew damn well about Big Ginny's bills since I was the one who paid them. "Yeah, all right. You got some hoodoo work lined up?" I dropped my voice to a conspiratorial whisper. "Did Miss Olivia finally figure out her husband ain't got no second job at night?"

But Big Ginny rolled her eyes, plopping down onto the couch and unpausing the television. "Mind your business. Go on, now. Don't keep Miss Opal waiting."

I stuck the paper in a pocket and left without saying goodbye.

NECRO SIS WAS a magical supply shop on the other side of town. Opal, the owner, was a necromancer like me, and Big Ginny and I had been buying supplies from her for years. Outside of my family, she was the closest thing I had to a friend.

The shop was a converted chapel in an older neighborhood. From the outside, it looked like any other tiny church, replete with steeple and keyhole windows. But inside, Opal had turned the sanctuary into her own boutique of the weird. Taxidermy hawks, owls, vultures, and ravens hung from the ceiling, their claws posed ready to nab their prey. The black walls were lit with flickering electric lamps that emitted a dim, golden glow. Oddities abounded: rattlesnakes and rats preserved in formaldehyde, skeletons peeking out of shadowy corners, elaborate sigils painted on the walls. I both loved and hated the Gothic décor; it was stunning and moody, but it also had nothing to do with necromancy or magic. It was just creepy.

When I arrived, Opal flashed me a huge smile and pulled me into a bear hug, patting me on the back and giving me a noisy kiss on the cheek. She had changed up her look. Usually, she wore Gothic, white gowns that set off her dark brown skin. Today, she was wearing a black gown with sheer bell sleeves and a silver spider choker at her neck. She was really going all out trying to recruit people to come to the store. She had even traded her platinum bantu knots for a sassy wash-ngo that made her look otherworldly and feminine. She still sported the black-lined eyes and dark lipstick. "Queen Kezia! It's good to see you. What you been up to?"

I gave a nonchalant shrug, but Opal had my number. "Girl, you *radiating* good juju. You ain't foolin' me. What you got going on? You meet somebody?"

I laughed, socking her in the arm with a grin. "Girl, no, you know I ain't got time for no man. I *do* have news, though. You got a minute to talk?"

Opal gestured to the empty shop floor. There was a time when her shop would have been filled with Black folks looking to receive their gifts — magical or psychic abilities channeled through a necromancer that gave Black people a little advantage in society. Common gifts were things like mind reading, clairvoyance, even preternatural likability and charm. The gifts lasted no more than a few weeks, and it was common for Black folks to get gifts from their local necromancer every month.

But lately, Los Angeles had seen a rapid increase of necromancers parceling out magic. It meant more magic to go around, but it also meant things were slower for Opal. Hence her new, wild outfit. "I got nothing going on. What's up?"

I bit my lip. "Guess where I'm heading?"

Opal raised an eyebrow, popping a hand on her hip. "Where? You don't never go nowhere."

I rolled my eyes, even though it was true. "Atlanta. I got an invitation from Evangeline Morris. I'm on my way to go stay at her place for a couple of weeks."

Opal's eyes grew wide, and she placed a hand on her chest, taking in a sharp breath of surprise. "No shit? You got an invitation from Evangeline Morris? Why?"

Part of me wanted to tell Opal the truth. In all the years we had known each other, I'd never known her to be a gossip. But explaining to someone who wasn't there that I killed a jinni that was locking dead people in a cult's sacred temple was a lot to recap, and I wasn't sure she'd believe me anyway. "Well, I've been emailing her for years, asking for her help with my affliction. I guess she finally felt bad enough to write back," I lied.

Opal's eyes narrowed, and she gave me a once over, her bullshit meter undoubtedly going off. Opal was sharp, and I was a bad liar. But to her credit and my relief, she let it slide. "That's crazy. So she's back?"

I frowned. "What do you mean?"

Opal's expression turned thoughtful as she crossed her arms over her chest. "Man, you need to read the news every once in a while. Evangeline dropped off the face of the Earth a couple months ago. Her church didn't close down or anything, but she stopped making public appearances. According to an article I read, you can't get an appointment for a gift anymore. She's not giving them out. Some folks speculated she had died, and nobody was saying shit about it." Opal shifted her weight. "You know, in her prime, I heard she was handing out a hundred gifts *an hour*."

I sucked my teeth and frowned. "Man, folks be making up shit. Ain't nobody granting a hundred gifts per hour. But they do be lining up around the block to get gifts from her. I saw that in *Essence*."

Opal nodded. Every necromancer alive had seen the spread in *Essence*.

"Well, maybe she's just taking a break. Seeing hundreds of people a day has to be exhausting. But you know how folks is. Can't let a thing be. There's rumors that it's something worse than that. Some folks saying she lost her touch. Others say she never had it in the first place — she's a charlatan."

I huffed. "Folks is trippin'."

Opal shrugged. "I don't see how anybody thinks a Black woman got as famous as Evangeline Morris without her past getting properly dug up. I bet if you look hard enough somebody knows what color underwear that woman puts on every day. Anyway. Who's taking care of Big Ginny while you're gone?"

"Lamont is staying with her."

Opal chuckled. "I bet his wife's not too happy about that."

We both shared a chuckle then. My sister-in-law, Nadine, wasn't exactly on Opal's and my shit list, but she wasn't far off. She was one of those people who thought necromancy came from the devil and refused to receive her gifts — a so-called Uncle Thomas Aquinas.

Yes, it was a terrible joke. I loved it.

Opal's giggles dried up first. "All right, so you just stocking up before you go? Anything you need in particular?"

I fished a piece of paper from my pocket and handed it to Opal. "Here. Big Ginny made you a list."

Opal eyed the list only for a few seconds before nodding and refolding it. Nothing Big Ginny had requested was out of the ordinary: several kinds of magical tea blends, colored candles, stones, raven bones. By tradition, hoodoo was a magical practice of found objects: anything lying around the house could be repurposed with magical intent. After all, it was a slave tradition, and it wasn't like enslaved people could just hop down to their local juju shop and pick up supplies. But Big Ginny and I were spoiled: we liked our incense blends, saint statues, fancy knives, and exotic feathers.

When it came to hoodoo, we were a little saditty. We owned that.

Opal clucked her tongue. "Yeah, I got all this in stock. I'll go gather everything up for you."

While Opal bustled around the shop collecting items from my list, I started thinking about the journey that lay ahead of me. I hadn't lied about writing to Evangeline over the years. There were only a handful of necromancers known to have cured their affliction, and Evangeline Morris was the first and most famous. I'd been writing to her for years, asking if she would take me on as an apprentice and teach me what she knew. It was a long shot, and I'd known that even back then. Evangeline ran one of the biggest churches in the country and had been on every talk show and magazine cover imaginable. Hell, she even did *podcasts*.

Whites and Blacks alike loved Evangeline Morris. With that kind of dedicated following, it wasn't any surprise she had never had the time for me.

But if Opal was right and Evangeline wasn't giving gifts anymore, what did that mean? I'd be lying if I said I wasn't curious. Her invitation seemed to coincide with her disappearance from the public. And I didn't believe in coincidences.

Opal appeared in front of me and handed me a small basket filled with all the items I had requested. "That's everything you asked for," she said. "You need anything else?"

I offered her a nervous grin. I didn't like asking people for things, not even when it was their job. I was the person who ate the hamburger with mayonnaise on it even though I hated mayonnaise because I hated asking the waitress to send the hamburger back more. I drew in a breath. "You don't think you could lay a gift on me, do you?"

Opal's eyes went wide as she smiled and cocked her head to the side. "You know I'm happy to do that. But if you're going down to visit Evangeline, why don't you just wait for her to give you one? You've probably had every single gift I have to offer about half a dozen times. What if she has something new you've never had before? Don't you want to find out?"

I shook my head. "First of all, I don't think it works that way. I don't think necromancers have unique gifts only they can grant. But second, I don't know. It seems weird to show up at her house after so many years of begging for a visit and then ask for a favor."

Opal gave me a pointed look. "That is our job, Kezia. As necromancers. You don't have your Godsend, so maybe you don't feel it yet. But giving a gift? It's not a hassle. It's one of the most joyous feelings in the world."

I knew that Opal was trying to make me feel comfortable in asking for a gift. But her words cut me to the quick. She was right — I didn't have a Godsend, the ability to grant gifts. I was what they called a green necromancer — someone who couldn't channel magic from the ancestors. Usually, green necromancers were young people who weren't ready to bear the responsibilities of caring for a community. But in my case, the problem went even deeper than that. For reasons nobody understood, I couldn't find my mother on the other side. And contacting your nearest departed progenitor was required to receive the Godsend.

"Still," I said, forcing a smile. "That's even more reason to get it from you."

Without speaking another word, Opal stepped forward and placed the palms of her hands on my cheeks. Almost immediately, I felt warmth spreading through my body. I felt at once loved and comforted, a deep peace filling my heart and spreading outward to my limbs.

When Opal took her hands away, I knew the rite was finished, and I had received the gift. "Well? What did you get?" she asked.

I opened my mouth to respond, but then quickly shut it again. I felt *something*. My body felt changed somehow, and that feeling of warmth and peace remained. The magic had worked. Yet I had absolutely no idea what gift I had received.

"I don't know," I stammered. "Whatever you gave me, I've never had it before."

Opal's brows drew together in confusion. "A new gift? Well, what can you do? Maybe I know the name."

The most common gifts had nicknames. Polygraph was the ability to detect lies; hacker let you read people's thoughts. I'd had these and many others over the years. But whatever I had now was new. "I can't explain it. I *feel* like I know something — how to do something — that I didn't know before, but I have no idea what it is."

Opal's expression drew into a frown. "Are you sure? Maybe it just didn't work. Here. Let me try again."

Once more, Opal placed her hands on my face, but this time, no warmth flowed between us. No magic triggered my endorphins. Opal sensed it, too. Her frown deepened as she stepped back. "I can't give you another one," she said. "So you must already have one on you."

When a person had a gift on them, they couldn't get a new one. If you didn't like the gift you'd been granted, all you could do was wait a few weeks until it wore off. So the fact that Opal couldn't grant me a gift meant I had an active one. I just couldn't tell what it was.

"That's the damnedest thing I ever heard of," I said. "Oh well. It's not the end of the world. Thank you for trying."

Opal sucked her teeth and shook her head. "Naw, don't give me that thank-you-for-trying shit. I didn't *try*. I *succeeded*. You *have* a gift on you. It's not my fault you don't know what the hell it is. But when you figure it out, let me know, okay? Oh, and one more thing."

"What's that?"

Opal gave me a sly grin. "Find out what her secret is."

I raised an eyebrow. "Who? Evangeline?"

Opal nodded. "I wanna know how she cornered the market. You know she's the *only* necromancer in the *entire* city of Atlanta."

"Right," I said, remembering. "I saw that in an interview with her. It's why she works such long hours handing out gifts. Too many Black folks and not enough magic to go around. A city with a Black population as big as Atlanta's should have necros poppin' at the seams, but she's the only one, poor thing."

Opal rolled her eyes. "Poor thing my ass, Kee. Her bank account got to be *bomb*. The collection plate probably the size of a dinner platter."

I chuckled, shaking my head. Charging for gifts or even outright asking for donations was considered tacky among necromancers, but they weren't above leaving out a tip jar. And it was considered just as tacky for a recipient not to leave a fat tip for her necro.

"Girl, you crazy. But I see your point."

Opal pointed at me. "Okay? All right, get up on outta here. I'll check on Big Ginny while you're gone. Have a good trip. And find out that secret! I wanna be the only necromancer in Los Angeles and make some fat cash!"

She dropped me a wink before disappearing into the back of her store.

By the time Lamont and I pulled up to airport departures, the morning's nervousness had shifted toward excitement. I unbuckled and was climbing out of the car when my brother placed his hand on my knee and squeezed. I turned to him, eyebrows lifted. "What is it?" I asked.

Lamont hesitated, his fingers tightening on my knee. "I'm really happy for you, Kizzie," he said, his voice husky. "And I'm proud of you, too. Is that okay to say? It's not too condescending, is it?"

I smiled, my throat tightening at his use of my childhood nickname. It had been a long time since we'd been close enough for him to invoke that moniker. "Naw. It's nice to have somebody feel proud of me for a change. Makes me feel like finally I'm on the right track."

Lamont grunted, returning his hands to the steering wheel and looking out the windshield. "Not everybody in your position would have made the same choices you made, but only a fool would pretend not to understand. You did what you did for your own reasons, and I don't blame you for them. But that's not why I'm proud of you." He drew in a deep breath, not daring to look my way. "It takes a big person to change their mind. I see you evolving. I see you learning to embrace the fate that you were dealt. I can't imagine what it must've been like. Growing up with your affliction and everything. Just you and Big Ginny in that house all day long every day. No school, no friends." Again, my brother sighed, and I saw the weight of regret pressing against his shoulders, dragging them low. My heart surged with emotion. "I know I haven't always been there for you the way a brother should have been, and I'm sorry. I hope it's not too late to say that. And I hope you take it the way I mean it. When you get back..." Lamont hesitated, heaving a sigh. His grip tightened on the steering wheel.

"When you get back, let's try harder. You and me, I mean. Let's try harder to be the family we were always supposed to be."

For a beat, maybe two, I just sat there in stunned silence, my eyes wide as saucers as I stared at my brother's profile. When I didn't respond, he turned his head to look at me, and that small motion broke the spell. I lunged forward and threw my arms around his neck, squeezing him tight. "We'll figure this out together," I said. "That means everything to me, Lamont. Thank you."

I pulled away, and Lamont cleared his throat, brushing imaginary wrinkles from his shirt before opening the door and getting out of the car. I followed suit and waited on the sidewalk for my brother to bring me my luggage. We stood there awkwardly for a few moments, unsure what to say to each other. Perhaps we had already said everything that needed saying.

Lamont kissed me lightly on the cheek before getting back in the car. He rolled down the passenger side window and waved. "Have a great time," he said. "Catch a ball game if you can. Bring me back a T-shirt."

I waved my goodbye, then turned to head into the airport, not wanting to stand there like a fool watching him drive away. Whatever had just happened between us, and why, I wasn't sure. But I'd have plenty of time on the airplane to think about it. In the meantime, I needed to get moving.

Atlanta, Georgia awaited.

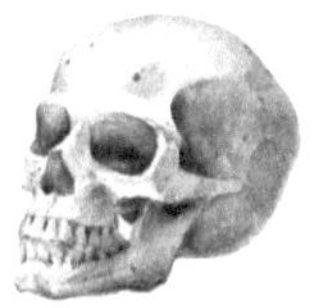

E VANGELINE MORRIS lived in the suburbs of Atlanta in a mansion that would've looked right at home in the opening sequence of a horror movie. The Victorian-style house was well-kept, its white paint pristine. A wraparound porch was furnished with a swing, a litter of plants and flower baskets, and several tables with chairs. On a different day, the tree-lined street would probably have been peaceful. But today, moving trucks and vans crowded the street. Up and down the road, people carried boxes in and out of the mansion, men pushed dollies, and dogs yelped and ran underfoot. I thanked my cabdriver and tugged my luggage out of the trunk. As the cab drove away, I stood on the sidewalk and stared at the mansion for a while. I was expecting Evangeline to meet me, perhaps. Or at the very least, I wasn't expecting to arrive at what was obviously the middle of a move. Tugging my luggage behind me, I went up to the front door, dodging movers and other people in office clothes as they came and went from the house. My expression must've betrayed my confusion, because a well-dressed man stopped me, offering me a small smile. "Can I help you with something?" he asked.

I gestured toward my luggage and then again toward the house. "I'm supposed to meet Evangeline today," I said. "But now that I'm here, I wonder if maybe we got our signals crossed. It looks like y'all got your hands full."

The man heaved a sigh and scrubbed his face with his hands. He was slender and professional looking — the kind of guy you'd feel comfortable telling your bank account number to. "Angie didn't tell me she was expecting anybody, but that doesn't mean you have your information wrong." I was going to ask what he meant by that, but the man quickly dug out a phone and began texting. When he slipped his phone back into his pocket, he jerked his head toward the front door. "Might as well follow me. If you're not supposed to be here, Angelo will take care of you."

I didn't like the sound of that.

Inside, the house was in as much disarray as the outside. Boxes were stacked everywhere, and friendly looking people were running about, moving things around, putting things in boxes, taking the boxes outside. Everyone I passed threw me a harried glance. I pulled my luggage closer to me, trying to stay out of their way. I suddenly had a deep desire to turn around and go home.

Not that that was really an option.

I cleared my throat. "So, what's going on?"

The man barely glanced over his shoulder as he addressed me. "We're moving."

"Oh. Evangeline's moving?"

The man sighed. "No. We're moving offices."

Again, these words made no real sense to me. "Oh." I paused. "Offices?"

Now, the man turned around and gave me a frown. "Look, I don't know who you are. You don't look like the reporters I see lurking around here, so maybe Angie did invite you. I'm about to find that out. If she wants to explain what's going on, she will. In the meantime, keep up, and try not to get in the way."

It sounded like good advice, so I kept behind the man without treading on his heels. I followed him through an anterior living room that looked to be serving as a lobby, a formal dining room, and finally up a staircase. It was here that the house began its transition. The front of the house, where we had come in, was borderline austere: modern furniture was accented with mass produced accessories probably purchased from IKEA. But as we walked up the stairs, the office-like coldness gave way to the warmer interiors of a woman's home.

Hardwood floors were traded in for worn carpet. The color on the wall was no longer office blue-gray but a dusty rose. Fluorescent lights were replaced with incandescent chandeliers, and the walls were lined with photographs — family portraits, mostly. Evangeline as a child, then a teenager, finally a young woman. I smiled at these; even as a young woman, she'd sported her signature long, lavender hair. I slowed my pace to take everything in. Even the air smelled different. The familiar scents of palo santo and copal swirled around me, accompanied by an undercurrent of freshly cut flowers.

I knew those smells. They'd been my constant companions since childhood. They were the smells of death.

Finally, the man led me to a small room where he held up his hand, indicating I should stop. "You stay there. I'll check in and make sure you're supposed to be here and if not..."

I nodded. "Angelo will take care of me. Got it."

"What's your name?"

I cleared my throat. "Kezia Bernard."

Satisfied, the man gave a curt nod before ducking into a room at the end of the hallway. He was gone only a few moments. When he returned, his demeanor had softened, and the tension melted from his shoulders. "All right. I'm sorry about before. It's just that you never know. Crazies say all kinds of things to get in here. I have to keep Angie safe."

I lifted an eyebrow. "Well, I guess you've done your job. She said she expected me?"

The man extended a hand, which I accepted and shook. "I'm Bradley, Angie's lawyer. Well, one of them."

I nodded. "Nice to meet you. You're her lawyer?"

Bradley laughed. "I've been with Angie for a long time now. I started out as her lawyer, and technically I still am. But I'm also her personal assistant, and I run the office." He gestured to a doorway. "She's waiting for you just in there. Please feel free to come find me if you need anything."

I was still confused about this whole office situation, but I didn't want to take up any more of this guy's time. Besides, now that all the weirdness was through, my earlier nerves had returned. I was finally about to meet Evangeline Morris, one of the few people in the world who might be able to help me cure my affliction.

And if she could, I would finally get my daughter back and reunite my family.

As Bradley disappeared down the stairs, I stepped into a bedroom. New smells accompanied the death smells from before: Nag Champa, sage, and rose attar oil were among the fragrances I recognized. There were others, too, that tugged at my memory: laundry detergent, baby powder, moth balls.

Evangeline Morris was sitting in an upholstered chair, her ankles crossed, a knitting project in her lap. When she looked up at me, her expression was open and smiling, but the smile didn't quite reach her eyes. She didn't look sad exactly; more like her happiness was unfinished. Interrupted.

She set her needles down and stared at me for a moment before saying, "Kezia. You made it."

I wasn't sure if I should shake her hand or offer her a hug or what. I wanted to do both and neither of those things. So I just stood there like an idiot, twiddling my thumbs. "Thank you for the invitation," I said finally. "Did I arrive at a bad time? Seems like there's a lot going on downstairs."

Evangeline motioned to the foot of the bed. "Want to have a seat? Let's chat for a minute."

I sat down on the edge of the bed. Evangeline watched me for a moment, her expression never changing. Up close and intimate like this, she did not meet my expectations. On television, she was always very polished and commanding, almost regal in her presentation. I normally saw her draped in pastoral robes in clips from her sermons or wearing a designer suit in interviews. But today, she didn't look like a personality. She was just a woman. She was perhaps in her late forties, though she could have been older. Long, softly curled lavender hair was pulled back into a low, loose pony-tail. Her skin, the color of sable, was unfettered by makeup. She was slightly plump, her figure suggesting a fondness for home-cooked meals but a distaste for exercise. She wore silver rings set with stones on each finger: moonstone, garnet, amethyst, and turquoise. Her jewelry looked inexpensive — the kind of thing you might buy from a Renaissance fair or flea market. She wore a long, gauzy skirt and a hoodie halfway zipped up, the left side slipping off her shoulder, revealing a colorful wildflower tattoo. If I didn't know better, I might guess that she taught yoga, or threw pottery, or worked in an independent bookstore. Her attire was artistic and carefree, unbefitting a leader of one of the largest churches in Georgia.

That was just my own prejudice. Even women of God could lounge about in inexpensive jewelry and hippie clothing.

Evangeline settled back into her chair, never taking her eyes off of me. "What's going on downstairs?"

I shrugged, a soft lift of one shoulder. "Bradley said y'all are moving offices, whatever that means." I looked around the room quickly. This didn't really look like Evangeline's bedroom. Maybe it was a guest room. I noted a lack of jewelry boxes, and the weathered vanity tucked in the corner was free of the usual accouterments one might find in a woman's bedroom. The walls were not bare, though. She had hung some art, but nothing personal — the kind of paintings you might find at Hobby Lobby, for example. Still, the smell of incense was strong. It was a moment before I realized those fragrances were coming from her.

"Do you work out of your home? Is that what's going on downstairs? Are people moving into the house or...?"

Evangeline shook her head. "Nobody is moving in. They're all leaving. We should have been done it a while ago, to be honest. But I enjoyed having everybody close. I liked spying on them if I'm being honest. In the beginning, it was just easier to keep everybody under my thumb. I had to make sure they were running the church the way I wanted it to run. I didn't want it to evolve into some kind of shady moneymaking opportunity. You know how that goes. People get greedy, they let their ethics slip. I didn't want none of that. So yes, we've been working out of the house. But recently, we've decided to change that."

She said this last part with a hint of bitterness, but I wasn't yet comfortable probing more into it. Instead, I waited for her to continue. "But let me ask you again. What's going on downstairs?"

I wrung my hands in my lap. "I don't know, I'm not sure what you mean. There's people moving stuff around, there's —"

Evangeline held up a hand, a sign to stop talking. "I'm asking you. You tell me. With your heart and your intuition or whatever you call it. What's going on downstairs? How does it feel?"

Ah, of course. I should have known she would test me. I felt foolish for not having understood from the start. Just because she had heard stories that I was a necromancer and that I had snatched the vital spark out of a genie didn't make it true. But unfortunately, my psychic abilities, if you could call them that, had never been powerful. I was damned good at sensing and directing the death current, that universal force of decay, decomposition, and deceleration that we necros relied on. But working with death energy didn't lend itself to the development of psychic abilities. When I worked magic, I had to be careful, almost clinical in my ministrations. The death current could carry me to the other side, and I could harness it to work spells, but it could also disintegrate my cells if I wasn't careful. As necromancers, working with death meant we had to intimately focus on our physical health and well-being. It didn't leave a lot left over for anything as frivolous as psychic abilities.

I sucked in a little breath. "I'm not very good at feeling out energies to be honest," I said. "But I mean...in general, people seemed stressed, frenzied." I paused, considering. "But there was something else, too."

At this, Evangeline leaned forward, narrowing her eyes.

"What else?"

I let my eyes flutter shut to better concentrate. I breathed in; the death smells were still there. Lemon pledge, palo santo, copal, cut flowers. I breathed them in and let the fragrances tell me what they wanted me to know. It was then that I sensed it, a vague but persistent undercurrent that tickled my stomach once I knew where to plug in.

"I think it's fear," I said, opening my eyes with a frown. "Or maybe anxiety. But people are worried." I watched Evangeline settle back into her chair, a satisfied expression on her face. When she still said nothing, I held my hands out before me, beseeching. "Did I pass?"

Evangeline picked up her knitting and moved it to the vanity. "You hungry?" she asked. "I'm hungry. Let's go downstairs and see what we can scrounge up." She eyed my suitcase. "You can leave that here. This'll be your room. You eat black-eyed peas?"

My stomach rumbled. "Hell yes, I eat black-eyed peas. Are there Black folks who don't?"

Evangeline grinned as she stood. "Can't trust nobody who won't eat black-eyed peas," was the only answer she gave as she led me out of the room and back downstairs.

A large dining room table was set buffet style, several entrees and side dishes set out for the taking. In the adjoining room, several people were already indulging in lunch, their plates piled high with meatloaf, potato salad, and black-eyed peas. Evangeline and I made our plates, and I followed her into the dining area.

We settled in and began eating without conversation. I was used to eating alone; sharing a meal with someone other than Big Ginny was foreign to me, but not unwelcome. The food was delicious, obviously made by someone with a lot of know-how and heart. You can always taste when food has been made by somebody without love in their bones. It just don't sit right in your stomach. Somebody cared about this food, and the people who ate it.

Weirdly, that gave me a great deal of comfort.

A woman approached, glancing only briefly in my direction. When her gaze fell on Evangeline, she tilted her head, sinking her hands into her back pockets. "Everything okay here?"

It was then that I realized the tilt of her head was to indicate me. I was the stranger she wanted explained.

Evangeline brushed her hands together as though clearing them of any remaining crumbs. She nodded. "Yes, everything's good. This is my friend, Kezia. Kezia, this is my friend, Rocky."

Evangeline must've said the magic words because Rocky's expression went from darkly scowling to damn-near bubbly when she turned her gaze in my direction. "Oh! Well, hi there. It's nice to meet you." She extended her hand, which I gladly accepted. The woman's smile transformed her face. She had large doe eyes, olive skin, and long, dark hair. She wore a white tank top that showed off sun-kissed, sculpted arms. Blue jeans tapered into her cowboy boots, and she smelled of girlish perfume and baby shampoo. She reminded me of my fourth-grade teacher — the one who died because I gave her the blues. Illogically, the associated memory filled me with guilt.

At the same time, a second emotion niggled at the back of my brain. I wasn't exactly sure what it was, but it felt... strangely good.

"I heard back from that property manager," Rocky said,

returning her attention to Evangeline. "Honestly, he's a real piece of work."

Evangeline nodded, almost with disinterest. "I'm sure. What did he have to say?"

"As long as we conduct our business legally, we're welcome to move in as soon as possible. But he wants us to know that he'll be paying attention to every financial statement the church submits and all the clientele who go in and out of his building." She shifted her weight to one foot and planted a hand on her hip. She narrowed her eyes at Evangeline, giving her head a small shake. "You sure about this? That guy is a complete asshole. I'm certain if you let me keep looking, I can find a better place for us to move to. You don't have to take the first place that comes along."

At this, Evangeline froze up. Her expression darkened, and she dropped her eyes to the side. "Yes, I do," she said. "Kezia, why don't you come with me? There's something I'd like to show you."

———

EVANGELINE LED me outside through a screened-in patio accessed through the back door. "This is my secret spot," she said, giggling like a schoolgirl. "Mosquitos can't even bother me out here. Everybody knows if I take to the back porch, means I need stillness." I thought she meant to entertain me here, away from the bustle of the move. But we passed through the screened-in area, emerging outside.

When we did, my breath caught in my throat.

Stretched out in every direction was an emerald-green cemetery, maybe an acre large. A mix of tombstones dotted the property, some relatively new while others were old and weathered, yet still they stood upright, unaffected by settling earth. Large oak trees provided dappled sunlight throughout the property, lending the cemetery an otherworldly, almost fairy-like atmosphere. In the middle of the graveyard stood a towering statue of an angel, its outstretched arm holding a lantern.

It was breathtaking.

"This is amazing," I cooed, my mouth gaping open. "It's... absolutely beautiful."

Evangeline took me by the wrist and led me down the patio steps that ended just where the graves began. "Everybody buried here is a family member," she explained. "I bought this property about five years ago. Obviously, the graves didn't come along with it." She chuckled as she said this, giving her head a small shake. "I had the graves transferred here — at no small cost, I admit." She said this with more than a modicum of embarrassment. "But in our line of work, having our ancestors at our fingertips is more than just a nice to have."

"I can feel their energy," I said, almost unable to believe the strength of it. I'd been in many cemeteries before. But something about this one gave me the all-overs in a way I'd never experienced. "It's like they want to speak. They're just looking for a voice."

Evangeline's voice was soft when she said, "Yes. Exactly so."

I started to step into the graveyard but was suddenly gripped by a sense of impropriety. I hesitated. "Is it all right if I have a look?"

My host said nothing, but swept her arm forward, motioning me to enter.

I took my time wandering through the graves, reading every name, date of birth, date of death, and any epitaphs included. There were so many people. I choked up thinking about all the magic captured here, the stories these people could tell, the wisdom they could impart. I felt the death current thrum around me as though it, too, were excited by so much love and family and possibility. I tried not to be jealous of Evangeline's abundance as the perfume of death swirled in my nose. I breathed in deep, comforted by the fragrances and energy. I was among my skinfolk; it was the closest thing to a homecoming I had ever experienced.

When I reached a particularly old headstone, I turned to Evangeline. "How did you find all these people?" I asked. "I mean, how did you know who your ancestors were? Most Black folks I know have a hard-enough time reaching back just a few generations. And it looks like you found everybody since America was colonized."

I thought my comment might add some levity to the situation, but Evangeline did not laugh. In fact, her expression was grave. "Money," she said simply. "If you have enough money, people working for you, and time, you can accomplish damn near anything. I had Bradley contact the Mormon church. Did you know the Mormons keep incredible genealogy records? I didn't," she said. "But over time, we traced most of my family, though of course not all their corpses were recoverable. But we did trace them, even some who came to America as slaves. We found their bills of sale." She tilted her head back, shoulders pressed low with reverence or grief; I wasn't sure which. "Can you imagine running across such an artifact? The bill of sale for a human being? Let alone an ancestor? Your family?" She turned her gaze to me then, her expression filled with sorrow. "You have to be prepared for that, you know. When you find them. You have to be prepared for all of their stories, including the sad ones. And believe me, girl, there's gonna be a lot of sad ones."

At this, I stopped in my tracks, my skin breaking out in goosebumps. "When I *find* them? How...how did you know?"

Evangeline cracked a small smile. "How did I know that you haven't been able to contact your people? Give me some credit. You don't think I invited you here without doing a minimal background check, did you?"

I started to object, to ask how one investigates something as intimate as that, especially since it wasn't exactly something I advertised. But if Evangeline had the resources to find and move dozens of people to her own personal cemetery, I guessed she had the resources to dig up the darkest secrets of a nobody necromancer living in Los Angeles.

Evangeline sidled up beside me, leading me again by the wrist through the gravestones. We were heading towards the large angel at the center of the property. "This is my great-great grandmother's grave," Evangeline explained. "Her name was Delia Rae Brown. She was an outstanding teacher from what I hear. Mostly taught stories out of the Bible, but all those stories were about how to find confidence, self-love, and a place in this world when you've got skin like ours." She trailed her fingers along the statue's contours, her expression full of love and reflection. "I come here a lot when I need to think. I want to be close to her so I can ask for guidance. Of course, you can always ask for guidance from the ancestors. Even if you haven't exactly made official contact with them." She looked to me then, her expression questioning. "Do you do that? Do you honor your ancestors as often as you can?"

I nodded. "I make an offering every day. I have two candles on my altar; one for Mama Fat, and one for Papa Jinabbott. Technically, they're not really my forbearers. They're the aunt and uncle of my stepgrandmother, but they're the closest thing

I have to ancestors since I know so many of their stories. I figure that counts."

Evangeline whistled. "Hell yeah that counts. And, frankly, if you've already figured that out, you're further along than I thought. I was a little afraid that you might be completely wet-behind-the-ears; a 30 something-year-old necromancer who doesn't know a goddamn thing about how this whole thing works." She smiled then, her expression softening. "But you don't strike me as any kind of dummy. Which makes me wonder why you're having so much trouble."

My heart seized under her scrutiny. Her gaze wasn't accusing, but it wasn't precisely friendly, either. She looked suspicious. I held my hands out before me. "I've done everything I could do," I explained. "I've been searching for my mother since I was a child. I don't know what I've done wrong. In fact, the more I search for her, the more I wonder if maybe this whole thing was a mistake. Maybe I wasn't supposed to be a necromancer. Maybe this fate wasn't for me. I don't know. I know so little of my family."

Evangeline was silent a moment, thinking. Then, taking a breath, she said, "Let me ask you a personal question. Your mother died giving birth to you, right?"

I nodded. "Yes, that's right."

"How do you know that? Do you trust with all your heart that this information is true, and your mother is dead? After all," she amended, "can't contact somebody on the other side if they're still alive. So. You sure she's passed?"

I blinked. "Yes! Absolutely. I've seen her grave. My brother Lamont is 10 years older than me. He remembers watching her die." My voice broke on the final word. I fought against the tears that tried to form in my eyes. Human emotions were so stupid. My mother had been dead my entire life. I'd never met her. So why did talking about her death cause me to well up like I'd lost something?

Evangeline heaved her shoulders and shook her head. "I had to ask. Sometimes, the simplest solutions are the truest. I won't lie to you. I considered the fact that maybe your mother wasn't dead, and that's why you couldn't find her. But if you have corroboration…Well, that's not *good*, but at least that's good *data*. Means your problem is something else. Something real."

I snorted. My problem was real, all right. More real than anything else in the world from my point of view. "Well, that's why I'm here," I said with a sardonic smile. "I'm here because I need your help."

Evangeline placed a hand on her hip and tilted her head to the side. "Yes, of course. That's why *you're* here. But that's not why I *asked* you here."

I was about to ask what she meant when a voice from behind us called out, stealing our attention. "Angie! Divina and Dominic are here. Want me to send them out?"

Evangeline looked over my shoulder, a broad smile plastered across her face. "No, thank you, Angelo. Kezia and I are just finishing up here. We'll be inside in not too long. Can you entertain Dominic for me? Or is Divina staying a while?"

Angelo shrugged, casting dubious glances in my direction. If this was the fellow Bradley had threatened me with, I could see why. He was barrel-chested with huge shoulders and arms, skin like burnished copper and close-cropped hair the color of autumn leaves. "I don't know. You know how Divina is. I'll take care of Dominic, get him something to eat. You need anything?"

Evangeline shook her head and waved her hand in a

shooing motion. "Naw, we good. Like I said, we'll be along in a little while. Thank you."

We watched the man turn and go back into the house. I readied my mouth to ask Evangeline why she'd asked me here, but the moment was gone. Whatever Evangeline was going to say to me would have to wait. I cursed inwardly, clenching my fists at my sides. But it was useless to be upset. We still had time. I'd been trying to end my affliction for years. A few more hours couldn't hurt.

As I followed Evangeline into the house, my thoughts wandered to the woman who had reminded me of my childhood teacher. It was only then that I realized why meeting Rocky had triggered a warm feeling in my gut that radiated out to my fingertips and toes.

It wasn't because Rocky reminded me of my teacher.

It was because when Evangeline introduced us, she'd called me her friend.

CHAPTER THREE

"MAMA!"

A ball of energy in the shape of a little boy hurtled toward Evangeline, arms outspread, crashing into her with the momentum of a freight train. Evangeline knelt to embrace him, wrapping her arms around his little body and pulling him close as she nuzzled his neck and plant kisses all over his face. "Hey baby boy! It's so good to see you! You have a good time?"

The boy peeled his way out of his mother's embrace, lifting his eyes to meet hers. "Yep. We went to get ice cream first, then we went fishing. At first, I didn't catch any fish, but then a man gave me some pink bait, and then I caught four fish." He held up the number four on his right hand.

Evangeline laughed as she ran her hands over the boy's face before planting a final large and sloppy kiss on his forehead. "I hope you brought them fish home! You know I love me some fresh-caught fish."

The boy grimaced and shook his head. "*I* don't. Can't we

have hamburgers or something like that? Divina said I didn't have to eat the fish if I didn't want it."

Evangeline looked up, casting a glance at the woman who had accompanied the boy in the living room. She was smiling, head tilted to the side as she watched their exchange. Her skin was almost my color, a rich, tawny gold, but she wasn't Black. If I had to guess, I'd say she was probably Native American. She had long, straight, dark hair, almond eyes, and a round, inviting face. She was about my height, slim but very toned, and wearing a plaid shirt and jeans. Fishing clothes.

"I did not *exactly* say that," the woman, who I suspected to be Divina, said. "What I said was if Evangeline didn't want the fish, I would surely take them off y'all's hands. All I have in my freezer is some pizzas."

"Well, I like fish," Evangeline said, returning her attention to her son, "and I don't think you even know what you like anyway. You ain't never had no fresh-caught fish. Where's the fish at, Dominic?"

It was Divina who answered. "The guy at the fishery cleaned them for us. I put them in your refrigerator. They're packed in ice, but you might want to put whatever you're not gonna eat tonight in the freezer."

Evangeline suddenly seemed to remember that I was there. "You eat fish?" she asked me.

"Sure," I lied. I really didn't like fish. But I was also not raised to be particular, especially when I was the guest in someone else's home. If Evangeline was going to make me some homemade fresh-caught fish, I was damn sure going to eat it.

From across the room, I noticed Divina shifting her weight as her arms crossed over her chest. "I don't know you," she said to me.

I sighed. "Yeah. I don't know you either." What was it with these people? Was everyone going to challenge my right just to exist?

"Difference is, I'm not standing in your house, but you are in mine."

I opened my mouth to object, but Evangeline beat me to it. "Y'all need to stop," she warned. "Divina, this is my guest, and you'll treat her kindly and with respect." She gestured between the two of us. "Kezia, this is Divina. Divina is Dominic's Big Sister. Divina, Dominic, meet Kezia. She's gonna be staying for a while."

Divina's expression didn't change. "Staying with us for how long?"

"As long as it takes," Evangeline said, more than a hint of steel in her voice. "Anyway, ain't no *us*, not from your perspective. You all packed up? You need to be ready for the movers. Yours are coming tomorrow. Or maybe those are Rocky's. Dammit, I need to check."

Again, Divina shifted her weight. "I know when they're coming. I just keep expecting you to change your mind."

Evangeline huffed. "Well, I haven't, and I won't." Slowly, Evangeline trod over to where Divina was standing, defeated, and gently put her arms around her. She held the girl for what seemed like a long time. "This is all gonna work itself out," Evangeline said, her voice low. "I promise. We're gonna sort this out. But right now, I just need to keep everybody safe."

I felt something bump into my legs, and I tore my eyes away from Evangeline and Divina to see that Dominic was walking past me, heading toward the stairs. Immediately, I smiled, enchanted by his adorable little face. Huge brown eyes were fringed with lashes too long and black for his own good. Skin the dark brown of desert hills at sunset. Head full of big, soft curls. He was probably seven or eight years old. Supposedly a great age.

I hoped to know that from personal experience soon enough.

"Hey, Dominic," I called out.

The boy stopped, turned a disinterested gaze in my direction. "Yeah?"

"What did you think about fishing?" I asked. "I've never been myself. Was it fun? Were the fish gross?"

Dominic's expression did not soften when he said, "I'm not supposed to talk to strangers." With that, he brushed me off and ran the rest of the way upstairs.

"Don't mind him," Evangeline said to me. "You know how kids are. He'll be back down when he gets hungry again."

Divina dawdled for a minute, occasionally giving me the stink eye before she finally made a move toward the stairs. "I guess I'll finish getting all my things together, and then I'll say goodbye to Dominic. Want me to come back tomorrow?"

Evangeline waved her hand like the question was of little importance. "You know you're welcome here any time you want to come around. I just can't have you being here *all* the time, things being what they are."

Divina almost smiled at Evangeline, but the expression melted into a scowl as her eyes drifted past me and she made her way up the stairs.

I crossed my arms over my chest. "So, that's Dominic's big sister?"

Evangeline nodded. "Yeah. Well, no, not big sister. Big Sister. With capital letters. From the Big Brothers and Sisters program. I adopted Dominic when he was a baby, but it wasn't as easy a process as you might think. For one, agencies weren't too thrilled to place a child with a necromancer. I guess you can't fault them for that, even though by then it was common knowledge that I had already ended my affliction. But what made the adoption even more complicated is that Dominic is half Creek."

I frowned. "Oh. What does that have to do with anything?"

"Well, there's been a history of non-Native people adopting Native children and taking them away from their home, depriving them of their ancestry, their people, all the culture and language and religion that's due them. Now, you might be laughing at that, given that your entire existence is wrapped up in bringing those very things back to our people." I offered an embarrassed grin, which Evangeline returned. "The irony wasn't lost on me, either. Historically, it was White families taking Native kids away from reservations and raising them in White households and White neighborhoods with White friends and White families. But today, adopting Native children out to *anybody* who's outside of the Nation can be problematic. I had to fight for Dominic, and in the end, I'm pretty sure I only got him because he's just half Creek. He's also half Black. My lawyer successfully argued that he has just as much right to his history and culture as a Black American as he does a Native American."

She paused then, her eyes tracing an invisible trail up the stairway, no doubt imagining Dominic in his room, sitting and chatting with Divina, happy as a clam in his own element. The love was evident all over Evangeline's face. "One of the concessions I made to bringing Dominic home was that he has contact with another Creek person that can help guide him towards finding his history and people. Divina is his assigned Big Sister in that regard. At first, it was kind of a strange relationship between the three of us, but over time, Divina became part of the family. Kind of like everyone else here, really. You met Rocky earlier. Rocky's been part of this household for the past 10 or so years, as has Angelo."

I wasn't sure what else to say, so I stretched and yawned, the universal sign that I wanted some alone time. Evangeline took the hint and made shooing motions, indicating I should go upstairs. "Go ahead and get settled in. Feel free to take a walk around the property, get to know the house. Talk to anybody you run into, and don't let anybody give you any lip. A lot of these folks are particular about me — protective, you might say. We've endured a lot of bullshit over the years, so don't take it personally if they don't open up to you right away. Things have been strange around here lately, and everybody looks at strangers with suspicion. Hell, these days, we're looking at each other with suspicion."

I couldn't contain my curiosity anymore, not now that Evangeline had so openly invited more questions. I rocked back onto my heels, unsure how to ask, but finally, I just went for it. "Evangeline, you've got to tell me. What's going on here? I'm no psychic genius, but it doesn't take one to know that things here aren't right. Everybody has been looking at me like I'm the enemy since I got here. Did I do something wrong? Am I not wanted? Is there some big pro-genie faction living here that I'm unaware of? Or something else I should know about?"

Evangeline hesitated, casting her eyes low before answering. "It's not personal, and it has nothing to do with you. And I promise I will tell you everything. Do you drink?"

I blinked, momentarily taken aback by the question, but then I eased into a smile. "Ma'am, I'm a bartender."

Evangeline laughed, a hearty sound that tickled my insides.

"Oh shit, you are, aren't you? How did I forget that? Hell, maybe you should make the drinks tonight."

I gave a playful shrug. "Happy to do it. You give me a bottle of good bourbon, and I can make all your worries disappear. At least until the hangover hits."

Evangeline joined me in my grin. "In that case, let's plan on an after-dinner drink, just you and me. We'll take our cocktails on the patio and have us a nice chat. In the meantime, go ahead and get settled in. Get to know the property. And come tonight, you'll have the answers to everything you want to know."

THE HOUSE TRANSFORMED once everyone had gone home or to their rooms for the night. During the day, the hustle and bustle had given the home a sense of frenzied chaos. Now, as I eased into a chair on Evangeline's back porch, the night was still, and even the house seemed to have settled in. Dominic, who had been a complete chatterbox since dinner, was hiding away upstairs watching a movie. The new sense of calm was welcome.

"God, I love a mint julep," Evangeline said as we clinked our glasses together in a toast. "I know it's a cliché, but it's my favorite drink. Used to drink them more often, but these days, I've been trying to keep my wits about me. Still, can't beat sharing a nice mint julep on the porch with a friend."

There was that word again, *friend*, and I felt ridiculous for the tingle that ran up my spine and warmed my heart. But something in the back of my mind was warning me. We weren't friends. Which meant one of two things: either she was super old-fashioned and Southern, or she was buttering me up because she wanted something.

Time and experience gave the second option much more weight.

"It's nice of you to invite me to stay down here," I began, settling back into my chair, and resting my cocktail in my lap. "I don't do a lot of traveling, so it's good to get out of my element for a while. I've never been to Georgia before. Are you from here originally?"

Evangeline nodded. "Yes ma'am. Born and raised. My family's been here for generations. That made moving the graves easier. Transporting bodies across state lines isn't exactly an activity for the fainthearted. In fact, I left a few that are buried in South Carolina and Alabama. Didn't have the fight in me for all that." She took a sip from her drink. "Where are your people from?"

I shrugged. "All over and nowhere. I was born and raised in Los Angeles, but my mother is from Ohio. Or was. My father is from Chicago but moved to Metairie when he was a pre-teen. He was raised by my step-grandmother, who is originally from South Carolina but lived a lot of her life in Louisiana. So like I said. We come from everywhere, but no place is really home. Don't really have any roots."

Evangeline hrmmed and sipped at her cocktail. "Kind of the story of our people though, ain't it?"

Well, I couldn't argue with that.

"So I guess it's about time I told you what you're doing here," Evangeline said. I looked over to see that her hands were shaking. The ice in her glass clinked together as her fingers trembled, and when I raised my gaze to meet hers, she looked anxious. Maybe it was just nerves. But suddenly I felt a roil in my stomach. Something wasn't right.

"As you noticed, things are changing around here. For the past few years, Rocky, Angelo, and Divina have been living at least part time at the house. It was a gradual shift, not something any of us outright planned, but Lord knows I had the room for it. Over time, we became a family, and everyone kind of made themselves a little nest here. And I loved having everyone around. But now, things've changed."

She blew out a hot breath, turning her eyes skyward. "I guess it started about six months ago, though at the time, I pretended I didn't notice the signs. My live-in housekeeper, Celia, got depressed. At first, I thought that maybe it was mid-life crisis, or maybe it was just the zeitgeist of the time. Living is hard, you know. But eventually, she showed some other signs, too. Listlessness, lack of focus…"

My blood went cold and I stilled, knowing what was coming. *No, no, no,* I thought, my fist tightening in my lap. *This can't be happening. Please, no.* "Eventually, she slipped into the fugue. That, of course, is when we realized what was happening." Evangeline dropped her head forward, staring down into her lap. "I don't know, maybe we knew it before then. Maybe *I* knew. But I didn't want it to be true. It had been *years.*" I sensed the slow boiling fury just beneath her words. "I guess you know what I'm trying to say. About six months ago, my affliction came back. My housekeeper Celia was suffering from necromantic exposure sickness, and last month, she died. I'm moving everybody out of my house — my colleagues as well as Rocky and them — so that no one else suffers."

My world began to spin. My eyes went unfocused and my hands numbed even as my spinal cord turned into pure fire. I was simultaneously freezing cold and burning hot as competing emotions vied for primacy at the core of my being. Terror. Fury. Confusion. My logical brain knew what Evangeline was saying, had even predicted it, but my emotional core couldn't accept it.

Evangeline was on a very short list of people known to have cured their affliction. And now she was saying that it was *back?*

The only thing keeping me going for the past few years was knowing that if I tried hard enough, if I performed the right rituals, I could end my affliction and finally get my daughter back. It was the only thing I wanted in this world.

And Evangeline's admission meant that even if I got it, I might not get to keep it.

The realization made me want to die.

Evangeline's eyes went cloudy. "There's more."

Evangeline bent forward and lifted the hem of her skirt. She stretched out her dark brown legs, turning so I could get a better look. My eyes followed a path from her ankle to her knee, and what I saw there sent me into another tailspin. Running the length of her leg were stark, black, serpentine veins. They looked almost like vines.

And they were undulating.

I looked up, my eyes wide in the darkness. "Evangeline, that looks like a hoodoo curse."

The woman dropped her skirt and nodded, folding her hands in her lap. "That's what I think, too. Whatever they are, they're keeping me here, trapped on the property. I can't leave. Haven't been able to leave since Celia died." She tried to chuckle then, but the sound rang false. "Divina calls it agoraphobia. I guess it is, though I always associate that word with people afraid to go out. Not people who physically can't."

I blew out my breath, my mind whirring with the possibilities. Agoraphobia, like many ailments of the body, *could* present in different ways — and it could have various causes.

The agoraphobia could be a psychological injury stemming from trauma. After I'd been attacked in an alley, I'd developed nyctophobia and couldn't be alone in the dark for weeks. And the vines could be some kind of pathology whose appearance just happened to coincide with the onset of agoraphobia.

Or, fuck, it could be a curse.

"You practice hoodoo, right? You're a Conjure woman?"

I leaned my head back, staring up at the lazily spinning blades of a ceiling fan. "I mean, that's a complicated question. My *grandmother* is a Conjure woman, and she's been teaching me hoodoo since I was a child, but I don't know if I'd call myself a Conjure woman. That just sounds pretentious."

"Then let me phrase it this way," Evangeline said. "Do you know much about working roots? Can you deduce anything from what you just saw?"

I sucked in a deep breath and lowered my gaze. "Show me again."

Once more, Evangeline lifted the hem of her skirt, and this time I studied the marks with academic scrutiny. They were slightly raised and gnarled like the branches of a tree. Properly speaking, they weren't black: they were a confusion of mottled purples, browns, and dark greens. The undulations were inconsistent, the skin crawling in different directions at once. As the veins moved, they pulsed. The overall effect was of dozens of insects slithering beneath her skin. The sight was ghastly. I held my expression together, and when I sat back and looked her in the face, I said with confidence, "Somebody good has been working roots on you for a while."

"Somebody good? You mean somebody accomplished? Somebody who knows what they're doing?"

I nodded. "Even people who know how to work magic like this mostly wouldn't do it because it's not safe. All the magic that you work in hoodoo has to be earned. If you work roots on somebody who doesn't deserve it, the universe turns it back on you. So even the most accomplished hoodoo workers must be certain that their targets are worth the spells they cast on them. Because the universe is watching, and it keeps its own tally." I motioned toward her legs. "The person who did this was either very sure that you deserved it, or they're just plain evil and don't give a fuck."

Evangeline took a deep drink from her glass, and I followed suit, my nerves jangling. "Whoever did this is responsible."

I frowned. "Responsible?" It took me a moment too long to realize what she was talking about. "You mean the person who's working these roots on you is the same person who brought your affliction back?"

Evangeline nodded. "They started right around the same time. And I don't believe in coincidences."

"No," I said. "Neither do I."

"So when I found out that you had killed a genie, you were necromancer, and you were Conjure woman in your own right no matter what you say, I knew you were the only person who could help me with this." Evangeline leaned forward and placed her hand on my knee. "I need you to find the person responsible, and then you need to reverse it."

I was quiet a moment, thinking. "Evangeline, you're the only necromancer in a city that should have hundreds. Do you know what happened to them?"

The woman shook her head. "Nobody knows, really. Different things. Some moved away or died. Others just stopped practicing. I met with a few of them. One fellow told me he just didn't want to practice anymore and didn't think he could if he wanted to. Another lady told me the thought of practicing necromancy made her sick."

I tapped a finger against my lips. "Is it possible that whatever happened to the other necromancers is happening to you, too?"

Evangeline frowned. "It's been years since anyone else besides me has practiced here. Why would it affect me just now?"

"I don't know, but sometimes, in biological systems, it takes a while for a sickness to ravage the whole organism. Think of gangrene, for example. Lack of blood supply to a toe causes the tissue to die, but the condition spreads. It might be a while before it reaches your knee, but it will get there."

Evangeline only shook her head. "If there's a sickness in the city, which there could be, that ain't what's wrong with me. I feel it in my bones. It's something else. This is personal. This is someone attacking me where it hurts me most. And that's why I need you to find them and put a stop to it. Please."

I ran a hand over my face, taking in all the implications of what she was asking. Beyond the obvious, I was in no way qualified to do this. I was shit at dealing with people, largely on account of not having a lot of experience with them. Yes, I worked as a bartender, and I could make small talk with the best of them, but when it came to having a proper conversation? I wouldn't know where to begin. Plus, investigative work was completely outside my wheelhouse. Even if Evangeline had a list of names, what was I supposed to do with them? Call them up and ask if they were working roots on Evangeline Morris? Fat lot of good that would do. It was an impossible request. I wasn't even sure how she managed the gumption to make it.

Until I thought of Dominic.

My eyes shot wide with understanding. "Everybody's moving out," I breathed. "Including Dominic? Is Dominic leaving?"

Evangeline opened her mouth to respond, then immediately burst into tears.

That was all the answer I needed.

I didn't know her well, but I knew her well enough. I leaned forward and pulled her into an embrace where I didn't let her go for a long time.

CHAPTER FOUR

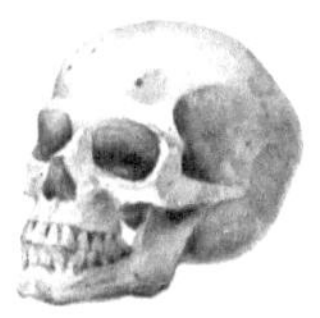

ARLY THE NEXT MORNING, I pulled myself from bed and struggled into the shower. I didn't travel much, so I was unaccustomed to sleeping in a strange bed. I had awoken sore and under-rested, but maybe that wasn't entirely the bed's fault. I'd been mulling over Evangeline's situation as I slept. My brain wasn't different from anyone else's in that regard. Always trying to solve problems when it was supposed to be resting.

I sighed, pulling an outfit from the drawers. *You've really done it this time, Kezia,* a voice in my head said. I recognized it immediately: my patron, Papa Jinabbott. He liked to appear just to torment me; he wasn't one to blow smoke. *Gone and bit off way more than you can chew. Heh. You proud, girl? Think you gonna get what you want?*

I slipped into shorts and a blouse, digging through my toiletry bag for a pair of earrings to complete the outfit. *You shoulda known she ain't ask you here out the goodness of her heart. What's Big Ginny always saying? Ain't no such thing as a free lunch!*

That voice came from Mama Fat. I scowled, planting a hand on my hip. "Double teaming me ain't fair," I grumbled. "What was I supposed to do? Tell her thanks but no thanks and go back home?"

I waited for an answer, but of course I didn't get one. My patrons were great at stirring up trouble. Not so great at bedding it back down.

Eventually I found the earrings I'd brought, but naturally, I only found one. I cursed, tucking the sole earring into a pocket. The earrings had been a gift from Marcus; I'd have to find the missing piece before I left. But now wasn't the time.

Right now, I had a real problem.

To help Evangeline with her curse, I needed to know everything about it: who had cast it, why, and the type of magic they used. Just looking at her skin wasn't enough — I needed to consult the bones.

Which, of course, I didn't have.

That's right, girl, Papa Jinabbott teased me from the other side. *Gone and left home without your tools! What was you thinkin'? Ain't we raised you better than that?*

I tried to ignore the voice, but he was right. Leaving California without my tools was stupid, but how could I have known I'd need them? Evangeline's invitation had mentioned nothing about curse-breaking. And anyway, packing a suitcase filled with raven bones, oracle cards, and my favorite candles and incenses seemed like a waste. I needed to pack light. Extra suitcases were expensive these days.

Still, to be effective, I needed to understand things. I needed supernatural insight.

It was still early, and I didn't know what hours the house kept. Emerging from my room, I stood in the hallway, silently listening for the telltale signs of wakefulness. But the house was still as stone; all I heard was a clock ticking in the distance.

I trudged down the stairs and checked all the rooms for signs of life. I could explain what I was doing if I were found out, but it was always better to not get caught red-handed digging through people's things. That was always uncomfortable, no matter your intentions.

When I was sure no one was awake, I started my search. For the work I needed to perform, I wanted an assortment of basic tools: playing cards, candles, incense, cloth, string, and, of course, bones. I smiled to myself thinking of how I had just bought tools like these from Opal and paid a pretty penny for them. Yet here I was, gathering everyday objects to imbue with magic, just as my ancestors had done. And while I still would have preferred to dig up fragrant incenses like frankincense or sandalwood, I was sure to find a cupboard of herbs and spices that could be burned to equal effect.

I found almost everything I needed easily, and I carried the assortment of materials to my room where I'd set up a makeshift altar on the small vanity.

The only things I still needed were bones.

Big Ginny always practiced her fortune-telling with chicken bones — the very bones left over from a chicken we'd eaten for dinner. I was more spoiled — I worked primarily with raven bones. But any bones would do. Chicken bones were convenient and easily obtainable, so that's what our ancestors used.

But even I wasn't about to go digging through the kitchen trash in the hopes these people had eaten chicken in the past couple days. Even the thought made me feel green around the gills.

I made my way into the kitchen to rummage through the

freezer. When I didn't find what I was looking for, I headed out to the garage, hoping to get lucky. Sure enough, Evangeline had a second refrigerator and a deep freezer tucked away behind a pickup truck and some kind of fancy sedan.

I pulled everything I needed from the freezer: a whole chicken, broth, and bags of frozen vegetables. Fresh would be better, but this would do. I carried the ingredients back into the house and got to work.

Some time later, I heard footsteps on the stairs. A fresh-from-sleep Evangeline padded into the kitchen, yawning and shuffling toward the counter where I'd already brewed a fresh pot of coffee.

"Girl, what you doing up this early?" she asked, pouring coffee into a mug as she yawned hugely. "And cooking already? Is that chicken soup?"

"I hope you don't mind," I said, lifting the pot lid to check the simmer. "I needed chicken bones. This seemed the best way to get them without wasting the meat."

Evangeline wasn't really listening. She was blowing across the surface of the coffee, tumbling into a chair at the island. "What are the bones for?"

Maybe she *was* listening.

"The thing about curses is that they're ornery," I said. "And if you untangle them wrong, they could blow up in your face. And since I have no idea what you've got on you, I want to do a reading. See if the universe will cough up something we can use. If the bones tell me it's a standard hoodoo jealousy curse, I can unravel that with a hand tied behind my back. But if it's something I haven't ever worked with before..." I let my voice trail off as I shrugged.

"Do you have everything you need, or should I send someone to pick up supplies?"

"I have everything for the reading. I searched around the house while you were asleep. I'll know more about what I might need once we see what the bones have to say."

Evangeline grunted. "What if the bones don't know?"

I put the lid back on the pot. "The bones always know."

As it turned out, the bones didn't know much.

We were sitting at the kitchen table, blood-smeared chicken bones scattered between us. Evangeline sat clutching a paper towel around a finger; I'd had to nick her with a kitchen knife, something I didn't like doing. I preferred a lancet, but I didn't have one, and I needed her blood to read the bones. I tried not to think about microbes waiting to attack the wound.

I opened myself to the death current, to the whispering of the ancestors in my blood. I sensed my forbears in my cells and DNA, hazy epigenetic memories breathing in my blood and bones. The dead inside me sent messages, inspiration, some-times knowledge. When I threw bones, the ancestors spoke using emotions and imagery — but often the message was jumbled and difficult to decipher.

"Well?" Evangeline's voice was ringed with anticipation. "What do they say?"

I shook my head, confused. "Something about the flow of water," I said. "Tides, maybe? Does that mean anything to you?"

Evangeline shrugged, deflated. "Not especially."

I leaned forward, trying to analyze the bones from another angle. "It's not hoodoo we're dealing with," I said, almost to myself. "The curse and I don't speak the same language, which means it's magic I'm not familiar with. Could be a type of shamanism, for example. But I do get the impression of people and water, and something to do with jealousy, secrecy, and questionable intentions." I pinched the tip of my nose as I thought. "But it's also possible that I'm being too literal. It might not be moving water but something having to do with movement: travel, or commerce, or..."

"That could be anything," Evangeline said, glancing up. "We need more information than that."

I picked up the playing cards that I'd found in a drawer, shuffling them blindly. I wasn't as deft in cartomancy as I was in osteomancy, but whatever the bones were trying to tell me wasn't coming in clearly. I pulled three cards off the top and laid them next to each other, adjacent to the bones: the 5 of hearts reversed, the ace of spades, and the 2 of hearts.

I thought for a moment before interpreting. "In a reading like this, hearts can mean blood relations, surgery, and some-times physical violence," I said, tracing the designs with a finger. "But I don't see that in the rest of your cards or in the bones, so I don't think this is about violence or cutting or blood. Five is the perfect form of a human: head, two arms, two legs. It represents personal freedom. And here it is, reversed. That's telling us that your personal freedom has been blocked, which we already know, since you can't leave the house," I said wryly. "And the ace of spades..."

I heard Evangeline's breath catch in her throat. "What is it?"

I clucked my tongue. "It's death, but that doesn't neces-sarily mean physical death," I hurriedly explained. "It often just means the end of a situation. And see, here, this 2 of hearts? This is the most sacred pairing or coupling in your world. If you were married, I'd say this was your marriage, but because you're not, I'd say —"

"It's motherhood," she said tersely, pushing away from the table, still squeezing her finger with the paper towel. "It's the cards telling me that if I don't regain my personal freedom, it'll be the death of my motherhood. Because they'll take Dominic away."

I opened my mouth to counter this argument, but the words wouldn't come. That wasn't how I was going to interpret the cards, but now that she'd said it, it made perfect sense. It didn't clarify the original message about flowing water, but sometimes the bones were just murky.

Unfortunately, the cards were so clear, even a non-practitioner could read them.

"We'll get to the bottom of this," I said, sweeping the cards into my hands and gathering the bones into a pile. "We'll keep thinking about what flowing water could mean. Water is associated with healing and intuition. Does that help?"

"I don't know," Evangeline said, rubbing her eyes with the heels of her hands. "I just don't know."

I was preparing an answer when Angelo wandered into the kitchen, sniffing the air. "Y'all already made coffee? *My* ladies!" he said with a grin as he made a beeline for the percolator. "Anybody need a refill?"

"Angelo," Evangeline said, brow creased, "*what* are you doing here?"

"I live here," he said, expression innocent as he poured himself a mug.

"You *don't* live here anymore. Not that I mind you coming around, but..."

The man plopped into a chair beside me, taking a long swig of his morning brew. "All my cooking stuff is packed away. Figured I'd come over here and whip up some eggs and bacon or something. Y'all hungry?"

"No," we answered simultaneously. Throwing bones always left me feeling a little under the weather. It looked like the reading had a similar effect on Evangeline.

"We were just finishing up reading the bones," Evangeline explained. "Trying to understand who might have put the curse on me."

Angelo's brows shot up on his face. "Yeah? What did y'all find?"

I held up my hands before me, unsure. "It's hard to say. The message wasn't clear. This curse looks very strong, which leads me to believe it's been cast by someone Evangeline knows." I turned to Evangeline then. "Or someone you *used* to know. Strangers can do this kind of work, it's just more difficult. The emotion you need to put words on someone?" I shook my head. "Hard to do that to somebody you don't know intimately."

At this, Evangeline leaned forward, resting her elbows on the table. "You're saying it's someone close to me? But I don't keep magic workers close to me," she said.

I shook my head. "No, I'm not saying it's a friend or family. Just someone you were close to in the past. A coworker, a neighbor, hell, a therapist or hairdresser. Someone who physically touched you or shared secrets with you. Combine that with somebody who has reason to hate you, and you've probably got a good list of suspects. Can you think of anybody like that? Anybody who would have a grudge against you?"

Evangeline and Angelo exchanged looks, but it was Angelo who spoke first. "We've always gotten a lot of hate mail ever since the church opened up," he said matter-of-factly. "Most of the mail we get is from right-wing types who don't like a necromancer leading a Christian church."

Again, I shook my head, my brow furrowed in thought.

"Those kinds of people don't usually have magic at their disposal. Especially not this kind of magic. This doesn't look like thaumaturgy or magic-for-sale to me. This looks more homegrown."

Evangeline nodded. "Well, I can agree with that. You know, I've never kept a list of people who don't like me. My mama always taught me you gotta let them chickens be. But there are folks who keep their ears to the ground, magically speaking. They might know something. Might've heard about grudges against me."

"Who?"

Evangeline leaned back and ticked the names off on her fingers. "The first person I can think of is Crystal Waters."

Angelo whistled, linking his fingers behind his head as he turned his gaze to the ceiling. "Angie, you ain't talked to them people for a hot minute. You think Crystal's still got your back after all this time?"

"Hold up," I said, raising a hand. "You know someone named Crystal...Waters?"

Evangeline chuckled. "Well, that's obviously not the name her mother gave her, though it is her legal name. I think beforehand her name was Erika or Eileen or something. She was the high priestess of our Wiccan coven back in the day," Evangeline explained. "I studied with her for a good long time. Before I embraced my own magic, she taught me hers."

I bit down on my lip to keep from laughing. "You were a *Wiccan?*"

Evangeline smiled. "I sure was. Everybody had a youthful period, didn't they? I bet you went through a goth or emo phase or wore plastic bracelets up and down your arms, right?"

I laughed. "Sure, everybody did some embarrassing shit, but..."

"Hey, don't knock it. You'd be surprised how good Wiccan magic can be."

I nodded, willing to let the topic go. "Okay, but *Crystal Waters?*"

"It was par for the course. And don't you laugh," Evangeline warned with a grin. "Back then, I called myself Semele VioletMoon."

I gaped, unable to hide my disbelief. "You're shitting me."

Evangeline nodded, but suddenly the mirth faded from her expression. "It was a different time in my life," she explained. "But I don't regret any of it. Hell, if nothing else, I ended up with this house. Crystal's the one who sold it to me."

"Really?"

"Well, she was the realtor, I mean. She's the one who told me it was for sale. We were close as sisters, and I learned a lot from her. About the world, about magic, and about myself. Anyway, who are you to sass me? You practice hoodoo. Are the two really all that different?"

I opened my mouth to retort that they were *wildly* different — all that Goddess religion stuff had little in common with the work Big Ginny and I did, but I decided against it. No good could come of my badmouthing her previous religious leanings. "Ok, so we'll talk to Crystal Waters, see if she's heard anything. Who else?"

Evangeline shifted in her seat. "The other one is Terrence Curtis."

I saw the color rise in Angelo's cheeks. "Terrence?" he asked. "Come on, Angie. You ain't even wanna go there, do you?"

My eyes darted between the two of them, taking in both their expressions. Angelo's face shifted slightly, his expression at once concerned and angry. Evangeline, for her part, remained stoic. "Why?" she asked, her expression unchanged. "Should I not go to Terrence even though he might be able to help?"

Angelo blew out his cheeks, giving Evangeline a doleful look. "You know why. You don't owe him anything, you know? Cauterize that wound. Don't let him —"

"Terrence isn't a *wound*," Evangeline cut in. "He's human, just like you, just like me. His path isn't for us to judge." She turned to me then, the lines of her face hardening. "Like most people, I have a past," she said. There was no ire in her voice and no apology. "Long time ago, I ran around with the wrong people. Got into trouble, did people wrong. But then I found Jesus and got my Godsend, and things are different now. But that doesn't mean the past just gets erased. I've paid my debts, don't get it twisted. But I also remember who my friends were. Are."

When neither Angelo nor Evangeline said anything more, I threw up my hands in frustration. "Who is he?"

Angelo turned to me, his lips pressed into a hard, thin line. "*Businessman*," he said, his voice run through with steel. "Not exactly...*legitimate* business, if you catch my drift. Definitely not the kind of guy you want to fuck around with."

I turned my attention to Evangeline. "Is he a criminal?"

Evangeline met my eyes but didn't answer. I decided not to press the issue. "Okay. And this guy has connections in the magic community?"

Evangeline nodded. "Yes. He has a relative — a second cousin, I believe — who practices Ghanaian wizardry. Powerful man. He's blessed every home I've lived in since I've been on my own. I feel his protection all around me, even now. Anyway, I don't think his influence is as large as mine," Evangeline said with a modest dip of her chin, "but magic workers know things. People talk when we place our hands on them. You'd be surprised."

I bit back a sour retort that tried to escape. I was sure she was right — one reason Opal and I were so close was because we shared intimate moments. When she placed her hands on me, I felt closer to her than anyone. She knew about my family, my daughter, my deepest pain.

But I didn't engender that kind of intimacy from others and wouldn't until I received my Godsend. For some reason, people just didn't form fuzzy bonds with bone readers smeared in blood, chatting up dead people on the other side.

I wanted to ask more about this, but just as I was preparing my question, Angelo pushed back from the table, his chair scraping across the floor. "I don't know about this, Angie. You never said anything about getting Kezia involved with a thug like Terrence. You send her nosing around into his business... I'm just saying he might not exactly like that."

"Well, good thing I'm not sending her *nosing* into anything," Evangeline retorted, something like weariness creeping into her words. "I'm *asking* her to talk with an old friend. That's all," she added before Angelo could respond. "But Angelo is right about one thing," Evangeline said, returning her attention to me. "Terrence can be volatile. He was never violent with me or anything like that, but it's true he's known on the streets as a dangerous man. Getting involved with him could put you on somebody's radar."

Angelo was pacing, lips pulled into a frown, a low grumble in the back of his throat. In honesty, I didn't like the sound of that any more than Angelo did, but as Evangeline spoke, a strange tingle started in the base of my spine, slithering its way up into my amygdala. I recognized the sensation, but I couldn't quite name it. I felt at once indignant but also confident, scared, and...*powerful*. And even though I knew that I should feel the same fear Angelo felt, I didn't. I was strangely calm. No, that wasn't right either. I was more than calm. I was serene. And part of me was...

...excited?

But that didn't make sense, either. I wasn't one of those adrenaline junkies who liked jumping out of airplanes or skin diving with sharks. I liked my adrenaline and noradrenaline in my adrenal glands where they belonged, not coursing through my body until my pounding heart increased my blood pressure and expanded my lungs, dilated my pupils, and redistributed my blood to maximize glucose to my brain, all of which was designed to help me kick ass or flee a dangerous situation.

Yet, as Angelo continued to rail on about how unsafe the situation was, I felt myself growing more comfortable not just with the idea of tussling with a criminal but the knowledge that I might have to.

The cognitive dissonance was dizzying.

"It's okay," I said finally. "I'll do it. Somebody has to for Dominic's sake."

At my words, Angelo and Evangeline turned toward me. Relief flooded Evangeline's face even as Angelo's expression grew dour. Her face broke into a smile and her eyes moistened with tears. "Thank you," she said.

"I have a daughter of my own," I said, my voice low. "I understand what you're facing."

Angelo sat back down in his chair with a grunt, arms crossed on the table. "Okay. So what's the plan, Angie?"

"You'll need some supplies," Evangeline said. "If we get lucky and find whoever's done this to me, we need to bind them and their magic, assuming it's not as simple as asking them to cut it out." She smiled when she said this, but I saw the soreness in it, like a wound that wouldn't heal. I couldn't imagine how it must feel to be the subject of a curse — to have someone wish you harm enough to actually do something about it. Especially someone like Evangeline who had dedicated her entire life to making people better. It must have felt like betrayal. "There's a magic shop across town, owned by one of my old coven sisters. The shop is called Well Met and Kismet, and the owner is a woman named Kismet Hanson. You're familiar with magic shops, right?"

I shrugged. "Sure. My friend Opal runs one called Necro Sis."

Evangeline smirked. "That's cute. Well, Wiccan magic shops are a bit...*different*," she said, dipping her chin. I suspected that the word *different* was doing a lot of work in that sentence, but I decided not to ask. I'd find out soon enough. "Still, if you tell Kismet I sent you, she'll help you. Tell her you want a binding spell."

I turned to Angelo. "You up for being my chauffeur for the day?"

The big man shrugged. "Drive a beautiful woman around town? Easiest job I've had in years."

I admit it; I blushed.

WELL MET and Kismet was like a "Live, laugh, love" Instagram post had come to life and taken up residence in a boutique on the edge of town. It didn't look like much from the outside, but the inside was another story. The walls were covered in unicorn and goddess art, with crystal balls, geodes, tarot decks and dream catchers cluttering every level surface. The shop sold everything from candles and incense to girl-power cocktail shakers and body oils, and an array of pseudo-spiritual wares in between. A basket of yoga mats sat next to a table with hand-blown glass pipes. It didn't feel like a magic shop. It felt like Anthropologie and a hippie sex-toy store had a very on-trend baby.

"If this is the kinda shit Evangeline was into when she was younger, it's no wonder she had to come to a stranger for help with magic," I whispered as I picked up a crystal ball and, turning it over, nearly passed out at the price tag. "This stuff is ridiculous *and* expensive as hell."

Angelo picked up a pair of furry pink handcuffs. "Do ladies actually like this stuff?"

I chuckled, shrugging a shoulder. "Different strokes, I guess. Evangeline doesn't really seem the type, but..." I glanced at Angelo and chanced a question. "You and Evangeline. Are you guys...?"

"What, together?" The surprise alone answered my question. "No. We're just...she's like my sister, I guess. As far as I can tell, Angie's asexual. Or maybe just aromantic, I'm not sure. But either way, in all the time I've known her, she's never had a partner or expressed an interest in one. She's pretty focused on work. She has to be. As the only necromancer around, there's a *lot* of work for her to do."

"And Rocky and Divina? What's their story?"

Angelo was examining a pair of magnetic bracelets. "Story? I don't know. Divina is Dominic's Big Sister. She's kind of a pain in the ass, but Angie cuts her a lot of slack because she's like Dominic — they were both adopted outside their tribe. I don't know why that excuses her attitude, but it's not my place to judge. Rocky met Evangeline in the ER one night when she got mugged on her way home from an event. Rocky used to be an ER nurse, but now she works full time for Angie and the church."

"And what about you? How did you meet Evangeline?"

Angelo shrugged. "Oh. Ah, well, I used to work at a gun range. I taught her how to shoot. She wasn't really any good at it, though, so then I became her bodyguard." He grinned and lifted a jade egg from its pedestal. "What do you think this is for?"

Before I could reply, a cheerful voice behind me chirped, "Let me guess: you're a Cancer."

I spun around, eyebrow shooting high on my face. "Excuse me?"

The woman grinned, eyes twinkling. "Your astrological sign. Cancer, right?"

I cleared my throat, squaring my shoulders and lifting my chin. "Capricorn," I responded, my voice sounding weirdly smug, even to my ears.

But if the other woman noticed, she didn't let on. "Dang it!" She stomped her foot and snapped her fingers. "I always guess the opposite." Her smiled widened, and she extended a hand. "Kismet," she said. "This is my shop! Welcome in!"

I had to bite my tongue from admonishing that she should have said "Well met" since that's what she named her store. But after a second, any inclination I had toward snark drained away. The woman standing before me was a poster child for what I believed Wiccans to be. She was fair skinned with bottle-red hair, too many piercings, and dressed in a halter top and a tie-dyed skirt. Celtic tattoos adorned her arms, and huge triskele earrings dangled from her ears. But she was also beguiling, with an almost grandmotherly intelligence that glinted from her eyes.

"Kezia," I said, accepting her hand. "Nice to meet you."

"You as well. What brings you in today?"

Angelo and I exchanged looks. "Well," I drawled, "we're looking for a binding spell."

"Okie doke," Kismet chirped. "Follow me right over here." She led us to a table of candles. She plucked a black one from the table, followed by a length of hemp twine. She pressed both into my hands. "You'll want to anoint that first," she advised, pointing a finger. "Depending on what you're trying to bind. I've got some *lovely* custom essential oil blends. I've got a lavender-patchouli blend that is to *die*." She kissed the tips of her fingers.

I handed her back the candle and twine, shaking my head. "No, I...think you misunderstand. We're not looking for, like, *New Age* magic," I said, hoping the disdain didn't seep too far into my words. "We're looking for the real thing. An actual binding spell."

At this, Kismet tilted her head to one side. "I'm sorry, but I don't think I know what you mean."

A hint of a smile feathered the corner of the woman's lips, and I couldn't help but grin myself. Like I said. Beguiling. "Evangeline sent me," I said.

But her expression didn't change. "Who?"

Now, I sucked in a breath, clenching my hands into fists at my sides. She was really going to make me say it. Evangeline was gonna owe me for this. "Semele VioletMoon," I said, my cheeks burning hot.

Kismet's eyes went wide as her mouth dropped into an *o*, and it was only then that I realized she hadn't been playing games. The name *Evangeline* meant little, but Semele Violet-Moon, she knew intimately. In an instant, her demeanor changed. All the coyness vanished, and in its place appeared a nearly stoic professionalism. She glanced over my shoulder and then waved for me to follow her as she disappeared into a back room.

Like Opal, Kismet kept her real magic in a dusty office. But unlike Opal, who was disorganized as hell, Kismet knew exactly where to find what she was looking for. Standing on tiptoes, she pulled a slender plastic container from the top of a metal shelf. She slid it onto her desk and lifted the lid, retrieving a small package containing what looked like red embroidery floss.

"I think this is what you're after," she said, holding out the package to me. I accepted it, but the skepticism must have shown on my face. "I *personally* worked the magic into those cords at the last blue moon." She said this as though it should mean something to me. "You'll have to activate them with the standard incantation," she said.

I frowned. "Standard incantation? What's that?"

Kismet's eyes narrowed as her brow furrowed. "The... power of three?" When these words failed to register, the woman sighed and dropped her head back. "You're not Wiccan, are you?"

I chewed my lips, suddenly embarrassed. "No," I admitted, "I'm not a witch. I'm not a stranger to magic, though. I'm a Conjure worker."

"A what?"

I faltered. "I practice hoodoo."

Kismet let her breath out in a whoosh. "Well, thank Goddess for that, at least. I swear, if Semele had sent me some wet-behind-the-ears muggle, she and I were gonna have words."

I grimaced. "So, how do I use it?"

Kismet reached for the package she had just handed me and peeled open the plastic, retrieving three individual cords.

"You only need one," she said, "but I sell them by the threes. Triads are more powerful," she explained.

"Triads?"

"One of the foundations of Wiccan witchcraft," she said. "Everything in life comes in threes. Maiden, Mother, Crone. Father, Son, Holy Ghost. Beginning, middle, end. Mind, body, spirit. Past, present —"

"Okay, I get it," I interrupted, staving off impending death by trinities. "Three is the magic number." In my peripheral vision, I saw Angelo choke down a laugh. "So I have to buy all three. How do I use it?"

Kismet took my hands in her own and placed my wrists together. Then, she wound a cord around my wrists in a figure-eight fashion. "You can't perform this spell from afar," she said, not taking her eyes off the cord as she spoke. "This kind of magic is personal, and you must work it just like this. If you want to hurt or heal someone, you do it up close and face to face. Feel the fear you inspire. Detect the trembling. Hear the weeping. Only then can you be sure that what you're doing is just. You must be a part of it. You understand?"

She looked up then, and when her gaze met mine, I saw that her eyes were all ice and steel. I'd seen that look before; it was the look of someone who wasn't playing around. What she was teaching me was precious.

"I understand," I said.

"You'll need to open yourself to whatever energy you can work with," she said. "I don't create spells for just anyone. I find it unethical and dangerous to give a loaded spell to any idiot off the street. To load the spell, you must use your own magic in tandem with the incantation."

Unicorn art and jade eggs aside, it seemed Kismet was a very sensible witch. "What's the incantation?"

She removed the binds from my wrists. "Better not speak it with the binds on you," she said with a smirk. Then, she cocked her head to the side.

"Three knots to find her,
Three more to bind her,
three knots to sever her spell.
One spell behind her,
two spells remind her,
three and her magic is quelled.
By the power of three times three, as I will it, so shall it be."

She blinked. "You need to tie three knots each time the poem mentions doing so. So, nine knots total. And, of course, it's *him* if you're binding a man. Can you remember that?"

"No worries," Angelo said, phone is his hand. "I recorded it."

"Good man," Kismet said, once again all smiles. "Now, there's one last thing you have to remember. Everything you put out to the universe comes back to you times three. So if you're going to bind someone, you better be sure they deserve it. Capisce?"

I nodded. "Similar principles apply in hoodoo," I said. Kismet handed the cords back to me, and I tucked them away. "Anything else we need to know?"

The woman shook her head as she led us back out into the main store. "That's pretty much it. I'll ring you up over here."

After we paid an exorbitant amount of money for the spell-work, I followed Angelo back into the car. He started up the engine and turned to me, his expression shadowed. "While you were chatting with that lady, I got a message from Angie. Right now, Terrence is down at the Blue Oyster Bar shooting pool. He's expecting us. You up to talking to him now?"

I sucked in a breath, beads of sweat popping out along my

brow. "I wasn't exactly expecting to do that today," I admitted, "but no time like the present, I guess. Let's get this over with."

Angelo was quiet as he studied me. "Listen. I know Angie says this guy is her friend. But Angie...well, she's too trusting. She doesn't always understand how people work, you know what I'm saying?"

I nodded. "You're saying I can't trust her instincts on this."

Angelo nodded. "Right. I know you probably think you can handle yourself," he said after a while, "and I hope you don't think me some kinda misogynist for this. But if at any point you don't feel comfortable or things go sideways, you get the hell out of there, you got me? Don't be brave. Just run and let me handle whatever needs handling."

I chortled as I buckled in. "You ain't got to ask me twice. I'm too pretty for a bar fight."

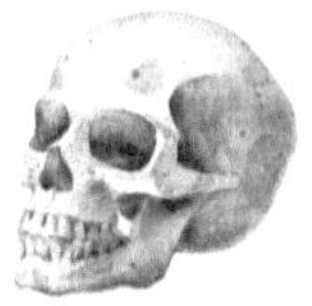

CHAPTER FIVE

THE BLUE OYSTER BAR was in the heart of a bustling, mostly Black neighborhood in Atlanta. Even at this hour, the bar was busy. As we stepped inside, I couldn't help but look at the surroundings from a business owner's perspective. I worked in my brother's bar, and if we had this many people in the early afternoon? Well, let's just say I might not have to work part-time in hospice anymore.

I followed Angelo's lead as he weaved through the crowds, heading toward the billiard tables. Eventually, Angelo drew up short, taking me by the elbow and pulling me against the wall. He motioned with a lift of his chin toward a billiard table on the far side of the bar. "You see that well-dressed guy over in the corner? Blue button-down shirt, dark slacks?"

I squinted into the bar's dimness and gave a little nod. "Yeah. I see him. That's Terrence Curtis?"

Angelo jerked his head to the side. "I'm gonna go sit at the bar and have a drink, but I'll keep my eyes on you. If anything happens, just make some noise, and I'll come running. You got it?"

I nodded. "I really appreciate you being here. But there's a lot of people around. I don't think anything's about to happen in a crowd like this."

Angelo snorted. "You don't know the things I know," was all he said.

As Angelo made his way toward the bar, I swallowed around the lump forming in my throat and squeezed my hands into fists. My palms were sweaty. I maneuvered through the crowds, keeping my eyes on my target. I was still several feet away when he called out to me, never once lifting his eyes from the table. "Don't come any closer."

I stopped in my tracks. "You Terrence Curtis?" I asked.

The man struck the cue ball, and when the shot landed, he grunted with satisfaction. "Might be. Depends who's asking."

I chewed my bottom lip. "My name is Kezia Bernard," I began. "I'm looking for —"

"I don't know you," Terrence interrupted. "Somebody send you? You got business here?"

"Evangeline Morris sent me," I said, refusing to be cowed. "I thought you were expecting me."

Terrence sucked his teeth and for the first time, flicked his eyes in my direction. "Her *friends* call her Angie," he sneered, taking aim at the 5-ball. "So you're not her friend. And you clear as *day* ain't *my* friend. So what the fuck are you doing here?"

I hooked my thumbs in the pockets of my jeans and cocked my head to the side. "You this welcoming to everybody trying to help your ex-lovers, or am I getting a special treatment?"

It had been a shot in the dark, of course. I had no idea

what Evangeline's relationship with Terrence was, but as soon as I spoke the words, something in Terrence's expression cracked. The tiniest ray of light peeked through that thug exterior and he grinned, revealing even, white teeth that gleamed against his dark skin. "You think a woman like Angie would get messed up with the likes of me?"

I shrugged. "Stranger things have happened," I said. "You got a minute, or am I interrupting?"

Terrence grunted and took his shot, missing the pocket by a micro-fraction. I winced; he should have sunk that shot. Irritated, he straightened, narrowing his eyes. "Who are you again?"

"Kezia Bernard," I repeated. "But you won't have heard of me. I'm not anybody. I'm not even a friend of Evangeline's."

Terrence's eyes narrowed ever so slightly. "You just said she sent you."

"That's right," I said. "She sent me as an investigator, I guess you could say."

Now, Terrence stepped away from the pool table, handing his cue stick to one of the men lounging behind him. He was a big man, with short, dreadlocked hair and tattoos on his cheekbones. I hadn't noticed until now, but several of the men standing around the table were eyeing me suspiciously. I guess I should've expected that. What self-respecting *businessman* went to play pool without an entourage in tow?

Terrence jerked his head toward the front of the bar. "Kwame. Did you put gas in the Caddy like I asked you to?" He directed this question to the dreadlocked man with the cue stick.

Kwame, shifting the cue stick from hand to hand, barked a laugh. "Had to, cuz. I made fifteen stops all over town just today." He sucked his teeth and gave me a once-over. "Them bitches was *hongry.* I'm wore the fuck out. And that Italian witch out in Peachtree Park? Girl is a *snack.*"

I rolled my eyes, unimpressed by boasts of sexual prowess. Fifteen in a day? Did he know how absurd he sounded? "Strega," I said. "Italian witches are called Strega."

Kwame narrowed his eyes at me. "So? You know what Ghanaian wizards are called?" He stepped nearer to me. "Daddy," he grinned.

I stepped backward, and he smirked at my discomfort. He must be the Ghanaian wizard Evangeline had told me about. I had never met one before; I had expected someone more refined.

Returning his attention to me, Terrence settled into a wide leg stance, crossing his arms over his broad chest. "And what is it you're investigating, Ms. Bernard?"

Terrence wanted to intimidate me, and it worked. I would rather be just about anywhere than here, but I had a job to do. "Somebody's making trouble for her," I said. "Magical trouble, I guess you could say. She thought you might be able to help us find the culprit. She thought maybe you'd heard something."

Terrence glanced quickly over his shoulder before taking a few steps toward me. As he closed the distance, my adrenaline spiked, and I dug my nails into my palms to keep myself centered and calm. "If you want my help," he said, "you're gonna have to give me more than that. Because from where I stand, it sounds like you're on a fishing expedition, and I'm not in the habit of divulging precious information to *people I don't know.*"

Terrence's expression was veiled but threatening, a thin veneer of detachment hiding a bomb underneath. Was it anger I detected? No, that wasn't it, but I wasn't far off. Hearing that

Evangeline was in trouble *worried* him. I needed to lean into that.

"It's about Dominic," I said. "Somebody put a curse on Evangeline that brought back her necromantic affliction and suppressed her magic. That's why she hasn't been making appearances. And Child Protective Services is onto the problem, and if she doesn't fix it, they'll take her son away from her. So when I say she's in trouble, I'm talking *trouble*. These people are coming for her *family*. They're coming for her *neck*."

Terrence gave a signal to one of his men and then motioned for me to follow him. My eyes flicked briefly to Angelo sitting at the bar, making sure he was watching. He was, his gaze following me as we meandered through the bar and away from the pool tables, toward an empty booth. I slid into the seat across from Terrence, who took his time getting settled in. When he was comfortable, one leg crossed elegantly over the other, he folded his hands on the table and leaned forward. "There's lots of folks in this town that have it in for Evangeline."

I blinked, surprised. "A *lot?* What do you know? What can you tell me?"

Instead of answering, Terrence leaned away from me, resting his arm on the top of the booth. "Why she send you? You said yourself y'all ain't friends, and I ain't seen you before. So who are you? Why are you helping her?"

"I'm a necromancer," I said, deciding to dispense with any ambiguity. "I have a daughter I haven't seen in person in five years," I explained. "She got the blues from me. That kind of thing doesn't happen. If a necromancer actually carries a child to term, that child doesn't get the blues. They're always immune. But in my case?" I couldn't even bring myself to finish the sentence, but I didn't need to. Those words softened the contours of Terrence's face, and for the first time since we met, I thought I saw a glimpse of something like warmth in his eyes. "I had been writing to Evangeline for *years* asking for her help. I wrote to everybody who cured their affliction, but Evangeline is the most high-profile. She seemed most likely to be able to help me."

Terrence nodded. "You know in the height of her career, she was spending more than 10 hours a day granting gifts to people. She lives for the work. They don't make them like that anymore."

I nodded. "I know. That's why I chose her, but she never wrote back. At least, not until recently. She heard about something I had done a couple weeks ago out in Los Angeles. Please don't ask me what it was because I can't tell you. But it impressed her, so she invited me out to her house. Said she'd teach me what she could to help me cure my affliction. But in exchange, she asked me to help her find her enemies and lift her curse. She can't lose her son," I said.

Terrence ran a hand over his face, nodding as resignation pressed his shoulders low. "Angie got her share of haters, all right. I'm not sure they would actually *do* anything against her. She's a powerful force in the community. But you know how people get. Petty. Jealous. I know some folks angry at her because the more gifts she gives out, the less...*vices* their customers need. You follow me?"

I grunted. "When people feel blessed, they don't really need risky sex or drugs," I summarized.

"That's right. So, yeah, there's folks out here wishing Angie harm. But I can't imagine them doing much more than wishing. Still, if it'll help, I'll ask around. See what I can find out."

I hadn't realized I was holding my breath until I suddenly

let it out in a big sigh. "I appreciate it," I said. "Let me give you my number. Contact me when you find anything."

As I pulled my phone out of my pocket to text Terrence my phone number, the other man waved the gesture away. "I know you don't think I got where I am by not knowing how to *find* people." He licked his lips and shook his head as I put my phone away. "If and when I have something to tell Angie, I will let *her* know."

I rolled my eyes as we both slid out of the booth, heading toward the bar's exit. I offered my hand, and to my surprise, Terrence shook it. "By the way," he said, without releasing my hand, "why do you think Angie didn't come down here to see me herself?"

I frowned. "She can't. She's developed agoraphobia. She can't leave the house."

I was about to slip my hand away and leave when Terrence's fingers squeezed against mine. I stopped, confusion twisting my face into a frown. But Terrence was smiling as though nothing in the world were wrong. "One more question, Ms. Bernard," he said, his smile widening. "She could have sent anyone to talk with me. Rocky, Divina, hell, even Angelo over there, pretending he ain't watching everything we do." He smiled with his eyes, and a blush crept up my neck at the realization that we hadn't been as smooth as we'd thought. "Not to mention she could've *called* me. So why'd she send you?"

I shrugged, my discomfort at Terrence's refusal to let go of my hand growing more pronounced. "Because I'm like her. Because I —"

"That ain't it," he interrupted, dropping his voice so it whispered against my skin like velvet. A shiver ran down my spine as he pulled me in, speaking words so softly only I could hear them. "See, my mama raised me right. I was in Tampa last weekend, and they got plenty of necromancers down there. I went to see one of em, so now I got True Colors on me."

He dropped my hand then, winking as he did so. "If I find out anything, I'll let y'all know," he said, too loudly. He dipped his chin and pulled away, disappearing through the crowds.

I watched him a moment, a quiet anger rising in my blood. He was an arrogant sonofabitch, but that wasn't why I was angry. He could have said nothing, letting me think I'd done my job. Instead, he wanted me to know that it wasn't *me* Evangeline trusted.

It was *him*.

By the time Angelo pulled up beside me, I was fuming. I bit my tongue as we pushed our way out the front door, and I managed to stay silent right until we slid into the car. But when he started the engine, I banged my fist on the dashboard. "This whole thing was a fucking test?"

Angelo had the decency to look abashed, refusing to meet my eyes. "I'm not sure what you mean," he lied.

"Before we left, Terrence told me he has the True Colors gift on him. True Colors. Meaning he can see people for what they are, their intentions and all. Evangeline didn't send me here to ask for Terrence's help. She sent me to him to get *read*."

"The good news," Angelo said as he backed out into the street, "is that you're still standing. So I guess you passed."

BACK AT THE HOUSE, we found Evangeline, Rocky, and Divina in the living room surrounded by piles of clothing, books, and household appliances. As we entered, Evangeline looked up and smiled, beckoning for me to come over. "You got here just in time," she said. "Help us fill up these boxes."

I stood before her, arms folded across my chest. "May I speak with you a moment?" I asked. "In private?"

Evangeline's expression didn't shift when she said, "If it's about your visit with Terrence, you can tell me now. We're all family here."

The other women kept working as though we weren't there, and in that moment, I knew everyone had been in on Evangeline's plan but me. The thought left me feeling naked and ashamed. "You could have told me you were sending me to your friend so he could tell you my true intentions. You could have said, *Kezia, I don't know you, so I don't trust you, so please don't take it wrong, but I need you to go get read.* I would've understood that."

But Evangeline barely looked up from the shirt she was folding. "Or," she drawled, "you might have hightailed it off to some unscrupulous cantrip vendor and bought yourself a little glamour and made yourself *look* like something you ain't. That wasn't a risk I wanted to take."

"Like I can afford to just run around buying glamours!" I exclaimed, my frustration and embarrassment getting the best of me. "Do you know how much a spell like that costs? Do you know —"

"Do you know how much I'd have to lose if you weren't what I believed you to be?" She was exasperated now, looking up at me with clear eyes that dared me to retort. I bit my tongue, refusing to take the bait. "I invited you into my home. I invited you to meet my *family*. Did you think I wouldn't do everything necessary to safeguard these people? This life? Ask yourself, Kezia. In my position, wouldn't you have done the same thing?"

I didn't intend to answer that, and judging by the way she went right back to folding clothes, she didn't expect me to. "Does Terrence even *have* connections to the local magical community?" I asked, unable to keep the last of the bitterness from my mouth.

"He definitely does. Terrence has his fingers in everything. Now, if you're done with all that, come over here and help with this."

The others smirked but said nothing. My only options were to walk away in a huff, which seemed counterproductive and juvenile, or join in whatever they were doing. The group was sitting cross-legged in a semicircle, so I swallowed down my pride and joined them. Rocky handed me an armful of T-shirts and motioned with her head to the large box sitting next to me. "Why don't you fold those and stack them inside? That would be a huge help, if you don't mind."

"Sure," I grumbled, forcing lightness into my voice, "but what are we doing? These definitely aren't yours," I said, holding a T-shirt up in front of my face and glancing between the tiny garment and Evangeline.

My host chuckled. "Nah, we taking these down to the women's shelter. Rocky's been out all morning collecting items from some folks in the community. I can't leave the house, but that doesn't mean the work stops." She winked at me. "People think being a pastor is drinking wine and giving a speech once a week. But mostly, it's just community service."

As I was folding the T-shirts, I heard footsteps coming down the stairs. I turned to see Dominic sauntering into the living room before hurling himself like a limp fish onto the couch with a grunt. He whined as he flopped onto his stomach, making puppy dog eyes at his mom. "What are you doing *now*? You said you was gonna come play video games with me."

Evangeline sucked her teeth as she loaded an armload of books into a small box. "I'll be up there in just a minute," she promised. "Don't you see we got stuff going on here? Just because you're bored don't mean women in our community don't still need our help."

Dominic scowled. "How come they always need *your* help? Can't Divina and Rocky help them?"

Evangeline huffed. "*Everybody* helps around here," she said. "You, too. You're getting big enough you can start taking part. Maybe next week, I'll give you your own assignment. You can help run errands on your bike."

Again, Dominic groaned, and I couldn't help but chuckle. "You might like it," I said, dropping another T-shirt into the box. "Won't it be fun to get out of the house for a little while?"

"No," Dominic said with a roll of his eyes.

"I'm gonna drop the stuff off at the shelter, Dominic, and when I get back, you and I can play *Magic the Gathering* together if you want. How does that sound?" Divina wiggled her eyebrows at the boy, and the smile he flashed back at her was toothy and genuine.

"You promise?"

Divina nodded. "Of course. Have I ever lied to you?"

Dominic glanced over at Evangeline. "Mama, you want to play? You can play with three people."

Evangeline ran a hand through her lavender hair. "Maybe some other time."

Dominic propped his elbow on the couch, leaning his head into his hand. "*What* other time? Ever since you got sick, you're here all the time, but you're not really *here*."

I recognized the complaint in his voice. It sounded like longing. I tried to catch his eye, to offer him a sympathetic smile, but he was staring at his mom, waiting for a response.

"Well, Dominic, you know your mom brought me here to help her get better," I said. "So pretty soon things are gonna go back to normal."

Dominic glanced at me only long enough to roll his eyes again. He was going to make a fine teenager someday.

"Dominic, I promise when we're done here, I'll play with you. And we're almost done. And while Divina's gone, we can play any game you want. But after that, you have to pack up your things because you're spending the night with Divina."

Dominic kicked the arm of the couch, not hard enough to do any damage, but with enough force to show he was frustrated. "Why? I don't want to spend the night at Divina's. I want to stay here."

Evangeline lifted an eyebrow. "What have I told you about getting what we want?"

The boy groaned and threw his head back into the sofa cushions. "Nobody ever gets what they want," he droned.

Now, Evangeline chuckled. "No, nobody *always* gets what they want. But you're in luck." She dusted herself off as she climbed to her feet. "I think the ladies can do the rest of this without me. So if you're done moping, we can go upstairs and play."

Dominic jumped to his feet and darted up the stairs with Evangeline close on his heels. When she was halfway up the stairs, however, she turned and planted a hand on her hip. "Oh. Divina, why don't you take Kezia with you down to the shelter?"

Divina glanced up from the shirt she was folding, casting a sideways look in my direction before answering. "That's okay. I've been there plenty of times on my own. I think I can handle it."

Evangeline drummed her long, lacquered nails on the

handrail, clicking her teeth. "That wasn't a request. Take her with you. I want Kezia to see how we do things here."

Divina opened her mouth to respond, but she quickly closed it. Not that Evangeline would have acknowledged the response, anyway. She had already disappeared up the stairs.

Rocky got to her feet next. "Okay, I'm going to go down to the church and make sure the doors are unlocked for the AlAnon folks. Can you guys handle the rest of this?"

Divina grunted. "Apparently, I have a helper today, so it should be no problem."

Rocky reached out to mess up her friend's hair. "So grumpy. You two have fun. I'll see you both for dinner."

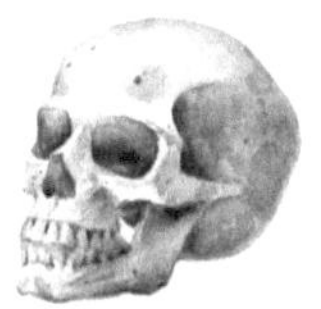

CHAPTER SIX

ONCE IN THE CAR, Divina ignored me for a full 10 minutes before I couldn't take her silence anymore. I turned down the radio and shifted in my seat to face her. "So what are you and Dominic doing tonight? Do you have any fun activities planned?"

Maybe Divina glanced at me from the corner of her eye, but if she did, I didn't see it. "Whatever he wants to do, I guess," she said grudgingly. "I don't usually plan for his visits. I guess I don't really know what kids like to do at slumber parties."

"Well, probably the same things you liked to do at slumber parties when you were young. Watch movies, eat treats...What did you like to do?"

I saw Divina's knuckles whiten as she squeezed the steering wheel. "I didn't really go to a lot of slumber parties," she said finally. "I wasn't allowed."

I nodded. "Sounds like you had folks like mine. I was raised by my step-grandmother, Big Ginny. She always said there was no good reason that a person needed to spend the night at somebody else's house. I was a teenager before I finally got rebellious and started doing it without her permission. She must've been wrong about all that, though. Because I turned out okay."

This time, I saw Divina glance at me sideways. "It wasn't my parents who wouldn't let me," she corrected. "It was the other kids' parents. There was an incident at a party one night, and it ended with everybody crying and going home early. They *blamed* it on me, so."

Sadness settled into the contours of her face as she spoke about that night, and something told me there was more here, something painful and seminal to the abrasive, distant woman I was talking to now. She wasn't unique in that; the injustices of childhood often left indelible marks upon us, even as adults.

I changed the subject. "So we're headed to the women's shelter?"

Divina shook her head. "We have a couple stops to make first. I promised Pamela I would help her move some furniture down at the Boys and Girls Club. I also need to pick up some painting supplies for the folks at First Baptist. We got some other stops to make, too. Just depends on how much time we have."

"You guys do this a lot?"

Divina quirked an eyebrow. "Do what? Charity work?"

I nodded.

Divina barked a laugh then, running her fingers through her hair. "That's pretty much all we do around here. Charity work. If we're not helping the folks at the Boys and Girls Club, we're running errands for the women's shelters, or dropping off food for Meals on Wheels. The only thing Evangeline loves almost as much as her son is feeling like she's doing something right for the community."

"It's got to be really fulfilling, doing all that kind of work."

"You don't do charity work, do you?"

I wanted to give Divina the benefit of the doubt, but I was fairly sure I heard judgment in her voice. I cleared my throat, shaking my head. "Unfortunately not."

"Let me guess," Divina sneered. "You don't have time. Is that right?"

My jaw fell open just as a spike of anger drove my heart rate through the roof. "As it turns out," I said, fighting to keep my voice even, "I don't have the *energy*. I work two jobs — I'm a hospice worker and a bartender. Plus, I take care of my grandmother. You act like everybody has spare time and energy, but *some* of us have draining obligations."

"Oh, I'm sure," Divina said. "And yet, the whole reason you're here in Atlanta is because you're hoping Angie can help you get your Godsend. So, once you get it, you'll have time for *that*, I suppose. Because giving gifts increases your own magic. So you're motivated when it helps you."

"Divina, you don't —"

"No, I do," she interrupted. "I know your type. Plenty of folks just like you come to Evangeline every day. Asking, asking, asking. Never giving. Never. Not once."

I stared at her profile, shaking my head more in wonder than in anger, though I was plenty pissed. She had no idea what she was talking about. I wasn't in Atlanta about my Godsend. I was in Atlanta about my *daughter*. But those words wedged in my throat; Divina hadn't earned the privilege of knowing my personal business. "Why do you dislike me so much?" I asked finally. "Did I do something to offend you?"

"I just don't know why you're *here*," she said, finally turning to me, her eyes narrow. "I mean, I don't know why Angie brought you here. You don't belong. We don't need you. There's nothing going on at the house that we can't handle ourselves."

I sighed, chewing my lip as I thought of the best way to answer this. "Divina, the curse Evangeline has on her is serious. She needs —"

"*You* don't know what she needs! That's my point!" The color was high in Divina's cheeks now. I could practically see the anger rising off her skin like steam. "Rocky and Angelo and I? We've been through *everything* with her. Break-ins. Physical assaults. Evictions. Celia *dying*. *That* was serious. Yet we handled all those things. As a *family*. So why did she bring an outsider here? Why didn't she just *trust us* to take care of her like we've done a hundred other times?"

"Because this isn't something you've dealt with a hundred other times," I retorted. "Divina, I've seen a lot of magic in my day. Curses, hexes, rootwork. And this thing that's eating up Evangeline is something I've never seen before. Never. She needs me because she needs a magic worker. Someone who can work with the currents. Someone who can activate magic — real magic. Why are you taking this personally when it's got nothing to do with you?"

For a moment, it appeared Divina might offer a retort. But the moment passed, and she snapped her jaw shut so tight the tendons stood out on the sides. I wanted to bridge the canyon between us, if for no other reason than we were going to be spending lots of time together, and the last thing I wanted was to share space with someone exuding negative vibes. But I didn't know what to say. So I shut up, shifting in my seat to look out the window in silence.

THE NEXT MORNING, I found Angelo downstairs in the study. He was lounging in an oversized armchair, his legs propped up on an ottoman. He was reading a magazine, but when I entered the room, he looked up with a smile. "There's hot coffee in the kitchen," he said as a greeting. "I can whip you up some eggs and bacon too, if you're hungry."

"Damn son, you're not married, are you? Because I'm in the market for a man who can cook." I flopped onto the couch across from Angelo who started to rise, but I waved for him to sit back down. "I'm only kidding. I'll make myself something in a little while."

Angelo shrugged and turned his attention back to the magazine. "Let me know if you need anything. I figure we have about an hour until we need to leave."

My ears perked up at this, and I threw Angelo a questioning look. "Leave for what? Where are we going?"

Angelo glanced up, his brow drawn in confusion. "Didn't I tell you? I could've sworn I told you."

"Tell me what?"

The big man dropped his feet to the ground, rested his elbows on his knees. "We have an appointment to go look at a house today."

I barked a laugh, shaking my head. "I was only kidding about looking for a husband. I'm definitely not ready to make that kind of commitment."

Angelo's smile broadened. "Well, we're just pretending to look at a house. I made the appointment so we could talk to Crystal Waters."

"Why the subterfuge? Why don't we just meet her for lunch or something?"

"Oh, it's not a trick," Angelo said. "I asked her to lunch, but she said she had a showing. But she invited us to come down, so I said we would. But like I said, we need to leave in about an hour. So I don't know what all you have to do, but..."

I groaned and got to my feet. "All right, you made your point. Guess I'll go get that coffee and then go have a shower. You need anything while I'm up?"

Angelo only grunted and waved me away.

WE LEFT EXACTLY AN HOUR LATER. The house we were visiting was tucked away in one of those cute intentional communities just outside Atlanta. I felt self-conscious as we pulled up to the gate, the guards peering into our car with a frown as they waved us through. I always felt overly aware of my skin wandering into neighborhoods like this. That wasn't a reflection of the other people who lived there. It was just my own personal paranoia. I didn't feel like I belonged. It made me nervous.

And I hated that it made me nervous. There was no reason for me to feel guilty for existing in my skin. But some things are hard to unlearn.

"What's the address again?" Angelo asked.

"1411 Jicama Ave.," I said, reading from the Zillow ad. "I still don't understand why you came with me. I don't think I need a bodyguard for this excursion."

Angelo adjusted the sunglasses that rested on the bridge of his nose, offering a carefree shrug. "Just don't feel right sending somebody new on such an important investigation," he said after a little while. "I know that makes it sound like I don't trust you, and I don't want you to get the wrong idea. But —"

I snorted at that, shaking my head as I folded my arms across my chest. "You don't have to say it," I interrupted. "Divina gave me the spiel yesterday. It's not that you guys don't trust me, it's just that you don't understand why Evangeline *does*. Even after I proved myself with Terrence, y'all are still butt hurt that I'm here. You're feeling left out and moody and you're grumpy about it. Is that about right?"

It took Angelo a moment to answer. "That might be how Divina feels, but it's not how I feel. This has nothing to do with trust. It's more that I don't understand how magic works. I don't know what's happening to Evangeline. And because I don't understand, I don't feel comfortable leaving any of this to chance. I never much thought of myself as a control freak, but here I am, trying like hell to control a situation I barely understand. Because that's my responsibility. To myself, to Angie, even to you."

A warm flush crept up my cheeks, and I suddenly felt damp at my hairline, my palms clammy. "I'm sorry," I muttered. "That was an asshole thing to say, and I don't even have an excuse."

Angelo gave a curt little nod. "I won't hold it against you. I think this is it."

1411 Jicama was a cute little ranch-style house with great curb appeal. The street was lined with emerald green, perfectly manicured lawns, with a handful of children running up and down the sidewalks or screeching on their bikes. If I were really in the market for a house, I would've been attracted to this one. Too bad I could never afford something like this.

We had hardly knocked on the door when it swung open, revealing a petite woman flashing us a thousand-watt smile. She was smartly dressed in slacks and a linen blouse, her salt-and-pepper bob flat-ironed to within an inch of its life. She was probably of an age with Evangeline, though she had long since shed any hippie fashion tendencies while Evangeline hadn't. Now, she'd aged into something altogether striking. She smiled pertly as she extended her hand. "Hello and welcome. Please come in."

Angelo and I followed the woman into the house, taking off our shoes so as not to soil the carpet. The house smelled like freshly baked cookies; even I knew that was an old realtor's trick. People liked houses that smelled like sweets. "Well, it's nice to meet you," she began. "My name's Crystal. I'll be showing you around today."

Angelo and I exchanged glances. "Well, uh, we're not here to see the house," Angelo said. "We spoke on the phone earlier? I'm Angie's friend. Angelo Rodriguez?"

Crystal's face lit up like a lightbulb. "Of course! So sorry; I didn't know you were bringing company." She offered me her hand. "Crystal Waters," she said.

"Kezia Bernard. Nice to meet you."

"I'm sorry I had to bring you all the way out here," she said with a sigh. "But, as you can see, this is a great property. I'm hoping for a tidy little commission when I sell this one." She dropped us both a wink, as though we were all in on a joke together.

"It's no problem," I said. "We're just glad you could make time for us."

"Any friend of Semele's," she said, suddenly sobering. She turned her attention to Angelo. "You said she was in some kind of trouble? You weren't very specific on the phone."

"Sorry about that," he said, looking apologetic. "Sometimes these things are easier to discuss in person."

Crystal hemmed and nodded, wringing her hands. "Well, what's going on? It's nothing serious, I hope?" She glanced between us. "To be honest, I thought she might come out to see me herself." I thought I detected a slight wobble to her chin.

"She can't," I explained. "That's...well, that's part of why we're here."

Even though I had already been through this once before with Terrence Curtis, I found I wasn't sure where to begin or how to explain. "It seems she's having some trouble of a magical variety," I said. "She's developed agoraphobia; she can't leave the property. And that's just the tip of the iceberg," I explained. "Since she can't leave, she asked me to make some visits on her behalf. She says you have your finger on the pulse of the community and a strong network. She thought you might be able to help."

Crystal held out her hands, supplicant. "Help how?"

"Just...Information, I guess? Have you heard anything? Do you know people who might have a grudge against Evangeline? Anything like that?"

Crystal heaved a heavy sigh and tilted her head back until her face was bathed in the sunlight pouring in from the living room window. "Agoraphobia," she whispered. "And she's sure a *person* did this?"

I wasn't sure what Crystal was getting at, but my skin prickled over instinctively. *I don't like the sound of that,* I thought. In the recesses of my mind, I thought I heard Papa Jinabbott bark his strong agreement. "What do you mean? What else could have done this?"

Crystal blew out a frustrated sigh, her expression darkening. "Shit. I was hoping to never have this conversation."

Angelo stepped closer, his presence looming large and intimidating over both of us. "What conversation's that?" he asked.

Crystal ran a hand over her face, somehow avoiding smudging her perfect makeup. "Did Angie tell you I sold her that property?"

I nodded. "Yeah, it came up. Why?"

"I don't want you to think I knew this at the time, because I didn't. But if Angie's developed agoraphobia, there's a good chance that *nobody* cast a spell on her. It's the property. The fucking property is probably cursed."

Angelo and I exchanged dark glances, but it was Angelo who spoke first, his voice gravelly and laced with concern. "Cursed how? What are you talking about?"

Crystal glanced around the living room. "Now I wish we *had* done this at a bar or restaurant so at least we can have a place to sit down. And a martini." She sighed again, and I saw despair all over her face. "I learned what she did to the place last year. Have you been out to the property? Have you seen it?"

I nodded. "I have. She's turned the front half of the house into an office. She's running her church operation —"

Crystal interrupted me with a shake of her head, raising her hand. "I'm not talking about the interior renovations. Have you seen the graveyard?"

"Oh. Yeah, I've seen it. It's gorgeous. I've never heard of anybody moving that many graves. It's really a stunning accomplishment."

"Did you know there used to be another family buried there?"

I blinked, glancing at Angelo, whose expression was blank. "Used to be?"

"Correct. As in, was buried there in the past, isn't anymore."

I shrugged. "No, I didn't know that. I knew she had her

family brought in, but this is the first I'm hearing about some other family moved out."

Crystal blew out her cheeks. "Well, they were. And I think their ghosts may not have been too happy at having their corpses moved."

I gaped. "*Ghosts?*"

Crystal hung her head, chagrin coloring her cheeks. "When we bought the house, the seller was this old fart — I couldn't possibly recall his name. His realtor told me that Old Fart thought the house was haunted. He *had* to tell me that — it's against the law to withhold information about a property. But I spoke with Old Fart, and the guy was certifiable. He was a complete crack pot. So I chalked up the whole 'haunted' malarky to old-people nonsense and called it a day."

Now, I was familiar with old-people nonsense. You couldn't work in hospice without getting a good dose of superstition, wives' tales, and even just run-of-the-mill dementia on the daily. But I also knew that sometimes, old people only *sounded* crazy. Like when they said they saw a ghost in their room moments before they themselves died. Lots of times, the families freaked out when their dying said these things. It was my job to comfort everyone and assure them everything was fine.

...Even when there really *was* a ghost in the room. Which, frankly, there often was. Ghosts sometimes appeared to their loved ones at their time of death. They rarely hung around, but they did appear.

"Well, anyway," Crystal continued, "Angie bought the house and I never really gave it another thought until now. But...you said she can't leave the property, right?"

I nodded. "That's right. When she tried, she had a complete panic attack. She doesn't even try anymore."

Crystal nodded, tapping a finger against her chin. "Right.

Well, listen, I'm not a curse expert, if such a person even exists. But here's a hypothesis: if the remains that Angie had moved weren't properly handled, that could incite a curse, especially if the place was already haunted."

"And by *haunted* you mean contained an unwanted astral imprint of the people who used to live there?"

Crystal's gaze shifted from me to Angelo as she held up her hands in confusion. "What's she talking about?"

Angelo smirked. "She's a necromancer." He said this like it explained something.

Which apparently it did, because a look of understanding dawned over Crystal's face. "I see. Well, sure. I just mean there were ghosts there."

I smiled. "Right. Ghosts are just astral imprints. Kind of like footprints. They're not the actual souls of the people who lived there. Their souls have moved on." Crystal didn't respond to this, so I kept going. "I've heard of a phenomenon called *involuntary torment* that can occur when a sacred place or thing is mishandled or mistreated. No one actively *places* the curse; the curse just *occurs* as the result of an interruption of natural processes. Like a pathology in the body."

"Yes," Crystal agreed, her head bobbing enthusiastically. "I don't know at all what that means, but it sounds good."

"Well," I began, warming up to the topic, "a biological pathology —"

"No, no," Crystal interrupted. "Please, don't consider me smart or interested enough for an explanation. I'll take your word for it."

Ignoring this entire line of conversation, Angelo cleared his throat. "Can it be cured?"

Crystal chewed her lips, a cloud of doubt passing behind her eyes. "I *think* the effects can be cured with the right spell — though please don't ask what that would be, as I don't know," she said. "But if you don't address the underlying cause and she stays on the property, something else could take its place. Some other...*pathology*, to use Kezia's clever word."

"So, her agoraphobia might be cured, but something *else* could go wrong?" I asked, incredulous.

"I really don't know," Crystal said, sympathy elongating her words. "Like I said, I'm no expert. But it might be smart to cure the current crisis — the agoraphobia — and then, you know." She leaned forward, dropping her voice even though there was no one around to overhear. "Get the hell out."

I sighed. "You mean sell. Sell a cursed house. That she'd have to disclose."

Crystal's frown deepened. "She could get lucky. The buyer could just not believe us. It's happened before." Her words were bitter with irony.

"All right," I said. "I guess the priority now is to try fixing the underlying problem. We should try returning the property to the state it was in when Evangeline bought it. We can't remove Evangeline's family graves, but we might be able to bring the previous corpses back."

Angelo lowered his chin to his chest as he thought, a cloud of concentration settling over his features. "I think Rocky handled the relocation," he said. "So if there were bodies on the property, she'd be the one who dealt with them. We'll have to talk to her to find out where they were moved to and how we might retrieve them."

I returned my attention to Crystal. "All right, this has been a good start, but let's back up for a minute. Let's assume that the house *isn't* cursed, and that an actual person consciously did this. Can you think of anybody who might cause magical trouble for Evangeline?"

The corners of Crystal's mouth dipped down into a frown. "Everybody loved Semele," she said, her voice soft. "I mean, yeah, there's people jealous of her success. Some people were sad that she left Wicca to start a Christian church, especially in the beginning. They called her a traitor and everything. But that was a long time ago. I can't imagine that anybody in the Goddess community is still ticked off enough to be casting black magic on her today. Besides, aside from me, there aren't very many people around who even have the talent."

I quirked an eyebrow. "Really?"

Crystal blushed, stammering out a response. "Not to toot my own horn," she said, "but most Wiccans are just dabblers. They couldn't perform a real magic spell to save their lives. But our coven was special. We were the real deal. Too bad none of us are still practicing — well, no one except Kismet. Semele became a pastor, Iris became a Buddhist, and Clover passed away a few years ago. Cancer," she added, eyes downcast. "But anyway, I'll keep an ear to the ground. And if you guys *do* decide to sell..." She gave an impotent shrug. "You know how to reach me. I wouldn't even take a commission. It's my fault she's in this mess, after all."

"We really appreciate your time, Crystal," Angelo said. "Thank you. And hey. I hope you sell this house soon."

"Oh, hell," Crystal said with a roll of her eyes. "At this point, I just hope this goddamn place isn't haunted."

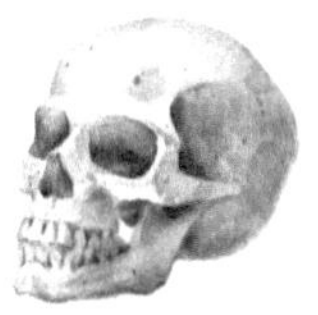

"GRAVES ON THE PROPERTY? Sure, of course I remember."

We were gathered on the patio, Rocky with her long legs draped over the side of a rocking chair as she smoked a clove cigarette, and Angelo and I standing with our arms folded over our chests. Rocky took a deep drag, then exhaled, peering at us through smoke that smelled like Christmas. "Why do you ask?"

Angelo quickly summarized our visit with Crystal, emphasizing the part where the removal of the graves might have caused Evangeline's curse. "So," he said, reaching the end, "we need to know what you remember about the graves. Do we have any records or anything?"

Rocky nodded. "Yeah, probably? I remember the whole thing being a *way* bigger hassle than it should have been because to move graves here in Georgia, you need an archaeologist present. It's like the law and stuff." She cocked her head to the side, squinting at Angelo. "You don't remember this?

Yeah, you remember, because I didn't have the first *clue* how to find an archaeologist, so I had to ask Devon for help. I had to get his number from you cuz Angie was busy."

Angelo cursed to himself, digging his hands in his pockets. "Right. I remember you asking for Devon's number. Shit. I should have remembered."

My gaze bounced between the two of them, waiting for someone to explain. When no one did, I cleared my throat. "Who's Devon?"

Angelo growled, his hands clenching at his sides. "Somebody I shoulda known better than to involve in anything that matters."

Rocky waved her hand, dismissing the complaint. "Angie didn't mind. She trusts Devon."

I opened my mouth to ask again who Devon was, but Angelo beat me to the quick. "Devon Curtis. Terrence's brother. Guess you could say theirs is a family business."

Ah. Another *businessman*. I turned to Rocky. "Okay, so what happened to the graves? Where did they get moved to?"

Rocky leaned her head to the side, her eyes listing upward as she smoked. "Well, I don't remember exactly. I was more interested in getting Evangeline's family moved in, not so much interested in getting the old families moved out. You know I'm saying?"

I sighed and ran a hand over my hair, giving Rocky a pointed look. "I really need you to think about this. If Crystal's right and we've catalyzed some kind of involuntary torment, I need to make that right. But to do that, I need to find those remains. I need to know who they were, where they went, where they are now."

Rocky tapped the end of her cigarette, letting the ash fall to the floorboards. "Yeah, I get it. *Involuntary torment*. I like that. Sounds like some shit Angie would say. You remind me of her," she said, lips curving in a smile around the butt of her cigarette. "You're smart like she is. I bet Divina *hates* you," she laughed, shaking her head, her shoulders quaking with her chuckles. "Anyway, I'll look into where they took the caskets. I keep good records, so I'm pretty sure I can dig up a name or something. It might take me a few days." She stretched and dropped the cigarette, crushing it out with the heel of a cowboy boot. "So, do you really think the property is cursed?"

I heaved a sigh, shaking my head. "You know what, I don't know. I don't even know what to hope for. Curses can be hard to break, but at least I have some experience with that."

Rocky's eyes went wide. "Yeah? You've broken curses before?"

I laughed, charmed by the admiration in the question. "My grandmother and I are Conjure workers. We practice hoodoo. I'd say about half of our business is dealing with people who *think* they've been cursed. Only about a quarter actually are. Still, it's enough that I've had plenty of practice."

Rocky's eyes grew even larger at this admission. "Man, that's so cool! I wish I had magic like you and Angie. She can do the most amazing things. Well, at least she could. Before she got sick."

Silence settled between us, growing thick and uncomfortable. Finally, Rocky stood up, dusting off her hands. "I'm gonna go smoke a bowl," she announced. "Anybody wanna join me?"

Both Angelo and I shook our heads. "Thanks," I said, "but I don't smoke."

Rocky tendered a limp shrug, heading into the house. "Suit yourself," she called as the front door shut behind her.

As Rocky disappeared inside, Angelo fell into the now-vacant rocking chair, rubbing his face with his hands. "I don't know why Evangeline lets her handle anything important," he muttered. "She doesn't take anything seriously."

"Well, maybe she's training her," I said, shrugging. "You know, trying to make the weakest link stronger."

Angelo snorted. "She's more than a weak link. She's a goddamned liability. What do you wanna bet she has no idea what she did with that paperwork? I mean, I love her, but jeez, she's a goddamned liability."

"Y'all talking about Rocky?"

We turned to find Divina coming up from the side lawn, smirking. She wore a wide-brimmed straw hat, overalls muddied at the knees, and rubber boots. "Why, what did she fuck up this time?" She peeled off her soiled work gloves and tossed them to the grass. When she saw me looking, she narrowed her eyes. "Weeding," she said.

It was probably just my imagination, but I felt like she'd just thrown down a gauntlet. Like, *Hey, I worked in the garden. What have you actually done since you've been here?*

Angelo gave Divina an exasperated look. "Did you know there was another family buried on this property when Evangeline moved her family cemetery in?"

Divina shook her head. "Really?"

Angelo nodded. "Apparently, Evangeline put Rocky in charge of relocating the graves. Problem is, she doesn't know where they were moved or what happened to them."

Divina removed her hat, wiped her brow with the back of her hand. "Yeah, that sounds like Rocky. But why is that a problem?"

Angelo glanced at me before answering. "Turns out all this trouble with Angie might be because the property is cursed. The curse resulting from Rocky inappropriately moving the graves."

Divina frowned, coming around to walk up the porch steps. "That doesn't make sense," she said. "That happened years ago. The stuff Angie's dealing with is new."

"It's not uncommon for these things to build up over time," I explained. "In phenomenon like an involuntary torment, it's almost like the property gets angry over time until —"

Divina guffawed, rolling her eyes. "The *property* gets angry," she repeated wryly.

"Come on, Divina," Angelo said. "Give her a break, huh? She's trying to help."

Divina squinted at me before returning her attention to Angelo. "Well, I guess it's not totally impossible. The thing about the curse, I mean. Most cultures have stern beliefs about how to treat the dead. I know I wouldn't like it if my ancestors were disturbed. Well, assuming I knew who my ancestors were."

I knew it was none of my business, and the smarter part of my brain was telling me to shut up and let sleeping dogs lie. But as a fellow person who didn't know much about the family who birthed her, I couldn't tamp down the emotions that Divina's wistful expression evoked. "Have you ever tried to find them? Your biological family? You're adopted, right?"

It took Divina a minute too long to answer, and for a moment I really wished I had listened to my smarter brain and kept my mouth shut. But to my surprise, Divina didn't bite my head off. "I tried once," she said, suddenly taking a keen interest in her cuticles. "When I was seventeen, I applied for a Creek Nation college scholarship, and I got it. I was feeling proud and unstoppable, so I reached out to the caseworker who handled my adoption to ask about my parents, but I didn't hear from her. Later, I got a letter with no return address that said I was better off not knowing who my folks were. I figured that was a sign, so I dropped it. Anyway, right around the time I was graduating with my degree in social work, my advisor told me that a Black lady was adopting a half Black, half Creek baby and was looking for a Big Sister to step in and be, you know, like a mentor. And I agreed. And that's how I met Angie and Dom and they've been my family ever since."

"I see," I said. "I've been looking for my mom all my adult life. Still haven't found her."

Divina offered a non-committal hrmm. "What about your pops?"

I grimaced, shaking my head. "He's alive, but my grand-mother — his stepmother — made it clear she wants nothing to do with him. That's a good enough warning for me. Not everybody is cut out to be a parent."

"I guess," Divina said, cutting her eyes and tilting her head. "Though I *do* think anybody who willfully walks away from their child deserves their place in Hell."

Her words lit my skin on fire; the thrum of my blood was a freeway in my ears. I couldn't know if she meant to aim an arrow directly at my heart, but before I could choose a direction for my emotions to run, Angelo climbed to his feet, clapping Divina on the arm. "Let's go see if we can help Rocky find those papers," he said. Turning to me, he added, "Let me know if you hear from Terrence or Crystal."

The two drifted inside, leaving me alone on the porch, shivering despite the heat. She couldn't have meant anything by it, could she? She had no reason to hate me enough to be intentionally cruel. Curing myself so I could get my daughter back was my singular mission in life. It was the entire reason I was *here*.

And yet. I *had* left. And sure, leaving was the right thing to do, because Lola showed signs of the blues. Staying would have been diabolical.

...But I could have kept in touch. I could have called, written letters, sent presents. I didn't have to go invisible. I didn't have to *abandon* her how I had.

I stood on the porch for a long time, staring out over the expansive front lawn, the sounds of the neighborhood echoing in my ears. But I wasn't really aware of any of it. All I saw and heard were tear-stained images of Lola, crying herself to sleep, wondering why her mother had never come for her.

SOMEHOW, I made it through dinner, through jaunty conversation and good-natured ribbing. Even Divina seemed in a bright mood as Evangeline and the others told stories about the past, carousing over roast beef, hot biscuits, and the brandy sidecars I kept refilling. I smiled and laughed in all the right places, but a broken record was playing in my head, filling my mind with thoughts of my daughter and Divina's bitter words. We finished the evening with slices of key lime pie, and after I helped with the dishes, I retired to my room, politely declining a post-dinner game of *Clue*.

I had barely changed into my nightgown and tucked my hair into a silk wrap when there came a knock on my door. I pulled it open to find Evangeline with a tray of tea.

"May I come in?"

I stepped aside mutely and Evangeline entered, setting the tray on the foot of the bed. She poured hot water and spooned some honey into a cup already prepared with a tea bag, which she handed to me. "Lavender," she said. "It'll help you sleep."

I accepted the teacup with a frown. "Thank you, but I'm not much of a tea drinker. Always preferred coffee. Besides, I seldom have trouble sleeping."

"You might tonight," she said, pouring herself a cup. She took a seat at the small vanity, leaving the more comfortable slipper chair to me. I sat down and sipped the tea to be polite. It tasted of flowers and sugar, but wasn't altogether bad.

"Why do you say that?"

Evangeline shrugged, took a sip from her cup. "You usually work nights, right? I imagine you're used to falling in bed exhausted after a hard night's work. I suspect being here hasn't been quite the same, has it?"

I curled my feet up underneath me, plucked the tea bag out of the water and set it on the saucer. "I guess," I said, though I suspected Evangeline wasn't telling me the whole truth. Maybe I hadn't kept as brave a face at dinner as I'd thought.

"How are you getting along with the others?"

There it was. I glanced up to see Evangeline peering at me, her expression curiously blank. "I'm used to being an outsider," I said finally.

Evangeline chuckled. "That's not really an answer, but I'mma let that slide." She set her teacup in her saucer and placed the whole thing on the vanity. "You're having trouble with Divina."

I liked that she didn't make it a question. It meant I didn't have to lie. "She doesn't like me much."

"She doesn't like anyone much," Evangeline agreed, "but I don't want you to take it personally. She had a rough upbringing."

"Name me one person you know who ain't had it rough at some point," I said. "My mother died giving birth to me. I don't know my father. My favorite teacher died from the blues when I was a child. I gave up a career in biology because my professor stopped believing in me, and then I lost my husband *and* my —"

My voice broke then, and I couldn't continue. I put the teacup on a side table, dabbing at my eyes with my knuckles. Evangeline didn't try to console me. She simply finished her tea before drawing to her feet. She gestured to my teacup. "Please try to finish that. You don't have to say it, but I know there's a lot weighing on you. That's my special blend. It'll help."

I scarcely glanced at the teacup, my vision gone blurry. "You know what will help?" I said before I could stop myself. "If we cured my affliction. We haven't even started on that since I've been here."

Evangeline paused, her hand on the doorknob. "I haven't forgotten," she said. "Good night, Kezia."

As soon as my head hit the pillow, I was asleep.

And I dreamed.

I was in Big Ginny's kitchen, the same kitchen that waited for me back in Los Angeles. But the paint on the wall was mint green, not baby blue, and that's how I knew I was standing in a much earlier version of that kitchen. I smelled coffee and Jean Naté. The sounds of gospel music drifted in from the living room.

It was Sunday.

I watched the scene like a movie, an outside observer peeping on my own life as a much younger me, maybe six or seven, skipped into the kitchen dressed only in a full cotton slip, the kind with the little pink bow at the neckline. I climbed into a chair turned away from the table set with Queen Helene's cocoa butter and Vaseline. Big Ginny came in behind me carrying a plastic hairbrush, a comb, a spray bottle, and a little baggie of rubber bands.

"You grease your face?"

Little me rolled her eyes and licked her lips. "Yes, Big Ginny," she droned. The shine of baby oil on her face told all the truth. "*And* I brushed my teeth." She said this with a little smirk, a psychic answering a question before it was asked.

"Don't get smart," Big Ginny said as she parted little me's hair, nimble fingers quickly braiding each section. "You got that dollar Miss Parker gave you for the collection plate?"

"I got it," the girl replied.

"Good. Go ahead and grease them legs, now. Them knees ashy."

I couldn't help but smirk as I watched this familiar exchange, a ritual Big Ginny and I must have performed hundreds of times. I didn't need to see down the hall to know that my brother Lamont was in the bathroom shaving his sorry excuse for a beard, after which he'd dab on too much aftershave.

As little me reached for the bottle of cocoa butter on the table, a flutter of movement from the corner of the room caught my attention. At first it looked like a trick of light, a thickening of shadow. But as I watched, I saw a form take shape in the dimness. I blinked, confused.

It was...a rabbit.

But even as the shape became clear, a chill ran down my spine. I had experience with dreamworld animals, and I knew that sometimes a rabbit wasn't just a rabbit. My own patron, Papa Jinabbott, was an animage who could turn into snakes, moths, spiders, whatever. Even from beyond the grave, he'd been known to manifest as an array of creepy nocturnal creatures. And so, while someone else might mistake the cuddly leporid for an inoffensive bunny, I was wary.

I thought for a moment the rabbit saw me, though that would have been strange since the humans in my dream didn't. But after a moment, I realized the rabbit wasn't looking at me at all. It was watching Big Ginny and little me, just like I was. Its ears angled ever so slightly toward them. I imagined it grinning.

My younger self's hair was in a giant poof all over her head, except for the locks my grandmother had wet down and deftly braided. My grandmother worked as little me rubbed lotion and Vaseline into her knees. My eyes flit to the rabbit in the corner. I still couldn't see any semblance of an expression — it was a rabbit, after all — but the careful way it watched little me and Big Ginny felt intrusive. Creepy.

Suddenly, for no reason I could articulate, I wanted to cloak the whole scene in darkness, blotting it from the rabbit's view. I didn't want it to see me like this, in my shift, my hair in my grandmother's hands. I didn't want it to smell the Queen Helene's mixed with coffee and Jean Naté. It was absolutely, positively ridiculous to have such strong feelings about a rabbit, but I couldn't help it. These were *my* memories. Memories that linked me to my past, my family, my people. They were an intimate part of me, and I didn't want to share them.

Not even with a rabbit.

I stepped forward, the reptilian part of my brain trying to protect the women of my subconscious from this interloper. But as my jaws unhinged and my tongue fell from the roof of my mouth, it wasn't my voice that broke through the dream.

It was a cry.

I cocked my head, my ears perking at the sound. It was a voice. A woman's voice.

A woman's voice crying out for help.

I awoke with a start, my eyes flying open in the darkness, my body suddenly on high alert. I held my breath as I listened. When I didn't hear anything, I threw the covers from my body and swung my legs over the side of the bed. It was a warm night, and I was damp with sweat, shivering against the air.

Again, I paused. Listened.

I reached for the phone on the nightstand. It was just past 2 in the morning. I grimaced as my bladder pushed me to my feet and propelled me down the hall toward the bathroom. But no sooner had I reached the bathroom door that I heard it.

The cry.

I froze, tilting my head as I strained to listen harder. Something was off. Something...

And then I understood. I wasn't hearing it with my ears. I was hearing it with the same part of me that allowed me to work magic and direct the death current and speak with the dead. The same part of me that smelled palo santo and lemon when death was near. I heard the woman's cry with my soul.

My bladder forgotten, I crept down the stairs, wincing at each squeaky step, afraid to wake the house. I made my way quickly toward the back door, easing it open. The night air was still, thick, and warm, and as I stepped into the night, I thought I caught the faint scent of magnolia and lavender tea.

I heard the cry again, louder this time. I followed my senses into the dark. Ambient light from the city blotted out the stars, but the moon was bright. Even so, my eyes took their time adjusting. Since I didn't know the layout of the cemetery well, I moved with slow caution, guiding myself with my hands as I shuffled across the grass.

After a few moments, the blackness gave way to gray as my pupils dilated. In the distance, two silhouettes stood unmoving amid the shadows. Men, judging by their size. Their backs were to me as they spoke to each other, a low muttering I couldn't quite make out.

I crept along the shadows, keeping myself out of sight. My logical brain was screaming at me to turn around and call the police, wake the neighbors, do *anything* but approach the two strange men doing God-knows-what in Evangeline's cemetery. But even as the thoughts materialized, I dismissed them out of hand. I didn't want to turn around. Stupidly, insanely, I felt with every fiber of my being that I needed to confront the men. That I needed to stop them.

I'd had a similar feeling that day I'd met Terrence Curtis in the bar. Though my brain told me to be afraid, my body acted like it could handle itself. Like it knew how to battle. Like I was five-and-a-half-feet of high-protein diet instead of five-and-a-half feet of Big Ginny's fried plantains. My body seemed to move on its own, on instinct. The adrenaline pulsing through my veins was making me shake, and I clenched my fists to steady myself. I didn't want to make a sound and alert the intruders of my presence.

When their mumbled mutterings became words, I slowed my pace even more to listen better. "Try again," one man was saying. "Don't trip over the words. He said you have to get it exactly right."

"Feel free to try it yourself, my nigga," the other man complained, the edge of his voice tilting toward agitation. "It's too damn dark out here to make the words out properly."

"Here." I heard rustling. "Use the flashlight on my phone.

Hurry up! We ain't got all night."

Then the first man began to speak. He was reading something in a foreign language, words I'd never heard before. My heart sped up, and I began to sweat as I realized what was happening. He was reading an incantation.

Suddenly, the ground jerked beneath my feet, throwing me off balance. Both men yelped and stumbled backward, losing their footing. Again, I heard the woman's cries, louder and more urgent this time. Her voice reverberated throughout my body and my eyes grew wide in the darkness as I searched for the creator of that awful sound.

"Holy shit, it's working!"

From my vantage point, I couldn't see what was happening. Crouching low, I strafed along the tombstones to get a better look.

Black holes like gaping mouths appeared in the grass. Each hole was ejecting stuff: pale objects of differing sizes and shapes that landed soundlessly on the grass. The men ducked, jumping out of the way of the projectiles shooting from the ground.

"He ain't said it would be like this!" one man said.

"I don't think you did it right! Do you see it yet? Do you see the skull?"

"It ain't come up yet! Shit!"

That's when I realized what was happening.

The earth was spitting out human bones.

For a moment, I stood in stark disbelief, watching the chaos unfold. But then, out of nowhere, I felt a lightning bolt slither up my spine. It was like someone flipped a switch, and suddenly, I went into fight or flight mode with the flight option crossed out.

Heart racing. Adrenaline coursing. Lungs expanding.

Well, Mama Fat said, *you just finna stand there or you bout to whoop some ass?*

Naw, Mama Fat. I ain't about to stand here, I thought back at her.

I was about to whoop some ass.

My body became a wrecking ball as I hurled myself at the strangers, the flat of my shoulder catching one man in the solar plexus. He grunted as he fell, carried by my momentum to the spongy ground. I reeled back, intending to pound him in the face, but a bone shot out of the earth heading for my head, and I rolled off my victim just in time to dodge. As I rolled over, the second man jumped on top of me, his hands digging into my hair, pressing my face into the dirt, trying to pin me down. With a scream, I rolled over, dodging more exploding bones, and elbowed my assailant in the nose. He screeched as he rolled off me, and I leaped to my feet.

The first man was on his feet now, lunging at me, grabbing me from behind. His arms hooked under my armpits, his hands clasped behind my neck. I couldn't see well from that position, but I didn't need to. I was a wild thing. I leaned into his chest, using him for leverage as I kicked hard, catching the other man in the stomach.

It all happened so fast. How was I doing this? I didn't know how to fight! But at that moment, bucking and kicking and growling, I was like a person possessed by a demon. I feared nothing and no one. Writhing and screeching and trying to jam my elbow in my attacker's midsection, my logical brain turned off. I was all adrenaline and lizard instincts.

"There! Over there! Grab the skull!" the man at my back shouted. The man I'd kicked was huffing and swearing as he staggered into the shadows, then leaned over to swipe something from the ground.

"Got it! Put her down, and let's get the fuck up on outta here."

I steeled myself for what I knew was coming. A blow struck me from behind, and my knees buckled as my vision dissolved into stars before going black. I sank to my knees before falling face first in the damp grass, the back of my head wailing in agony.

I curled onto my side, gasping and furious. My body ached, and by the time the two men ran off, I was near exhaustion. I listened as they disappeared through the side yard. I didn't see where they went. For now, it was enough that they were gone.

What the hell had just happened?

Magic, I realized. And not just magic, but my *gift*. As soon as the thought materialized my brain, I recognized it as truth. I'd never *heard* of a gift that commanded the body to fight like that. Most gifts involved psychic abilities or preternatural charisma, things like that. But there was no doubt in my mind that I had fought those men off because of a gift granted to me temporarily by my ancestors.

I sat up, looking around at the carnage. It was too dark, and I was too ignorant to know whether any of the bones had been damaged in our scuffle. I climbed onto all fours, preparing to stand when I heard the woman again, her cries less urgent. And suddenly, without understanding how, I realized that the bones scattered on the ground belonged to the woman wailing in my mind.

I didn't want to, but I couldn't stop myself. I reached out and touched the bone closest to me, a femur, my fingers curling around its diameter, clutching it against my palm. Pain surged through my body, followed quickly on by anguish, fear, and anger. Images flashed through my mind, too fast to comprehend. I saw faces, smiles, sunsets, hands, darkness, tears. In an instant, a lifetime of her memories tore through my body, leaving the delicate imprint of her life on my soul.

I looked to the angel, its vacant, stone eyes refusing to meet mine as it held aloft its lightless lantern. *So much for protecting the dead,* I thought bitterly. Climbing to my feet, I sought out the tombstone, struggling to read the name by the moon's meager light. *Delia Rae Brown,* it said, and I recalled that this was Evangeline's great-great grandmother, likely the oldest grave onsite.

I let go of the bone, her sadness giving way to my own sobs. I buried my face in my hands as I cried, letting Delia's sadness course through me. She had no physical body to cry with, not anymore. In that moment, I was the physical expression of her despairing over this callous and grotesque treatment of her earthly body.

When the tears subsided, I wiped my face with the hem of my nightgown. Whoever those men were, they'd come prepared. It didn't take a genius to see those two had not a magical bone in their bodies. They must've purchased a loaded incantation from someone. Which meant this attack was premeditated. But what were they planning to do with Delia Rae's skull? And where would they have gotten a bone summoning spell? Bone magic wasn't illegal, but it was highly restricted. The only people allowed to practice were paleontologists, archaeologists, and anthropologists.

I made my way back to the house, my mind reeling from so many questions. I changed quickly out of my dirty nightgown and collapsed into bed where I fell instantly asleep. There, I dreamed of my brother teaching me to play basketball while Big Ginny worked up a batch of honey biscuits in the kitchen, and all the while, the rabbit watched, cataloguing my memories, and I could do nothing to hide them.

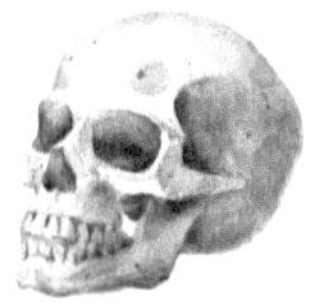

CHAPTER EIGHT

"JESUS CHRIST, this is awful."

It was early morning, and Angelo and I were standing in the cemetery, surveying the damage last night's looters had caused. Under the glare of the sun, the bones looked vulgar and vulnerable. I felt indecent witnessing something meant to be private. Human bones weren't meant to be seen this way. Skeletons were supposed to be complete and cared for with reverent tenderness, not tossed about helter-skelter on the lawn. "It's an absolute sacrilege," I muttered. "I can't imagine what would cause a person to do such a thing."

"Do you think it was a person, though?" Angelo asked. "What if it's...you know. That curse."

I folded my arms over my chest, giving myself a hug. When I'd found Angelo in the kitchen, I hadn't told him what had happened. I'd only asked him to follow me into the cemetery. "It wasn't a curse." I exhaled the words more than spoke them, grief pressing against my lungs. "It was two men. Something woke me in the middle of the night. It sounded like — I don't know, wailing. A woman's wailing. I followed the sound outside where I found these two guys. They were summoning bones from the cemetery. When I realized what they were doing, I fought them off."

Angelo's head whipped around, his eyes at first going wide and then narrowing in suspicion. "You fought them off," he repeated. His voice remained flat, not rising into a question, but I could read that disbelief at a hundred paces.

"I wouldn't believe me either. Even as it was happening, I wasn't sure *I* believed it. But before I came down to Georgia, I went to see a necromancer, and she gave me a gift. Now, I've received lots of gifts over the years, and I've had most of the common ones. But this time, when she laid hands on me, I didn't know the gift I had received. I felt different, and I knew I had received something, but I couldn't name it. Fast forward to last night. When I came outside, it was like something took over my body. Like the universe was controlling my movements. I kicked those two guys' asses, Angelo. But it wasn't me. Not really. It was the gift."

Suspicion hadn't yet left Angelo's face. "I've never heard of a gift like that," he said.

I heaved a sigh, lifting my shoulders in weak resignation. "Neither had I."

"I do. I know that one."

I felt movement at my side and looked down, surprised to find Dominic standing next to me, his eyes latched on the bones. Instinctively, I reached out, placed my hand on his shoulder and pulled him back. "What are you doing out here?" I asked. "You should be in the house. This isn't anything a kid should see."

But Dominic ignored that. "I know that gift you got," he repeated. "You got Terminator."

My brows shot high on my face as I looked down with new interest at the boy by my side. "Terminator?"

Dominic nodded, not taking his eyes off the bones. "Yep. That's what we call it, anyway. My friend's big brother gets it sometimes." He shifted his weight, his thumbs hooked in his pockets. "He's got a bad stepdad," he said, his voice soft.

A lump formed in my throat as the implications became clear. No one I knew had ever received this gift because physical danger was not a regular part of our lives. But someone Dominic knew — a friend's brother, a *child* — lived with enough violence that the ancestors had given him a way to defend himself and his family.

The world's horrors never ceased to sadden me.

"Terminator, huh?" I said, trying to keep my voice light. "Like that Arnold Schwarzenegger movie?"

Dominic nodded, finally turning his eyes away from the bones to look me in the face. "If you got it, you prolly need to watch out."

I opened my mouth to respond, but Dominic had already moved on, turning his attention to Angelo. "That's Aunt Delia, huh?"

Angelo's breath hitched in his throat, and the big man wiped a palm over his face as though to hide his own grief. "Kezia's right, Dominic. You should get back in the house. You don't need to see this."

"Well, I already seen it," Dominic answered matter-of-factly. "Is it? Is it Aunt Delia?"

Angelo sighed. "We think so. Now, please. Go back inside."

Again, Dominic didn't move. "Did this happen last night?"

Accepting the fact that the boy would not do anything we

told him, I placed my hands on my hips and rocked back on to my heels. "Yes, last night." I glanced over my shoulder, toward the house, looking for Evangeline. I didn't want her to see this.

"Did you see it?"

My attention snapped back to the boy as I chewed my bottom lip, unsure how to answer. I didn't have a lot of experience with children, but my gut told me it wasn't a good idea to lie to them. On the other hand, there was such a thing as too much truth. "Unfortunately, yes. There were some bad people here last night," I answered slowly. "They were using magic they shouldn't have been."

Dominic didn't seem bothered by this answer. "How come you saw them? Weren't you asleep?"

It was only then that I noted the hints of steel in the boy's voice. If I didn't know better, I might think he was accusing me. My eyes flicked to Angelo, and I didn't like the way he was looking at me, as though Dominic's suspicion were contagious. I drew in a quick breath. "I *was* asleep, but the noise woke me up. I was glad to be awake because I was having a weird dream."

Now, something changed in Dominic's expression. His eyes became softer, his mouth rounder. "What kind of dream?" he asked.

I ran a hand over my hair. "Ah, well, I was remembering something from my childhood — getting ready for church. But there was...I don't know, something there that wasn't part of my memories. It just kind of...spooked me," I finished lamely, dropping my eyes to the ground.

When I looked up again, Dominic's gaze was intense. I'd never seen a child look so old and wise. "You saw Roger."

"Roger?"

Dominic rubbed his nose with his palm. "That's what I call

him, anyway. The rabbit. You know. Roger Rabbit?"

I stopped breathing for a moment. "Roger Rabbit," I chuckled. "From the movie. Yeah, I saw a rabbit. How did you know?"

"I dream about Roger sometimes. A lot more, lately." Although the sun was shining down on us, the boy shuddered. Goosebumps prickled along his skin. "Everybody who stays in our house dreams of him. Mama says he's our guardian."

I hesitated, blinking in my surprise, and not just because I thought a rabbit was a shitty guardian. "*Everybody* dreams of him?"

Angelo cleared his throat, edging closer to our conversation. "Hey, Dom —"

But Dominic ignored him. "*Everybody*: me, Mama, Rocky, *and* Angelo." He gave Angelo a look then, like he was challenging the big man to disagree with him. Angelo blushed and dropped his gaze to the ground. "Divina says she doesn't, but I don't believe her. Divina lies sometimes."

"That's not a nice thing to say," I said automatically. "Besides, everybody stretches the truth sometimes."

Dominic snorted, a half-smile curling over his lips. "Yeah but Divina lies about *dumb* stuff. She says she doesn't believe in magic, but she has a book called *Alchemy of Souls* in her car. I looked at it once when I was waiting for her to come out of the dry cleaners. It's all about dreaming down, and dreaming down is *definitely* magic."

I wrinkled my brow, not sure I was following the twists and turns of this conversation. "What's dreaming down? I've never heard of it."

"Well *duh*," Dominic said, flashing me a smile. "That's because I made it up."

I chuckled. "Oh, okay. Well, what is it?"

The boy sucked in a breath, tapping his chin with a finger. "You know how sometimes when you have really good dreams, you wake up knowing something you didn't know before? Like maybe you never knew how to spell *invisible,* but one day you wake up and you can just do it?"

"Of course I know about that," I said with a laugh. "Anybody who visits necromancers knows about that. Sometimes when you get a gift, it awakens something in your genetic memory — something old that we used to know, but forgot before we were born." I smiled at a memory of my grandmother telling me she needed to go to the local African market because she had an overwhelming need to cook moamba de galinha — something she had never even eaten before. Now, she could cook like an old Angolan grandmother even though she'd never set foot outside the United States.

"My sister Letty woke up a memory of traditional Bata dance," Angelo said, smiling. "We found her outside, dancing in the driveway. She looked beautiful, but also possessed. We didn't know what was happening." Angelo chuckled then, rubbing the bridge of his nose as he conjured up the memory. "We didn't figure it out for a while. But then my sister built an altar to a thunder god called Sango, and Moms about passed out. Her, a God-fearing Christian woman finding a shrine to a thunder god in her daughter's bedroom. But anyway, that's how we found out that Bata dance is dedicated to the god Sango. Moms bought Letty a Bata drum and told her to take down the shrine."

"Did she?"

Angelo shook his head. "Nah, she just hid it in her closet."

Dominic laughed at that. "Do you got one, Angelo?"

The big man just shook his head. "A genetic memory? Nope. Doesn't happen for everybody. Kezia? You got one?"

I, too, shook my head. "Nothing. Just another piece of magic the universe doesn't want me to have."

I said it lightly, but I felt the denial like a hole in my heart. But then again, I wasn't being entirely fair. Genetic memory wasn't *really* magic, but it wasn't really science, either. It was a rich field of study for psychologists and spiritual gurus, but the hard sciences had little use for it. Genetic memory was considered nonsense to most, yet my grandmother had experienced it, as had Angelo's sister. I knew Big Ginny wasn't crazy, and I had no reason to doubt Angelo. So if it wasn't science, and it wasn't magic, where did that leave us?

"But anyway, that's not what I'm talking about," Dominic said. "I'm talking about stuff you learn from *dreams*. Not from the ancestors. You know?"

"Sure, I guess so," I said, nodding. "Sometimes when I have a problem I don't know how to solve, I sleep on it, and when I wake up, I know what to do."

Dominic considered this a moment. "Well, that's not really the same thing, but it's close enough. Anyway, when you dream about stuff and you wake up knowing how to do something new, that's dreaming down. You dream that stuff down into your brain."

I nodded like he was right, but technically, the phenomenon he was describing had nothing to do with magic — it was pure science. Our brains held onto all kinds of information that we weren't consciously aware of — and it discarded information that it considered worthless. But during sleep, brains did another fascinating thing — they replayed information gained during the day, processing it and deciding what was worth making available for easy access and what could be stored away in the deeper, less accessible halls of memory. That was likely why Dominic would fall asleep unsure how to spell *invisible* but wake up certain. His brain had analyzed the pattern and deemed it necessary.

But to a boy of eight, it wasn't any different from magic.

That was fair.

"Okay," I conceded. "And that's what that book was about?"

Dominic nodded. "Yeah. It's all about how your soul and the special stuff you can do — like your talents — and your dreams are all connected. Or more like, tangled in a big messy ball. The book says if you learn stuff in your dreams, it changes who you are as a person because your dreams and your soul are tangled together." He shrugged, rubbed his nose again. "That sounds like magic to me. Even though I don't have any talents."

"I'm sure that's not true," I said with a chuckle. "You're just little; you ain't figured 'em out yet. But anyway, you're right," I said. "That dreaming down stuff does sound like magic. But just because you found that book in her car doesn't mean Divina believes in it." I bit back my true thoughts, which were that being surrounded by magic every day *without* believing meant she must be performing some Olympic-level mental gymnastics. "Sometimes people can study things they don't believe in."

"No," Dominic said, shaking his head. "I'm telling you. She's lying about that. She believes, she just *mad* about it."

"Mad? Why?"

Dominic sighed. "Cuz she ain't got it. She can't get gifts like we can. Everybody else in the house can get gifts, even Rocky, and she don't even *look* Black. But Mama always says the bones know." He laughed then. "But Divina's bones don't know nothing, I guess."

Ah. A pang of understanding softened my heart, and for a moment, I allowed myself to feel sorry for Divina. At least that explained some of her prickliness. Over the years, I'd met plenty of people pissed off that they couldn't receive necromantic gifts. They'd hoot and holler and say it was rigged and racist, but the thing was, necromancers didn't control who could receive gifts and who couldn't. Mother Nature did that. Divina hadn't struck me as one of those folks, but what did I know? She was a Native woman adopted by a White family. I could see how a person like that might harbor grudges against the choosiness of necromancy.

Still, it felt wrong to talk shit about Divina behind her back, so I changed the subject. "You and Divina are pretty close, huh?"

Dominic grinned wide, showing his perfect jack-o-lantern teeth. "Yeah. We do everything together. Last year, she had a mixed martial arts tournament in New Orleans, and she took me with her. Divina's a badass. But Mama won't let me learn to fight. She says I'm too young." He sighed, rolling his eyes. "I think she just doesn't want me fighting so I don't end up like the guys she grew up with." Then, without saying anything more, he turned to head back into the house.

"You can't take everything Dominic says at face value," Angelo said once the boy had gone inside. "He's a kid. He sees things...in an exaggerated way."

I lifted an eyebrow. "Is that right? Do *you* dream of Roger Rabbit, or was that also an exaggeration?"

Angelo was readying his mouth to answer when my phone rang. "It's Rocky," the voice on the other end said. "I tracked down that archaeologist who helped disinter the graves. He lives out in Marietta. His name is David Pope. He says he has some documents for us if we're interested, but he doesn't want to fax them over or whatever." I could almost hear Rocky rolling her eyes on the other end. "Do you have time to meet with him today?"

I turned to Angelo. "Rocky found the archaeologist. He lives in Marietta, and he wants to meet with us today. Your schedule open?"

Angelo gestured toward the house. "Never a dull moment around here," he said. "After you."

DAVID POPE LIVED IN A LARGE, impressive Tudor house in an affluent neighborhood in Marietta. Angelo whistled as we pulled up, admiring the old-style English architecture. I, too, was stunned at the grandeur; it was much more lavish than I expected.

David met us at the door, all grins and warm handshakes as smile lines crinkled around his eyes. "Hello!" he boomed as he pumped my hand up and down with enthusiasm. "So glad you could make it. Please come in." He ushered us into the living room where we settled into plush, comfortable couches. David sat across from Angelo and me in an ornate bergère chair upholstered in silk velvet, one leg crossed casually over the other. "I'm sorry to make you come all the way out here," he said, his expression genuine. "But considering your inquiry, I thought it appropriate for us to converse face to face."

"We're just glad you could meet with us at all," I said. "Especially on such short notice. And the drive out here was quick. Easy."

I thought Angelo might contribute something to the conversation, but the big man just leaned back into the cushions, content to let me do the talking. "So, what can you tell me about the cemetery that was moved? Do you remember that day?"

David nodded enthusiastically. "Oh, sure, of course. You don't really forget something like that. To be honest, I haven't moved very many cemeteries over the course of my career. There aren't that many archaeologists in Georgia, but then again, there aren't that many cemeteries being moved, either. The government far prefers to keep cemeteries intact where possible. But the world changes and development happens. So I was honored to be selected to oversee such a delicate and emotional endeavor."

I raised an eyebrow. "Was it emotional?"

David smiled. "Whenever you deal with the past, especially where humans are concerned, it's always emotional. We were digging up what was supposed to be a *final* resting place. It's an inherently violent process, and Ms. Morris fretted over it the whole time. So yes, emotions were high." He gave a little shrug. "Let's just say that aside from myself, suffering from an unhealthy amount of professional curiosity as I do, nobody wanted to be there that day."

I nodded. "Before the graves were moved, was there any attempt to find living descendants?"

"Of course, as required by Georgia law."

"And do you know who handled that? A genealogist?"

David smiled, flashing pearly white teeth as he nodded. "That would be yours truly. Lucky for everybody, I am a professional archaeologist and an accomplished though amateur genealogist." He handed me a folder then, which I placed in my lap without opening. "The deceased buried on that property were Joseph and Cordelia Scarborough and their two children, Emilia and Rupert Scarborough. They had only one living descendant: one Erin Scarborough. I contacted her to let her know that the graves were being moved to a public cemetery nearby." He leaned forward, gesturing toward the file in my lap with a small nod. "I don't recall the name of the cemetery, but it's in the file. Along with Erin Scarborough's signature on the letter of intention I sent her. I keep meticulous records of everything," David added proudly. "After all, proper documentation is the archaeology of our day, is it not?"

I didn't have an opinion on that, but I smiled anyway. "So everything went fine, then? This Scarborough woman wasn't upset or anything?"

David hrmmed, wagging his head from side to side, dithering. "Well, I wouldn't say she was happy about it," he admitted. "She said those graves were sacred, and it violated the natural order of things to move them."

Nope, that didn't sound like she was happy. "And then what?"

David shrugged. "And then nothing. I asked if she wanted to file an appeal to get the state to rescind the disinterment license, but she said she didn't have the finances for that. I promised her that the bodies would be well cared for, and she seemed to accept that. At least, I never heard from her again."

I finally looked down into the folder on my lap, flipping the cover open. Old photographs accompanied photocopies of birth certificates, family trees, and what looked like marriage licenses and name change documents, none of which especially interested me. I flipped the folder closed and raised my gaze once again to David. "The reason I wanted to speak with you," I said finally, "is because it seems someone wasn't very happy with the removal of the cemetery. We've had..." I sighed, unsure how to frame it. "...problems. Do you remember anyone starting shit around the time that the graves were disinterred?"

David clucked his teeth and leaned his head to one side. "If I recall correctly, the only person besides Ms. Scarborough who was irritated by the removal of the graves was the previous property owner. He was furious and told me it had been an honor to be the caretaker of the Scarborough property. He wrote a couple articles for the local paper trying to stir up resentments, but that was about it. But aside from him, I don't remember anybody causing us any trouble. Those articles are in the file."

"So this is everything, then? The graves were transferred to a local public cemetery, the next of kin, a woman named Erin Scarborough, was notified of the transfer, and the only person upset was the previous property owner. Do I have that right?"

David nodded. "That's about the size of it. But again, it's all in the folder for your records."

All of this information added up, but something was niggling at the back of my mind, something I couldn't put a finger on. As I pondered the facts, I let my attention wander the room. The drapes were silk jacquard, the candlesticks real crystal. There was a lot of money in this house, and the Popes obviously enjoyed showing it off. But something about it didn't sit right with me.

"Mr. Pope —"

"Ah, *Dr.* Pope or David, if you don't mind," our host interrupted. "I know it's childish but I'm proud of the accomplishment. I was the first in my family to go to college, let alone enter a professional career."

Well, I understood that. I recalled how despondent Big Ginny had been when I dropped out of grad school. I would have been the first in our family with a master's degree, and though that designation had meant little to me then, I saw the importance of it now. Maybe she hoped we'd end up in a house like this, breaking the cycle of generational poverty.

"Sorry, of course," I said, dipping my chin. "*Dr.* Pope. How long have you been an archaeologist?"

"All my career," he said. "And I'm fifty-seven now, so I'll let you do the math."

"And your wife? What does she do?"

"Regina? She's never worked. She's a stay-at-home mother to our three boys. She resisted at first. She comes from modest means, as do I, and she believed that it was a woman's obligation to be able to provide for herself. But the first pregnancy was difficult for her, and she never recovered." He laughed then, color rising in his cheeks. "I'm sorry, I don't know why I just said all that," he admitted, embarrassed. "Regina would have my head for airing all our laundry like that."

I started to say that I agreed when my eyes landed on a framed document on the far wall.

"Is that your certificate?" I asked, motioning toward the paper with a lift of my chin.

David turned to look and smiled, his expression proud. "I graduated from the University of Georgia with a double degree in Archaeology and Arcane Magic," he said. "It was a passion pursuit, really. I wanted to understand the history of magic in human societies. Your people, for example, have necromancy. I felt then, as I do now, that magic has an important place in human culture. We like to pretend that we replaced it with religion and science. But I don't believe that. I think magic lends a mystery that humans need. We *need* a puzzle that we can't solve. We *need* to chase that power. It's what gets us out of bed every morning."

I leaned forward and squinted, trying to read the small

print on the document. But I didn't really need to read it. My intuition was screaming so loudly, I was sure the neighbors could hear. "And what did you study, Dr. Pope? As an archaeologist, you were allowed to study bone magic. Did you?"

David smile broadened and his eyes twinkled. "I did, in fact! There are damn few archaeologists in Georgia, and even fewer with a certificate in osteurgy. It's too bad, really. With the way the world is progressing and the middle class shrinking, fewer people have the means to move their families to private locations when their ancestral plots are sold to developers who want to raze the ground to build their million-dollar buildings." He sighed, giving a rueful shake of his head. "Osteurgy, or the colloquial *bone magic,* allows archaeologists to help those who are less fortunate."

But I wasn't interested in his tales of lifting the downtrodden. "Do you craft those spells? And maybe sell them?" I gestured vaguely around the room. "You don't afford something like this on an archaeologist's salary," I amended with a sardonic smile.

Now, David Pope's face grew dark, his lips pulling into a frown. "What are you suggesting, Ms. Bernard?"

I leaned forward and cut my eyes at the archaeologist. "Last night, two men broke onto Evangeline's property and performed a bone summoning spell in her family cemetery. They exhumed her ancestor's bones. As we speak, the county corner is gathering the pieces, and the local police are doing whatever the hell local police do at a crime scene." David squirmed in his seat, his expression forlorn as color rose in his cheeks. "You yourself said there aren't very many archaeologists in Georgia, and even fewer who know how to work bone magic — or, excuse me, *osteurgy*. I saw the two men who performed the spell. They had no idea what they were doing.

They *bought* a spell from someone. So I need you to tell me. Have you sold bone summoning magic?"

David rose from his seat, running his hand through his hair as he began pacing around the living room. He wouldn't meet my gaze as the words rushed from his mouth. "Understand that there are perfectly good, pragmatic reasons a person might need a bone summoning spell," he began. "It's not cost effective to move graves the legal way. But people have a right to the remains of their family members. Sometimes the best way to get those bones out of the ground without government involvement is to summon them."

"David," I said, letting my voice turn syrupy sweet, "how much do you sell bone magic for?"

The archaeologist sputtered. "I don't see what —"

"Because either you sell a *shit* ton of cheap magic to poor people, or you make a few healthy transactions with the wealthy. So, when I tell the police about this black market you're running, you can either be on the hook for hundreds of crimes or a few."

"All right!" His face was bright red now, whether with anger or indignation I couldn't be sure. "Yes, I've sold them to a few high bidders over the years, but only enough to provide for my family."

I choked back a guffaw. *I* provided for my family, and we lived in a bungalow purchased in the 60s and shopped clearance racks to get by. This was something else altogether.

This was *pride*.

"Dr. Pope, who have you sold bone magic to?"

David exhaled heavily and returned to his chair, slumping sideways, resting his forehead in his hands. "I don't know," he said. "The transactions are handled by a private auction house. I don't interact with the buyers at all."

"How many have you sold?"

He gave a limp shrug. "Ten? Twenty? Something like that."

"And how much do you sell them for?"

He closed his eyes so he didn't have to look at me when he said, "Bidding starts at $100,000 each."

Finally, Angelo came to life, whistling low and leaning forward onto his elbows. "You go to big boy jail for money like that."

Sitting in his expensive chair and draped in a silk smoking jacket, David Pope trembled. "I can't go to jail," he breathed. "My reputation...my family..."

"Nobody's going to jail," I interrupted. "Because Angelo and I aren't going to tell anyone about this. Are we, Angelo?"

The big man blinked. "We're not?"

I grinned, but the expression was devoid of mirth. "No. Because we're going to get a favor from Dr. Pope in return." I turned to the archaeologist, a glimmer of hope shining behind his eyes. "If you can craft a summoning spell — a *disinterment* spell — I assume you can craft an *interment* spell?"

The doctor stammered, blinking rapidly as he processed what I was suggesting. "A spell to return bones to their grave? Yes. Yes, of course I can do that. Is that all? Is that —"

"Give us an interment spell," I interrupted, "and nobody will go to the cops. Assured mutual destruction," I said. "After all, it wouldn't be legal for *us* to have bone magic in our possession, either. But I think in this case, we can all agree that it's the right thing to do. Nobody wants to dig up the property again just to return the bones to their casket by hand."

David was already drawing to his feet. "Of course! The right thing to do! Yes. I can have the spell ready by next week. I —"

"We'll leave here with the spell *today*," I cut in. "And I'd like to be home by dinner."

"That's absurd," David spat, the color draining from his face. "The sheer hours alone —"

"I guess you should get started then," Angelo said, also climbing to his feet. He didn't need to do more than that. His size was enough to cow the archaeologist. Or anyone, really.

David's face pinched as resignation settled in. "Very well. I guess you may as well come with me," he said. "Just keep your hands to yourselves, please. Some of what you're about to see is precious to me."

As I stood, David jerked his head, an invitation for us to follow him. He pushed open a door in the kitchen, revealing a staircase leading into the basement. He flipped the light switch and stood aside, beckoning. But Angelo and I both laughed, shaking our heads. "We wasn't born yesterday," Angelo chuckled. "Not about to lead a White man into his own basement. You first. Please."

David rolled his eyes with exaggerated annoyance but didn't argue. He thumped his way down the stairs, and Angelo and I followed behind.

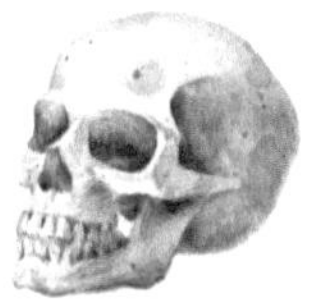

CHAPTER NINE

THOUGH DAVID HAD turned the lights on, the lamps did little to erode the darkness that met us at the bottom of the stairs. The air smelled close and stale with an unidentifiable grit that tickled my nose and the back of my throat. The walls hummed with the death current, and my hands felt hot, wanting to grab on and mold it. The scents of palo santo, copal, and lemon were so thick I could nearly chew them. I couldn't recall the last time a room had contained so much death energy. Not even the hospice was this rife with death.

But then my eyes adjusted to the warm glow emitted by low-watt incandescent bulbs, and when I recognized what we had descended into, I drew in a sharp breath.

"What the hell is this place?" Angelo's voice sounded strained; I couldn't tell if the dryness in his throat was confusion or awe. Or maybe it was pure disgust.

"It's an ossuary," I answered. "A place to store and care for human bones."

Angelo gawped wide-eyed as he explored the room. "It's like some kind of fucked-up museum."

It was an inelegant way to put it, but he wasn't wrong. Shelves and bookcases crammed with human bones lined the crumbling walls. Some bones were pristine; others looked like they'd been dug from the muck of the bayou or maybe the Nile. Two adult-sized skeletons flanked the bottom of the staircase, one with a tennis visor on its head. On the desk in the room's corner sat a machine that looked like an industrial meat grinder.

That's when I understood the grit in the air. Bone dust.

"This is my sanctuary," David announced, turning on his heel to face us. "This where I do most of my work. You already know I'm an archaeologist, but more specifically, I'm an *osteoarchaeologist*. I study the bones of humans to travel into the past and better understand our forebears — their culture and way of life. How did they behave? How did they move? Did they dance? Did they fight? Did they sing?"

Angelo frowned. "You can tell all that from bones?"

"Oh, certainly," David answered, rubbing his hands together. "Your entire life leaves its mark on your bones. Every serious injury, every nutritional defect…these things scar the bones, leaving stories for scientists to find and decipher long after you've passed on. They're the truest echoes of a past we can't see or touch."

"Not the truest," I said, not even realizing I would speak until I did. I was examining a pile of vertebrae covered in a thin layer of dust. Next to the vertebrae was a skull with some kind of medicine bundle stuffed into the left eye socket. Something about it prickled at my subconscious. "*Necromancy* lets us hear the truest echoes of the past. We raise the dead." I turned to him, half smiling. "We raise the dead that live in your bones and in your blood. We reincarnate their memories. Their dreams. Their abilities. *Those* are the truest echoes of the past."

Now, David's eyes grew round as saucers as he padded over to me, stopping just short of actually touching me. "You're a necromancer?" he asked.

"I am."

"Fascinating," he breathed. "And I suppose you're right. What you can do is far greater than what I can do, science be damned." He smiled crookedly, his gaze moving now to the bones I had been looking at. "And I see you've found Agnes. Well, her skull and spine, anyway. She died in the early 1800s of an atlanto-axial dislocation."

I raised an eyebrow. "Pardon?"

David's gaze didn't stray from the bones when he replied, "Broken neck."

Next to Agnes was a reconstructed leg. I leaned in, my professional curiosity getting the best of me. "I think I recognize this one," I said. "Distal fibula fracture."

The archaeologist did touch me then, pressing his palm against my shoulder blade in a tentative attempt at camaraderie. "You know bones?"

"Only a little," I admitted. "I studied biology in grad school, but cells. I work in hospice, though, and the patients suffer their fair share of breaks. I've accumulated a bit of anatomical knowledge by osmosis." I grinned. Cellular biology joke.

But if David got it, he didn't let on. His smile faltered when he said, "But you're a necromancer?"

I frowned, letting my eyes meet David's in the dim light. "That's right. What's that got to do...?"

I let my words trail off as David clucked his teeth with a

sad little shake of his head. "You said yourself you can raise the dead in others, your way of looking for the past. Sometimes, perhaps, even finding it. But if you wanted to know your ancestors, I don't know why you chose to study cells. You should have studied bones."

It wasn't the first time someone had scorned my field of study, and I had to grind my molars to keep from putting the doctor on blast. Even Angelo sensed my frustration, reaching out to wind his fingers around my wrist, applying a gentle pressure I easily interpreted. *Stay focused. He means nothing by it.*

"Bones tell the stories of human life more powerfully and with more poetry than anything else in the universe," David continued, turning to face the two skeletons at the bottom of the stairs. "If you understand bone, you understand the body, and from the body, the activity and diet, and from there, culture. Take Andre here," he said, gesturing to the cap-wearing skeleton. "Examine for a moment the thoracic cage. If you look closely, you'll see that Andre broke his first rib here." He indicated the top of the skeleton's rib cage with his pinky finger. "But the bone didn't knit back together properly. See, bone is miraculous. We think of bone as something inorganic like rocks, but nothing could be further from the truth. Bones are living tissue. And even after a clean break like Andre suffered, the broken ends will still reach for each other, trying to again become one."

The poetry in that sent shivers down my spine. I often thought of myself — of all necromancers, really — as people reaching across time for our forebears, trying like hell to mend the breach in history that separated us.

I squinted in the shadows, trying to make out the break David referred to. "And what story does this tell you about Andre?"

"Well, Andre suffered a pathology called *pseudarthrosis* where the bones reach for each other but never quite make it. And because it happened in the first rib, it indicates that Andre may have been an overhead athlete — probably a tennis player." He mimed an overhand serve. "Hence his name." He grinned. Tennis joke.

But the joke was lost on me, as I never had much of a head for sports. Angelo, however, chuckled like a little boy. "Andre Agassi," he said. "Good one, doc."

"Thank you," David said, beaming now. "I admit I was proud of that." He turned to me then, eyebrow raised. "You know, a similar evaluation could likely be made of your friend's bones."

"What friend?"

"Ms. Morris," he said. "She holds a peculiar posture when she hands out gifts. She stands on a raised platform and places her hands on her recipient's cheeks, cupping them. Then she leans her body forward and down — creating a curvature in her spine and a forward roll of her shoulders. In a skeleton, we might observe a compressed rib cage and an anterior pelvic tilt. We wouldn't know exactly what caused her poor posture from those conditions alone, of course, but it would give us very important clues. If we knew she was an African American female, for example, an astute osteoarchaeologist might recognize one granting necromantic gifts."

I hrmmed, thoughtful. "Well, but maybe not," I said. "If they knew the time period and that the skeleton was from Atlanta, they might recall the dearth of necros here, leading them to a different conclusion."

The archaeologist looked impressed. "A *brilliant* observation," he agreed. "You know, the lack of necromancers in Atlanta is such a strange case. I suspect one day it will make a fascinating case study. Did you know that compared to African Americans in the rest of the country, those residing in Atlanta are thirty-five percent less likely to own a house, thirty-two percent less likely to go to college, forty-four percent less likely to own a business and seventeen percent *more* likely to die in childbirth?"

I had never heard those statistics, and my mouth gaped at the recitation. "Is that true?"

"It makes sense, unfortunately," David lamented. "Necromancy evolved to grant certain advantages to your people since the system is — intentionally or not — rigged against you. But since those who live here have a much smaller chance of receiving their gifts, they're not thriving like their counterparts in other cities who receive gifts regularly, even adjusting for cost of living and whatnot. It's terrible."

"That *is* terrible," I agreed. "I never thought of that." I thought of Opal, wishing to the be the only necromancer in Los Angeles. If she were, she might've made a killing, but at what cost our local community?

"It's also biologically unlikely." David crossed his arms, frowning. "The lack of necromancers, I mean. Evolution doesn't make mistakes like that. Which makes me wonder whether an outside force is at work."

"What outside force?" Angelo asked.

"Could be anything. Social mores, behavioral adjustments, even other biological conditions can influence biology. Think about how your shoes alter the shape of your feet, or how ginkgo trees change sex in a single-sex environment. But I wonder if, in the case of absent necromancers in Atlanta, the simplest explanation isn't truest."

"And what's the simplest explanation?"

David shrugged. "Magic." His eyes flicked briefly toward his bone-clotted shelves.

I blinked. "You think someone might have Atlanta under a spell to prevent necromancy from flourishing here?"

David's eyes narrowed. "Truth is stranger than fiction, Ms. Bernard." His gaze was intense, and I felt there was something more he wanted to tell me. But the moment passed, and he shrugged. "All I can say for *sure* is that it's unusual."

My brow furrowed. "But Evangeline hasn't been affected."

Now, David blew out a breath. "Are you sure? Because by my measure, it seems she has."

No one spoke for a moment, and the air hung thick between us. Finally, I shook myself, returning to the matter at hand. "All right," I said, turning away from Andre. "While I appreciate the osteology — and tennis — lesson, I think you have work to do?"

Disappointment clouded David's face. "Of course. Well, I'm afraid the accommodations down here aren't very comfortable, but if you insist on waiting, it'll have to do. I don't want you upstairs bothering my wife and children." He sucked in a breath, holding it for a minute before saying, "I hope you aren't squeamish. Crafting bone spells isn't for the faint of heart."

"I'm not squeamish," I said. "In fact, I'm curious. Would it be too much of an imposition if I watched you work?"

The bone mage's eyes grew wide, a smile dancing over his lips. "Not at all. Why don't you hand me that patella and mandible from the shelf behind you, and then we'll just get started?"

Hours later, after we'd watched David Pope grind a dozen different bones down to powder, use that powder to create ink, and then use that ink to draw symbols onto bone, the spell was finally complete. The whole time he worked, I felt the death current surging and swelling, dancing about. David worked the current, using its pulses and vibrations to imbue his work with wizardry I scarcely understood.

We had been in David's basement for nearly seven hours. The archaeologist looked exhausted; huge bruises had formed under his eyes, and his skin was pale. Working so much magic in a short time had drained him, and I felt a pang of sympathy — I knew how tiring going through the veil was. David looked like he'd gone through the veil several times in one evening. Unthinkable.

"It's finished," he croaked, pressing into my hand a strange, U-shaped bone that was only a little larger than my palm. "Meles meles pelvis — the pelvis of a common, underground-dwelling badger. With this talisman and the cantrip I'll give you in a moment, you'll be able to return the bones to their resting place. Be advised, however, that this spell can't inter bones for the first time. They can only return to their original grave."

The bone was beautiful, if strange, and magic hovered around it like morning fog over the ocean. It was so delicate — how could something so fragile be so powerful?

"Thank you," I said, cupping the pelvis against my chest. "I appreciate how much this cost you." I lowered my voice to add, "And you know I don't mean money."

The archaeologist merely nodded, too weary now to speak. He slumped back down at his workstation, and I reached for Angelo's elbow, guiding him toward the stairs. "It's time to go," I said.

We ascended the stairs and made our way outside, our lungs grateful for fresh air free of dust and bone grit. We slid into the car, and I stowed the pelvis safely in the glove box before Angelo started up the engine.

We had been on the road about ten minutes and my eyelids had turned to lead. I must've been falling asleep when Angelo's voice woke me. "Can I ask you something?"

"Go ahead."

"Back at the house. You said you appreciate how much it cost him. What did you mean by that?"

I yawned, pressed a knuckle to my eye. "I didn't know it until he started working, but he uses the death current to work his magic. It's the same energy we use in necromancy. It takes things apart and promotes entropy — disintegration and decay. If you don't handle it properly, it decomposes your own cells and vital energy."

"The closer you get to death, the closer it gets to you," Angelo intoned.

"Exactly. He worked with the current for hours without stopping to recharge, re-shield, or breathe fresh air. Nobody can do that without repercussions. If I had to guess, I'd say we just cost Dr. David Pope about a year of his life."

Silence. Then, softly, "Jesus."

"Ain't no such thing as a free lunch," I said sleepily, sinking down into the seat. "Every magician needs to know the costs of his magic. Somebody always pays. Every time."

I was glad Angelo didn't want to discuss further because almost as soon as I finished talking, I was asleep.

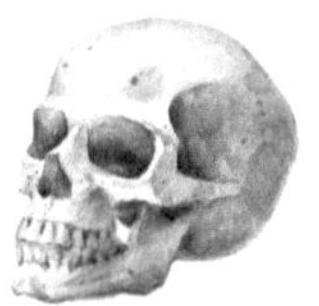

CHAPTER TEN

THE NEXT SET OF MOVERS arrived several days later. Evangeline hadn't wanted to waste the spell returning Delia Rae's bones until we had retrieved her skull. I didn't have the heart to tell her we might never get the skull back — that whoever stole it may have already damaged or destroyed it while working whatever mischief they had taken it for. But Evangeline was stubborn, and so I had placed the enchanted pelvis on the vanity in my bedroom until we were ready to help Delia Rae rest once again in peace.

The chaos in the house was palpable. I wasn't even the one moving, and the stress was already getting the best of me, setting my teeth on edge as I picked my way to the kitchen, doing my best to avoid people carrying boxes and pushing dollies. I found Evangeline directing traffic in the dining room. She looked haggard. "I swear these people ain't never loaded a truck in their lives, and they're *movers*." She cursed, tiny beads of sweat popping out on her brow. "If I didn't have this curse on me, I swear I'd just do it all myself."

I chuckled, trying to imagine Evangeline moving three people into three separate houses on her own. "Well, it's a good thing you can't do it because that sounds exhausting. Speaking of. Is there anything I can do?"

The sound of tinny gunshots drifted into the room, grabbing our attention. We both turned to see Dominic shuffling up to us, a portable video game console in his hand. "I don't know," he said, his voice pitched strangely low, his eyebrow comically cocked. "Is there anything you can *do?*"

I laughed, recognizing the line of dialogue even though it surprised me coming out of a child's mouth. "You been watching *Aliens?*" I asked. "That's a great scene, but you kinda young for that, ain't you?"

Evangeline snatched the device from Dominic's hand with a quick swipe, and the boy's face darkened, his brows knit together. "Hey! Mom! What's that for?"

"You been watching movies you ain't supposed to watch? What's Kezia talking about? What movie?"

Dominic growled with exasperation as he threw me a dirty look, his hands still reaching for the device his mother dangled beyond his reach. "Keziaaaaa," he whined, "can't you keep nothing to yourself?"

I held my hands up, surrendering. "Whoa, I just meant that movie came out long before you was even a twinkle in your mama's eye. I didn't mean —"

"You know you're supposed to *ask permission* before you watch a movie on this thing," Evangeline said, shaking the device. "Did you ask?"

But Dominic just stared, incredulous. "I ain't do nothing! Mom, you can't even *watch* movies on that!"

Evangeline turned her attention to me, expression questioning. "Can you? Can you watch movies on this?"

I waved both hands furiously before my face, shaking my head. "Nuh-uh, my name Paul, and this between y'all," I said.

Again, Dominic shot me a dirty look, and for a moment, I felt bad that I hadn't taken his side. But I had no idea if you could watch movies on that thing, and I didn't want to look stupid.

"I'll ask Divina about it later," Evangeline said, placing the device on a cupboard out of Dominic's reach. "In the meantime, why don't you go read a book?"

"But Mom —"

"Don't but mom me," Evangeline warned, "You 'bout to hit my last nerve, Dom. I ain't got the patience for it today. You see all this shit I got to deal with? Go read a book and stay out my hair. I'll bring you back your game thing later."

Dominic rolled his eyes as he skulked out of the room, but not before he stuck his tongue out at me and darted away.

Evangeline turned to me, eyes refocusing like she was only just remembering I was standing there. "Think you can help Divina and Rocky with some deliveries today? I got a call from Claudia Buchanan this morning down at the women's shelter. They got a big delivery from a couple of the local churches, and they need some help sorting out all the items. I volunteered my services, but I kind of have my hands full." She grinned, but the expression slipped away just as quickly as it had appeared. "Not like I can leave anyway. I told Rocky and Divina to handle it, but I'd like you to go, too."

I hesitated. "Well, of course I don't mind, but..." I chewed my lips, my stomach doing a flip. "Are you sure it's safe? I've been seeing a lot of them lately. And the whole reason you've got them moving..."

For a moment, I thought Evangeline had forgotten that I was like her. Or maybe she had lived so long *without* her affliction that she'd forgotten that most of us still had to think about how much time we spent with normal people. Then she smiled, patting me on the arm. "You're right," she said. "It might not be safe. Why don't you *ask* them if they feel comfortable with you tagging along?"

"I could," I agreed, "but I've found that puts people on the spot. I don't want —"

"Ask them," Evangeline interrupted, her attention already returning to the chaos she was trying to manage. "No, *do not* roll those up like that! Christ the Savior, let me show you." She marched toward the offending worker, pausing only long enough to call over her shoulder to me, "Just ask them."

I found Divina and Rocky in a now-empty front office, Rocky with her arms folded across her chest, and Divina with a finger pointed in her face. "... So if you didn't know what you were doing, you should have *asked* someone for help. You should have —"

As I stepped into the room, both women turned to me, their expressions embarrassed. I feigned a smile. "Did I...interrupt something?"

They were both quiet a heartbeat. Then, "Yes," Divina said, eyes narrowed, at the same time that Rocky piped in with, "No!"

Divina flashed the other woman a dirty look, but Rocky looked glad for the interruption. "If you're looking for a quiet place to escape, this room ain't it," she said, rolling her eyes in Divina's direction. "I recommend getting the hell out of here and going for gelato. There's a great little place not too far from here over in Castleberry Hill. Hell, if we weren't so busy today, I'd take you myself." Then, under her breath, "Sure beats putting up with *this* shit."

"If you have something to say to me," Divina put in, "I suggest you —"

"Hey," I interrupted, a dull ache forming behind my eyes. "Evangeline said y'all are heading out to the women's shelter. Do you mind if I come? She asked me to go."

Divina cocked an eyebrow at me. "Angie gets what Angie wants, so why are you asking *us* for permission?"

But as soon as the words were out of her mouth, she seemed to understand. "Oh," she said, her voice dropping an octave. "You're worried about the blues."

I nodded. "Yeah."

Divina and Rocky exchanged looks I couldn't read. Finally, Rocky looked over to me, her mouth pulled into a small moue. "If Angie wants you to come along, you should come along."

"It's...not really her call," I said, wringing my hands. "If you get sick, that's on *me*. I'm not willing to put anybody in danger who doesn't want it. I know the risks are small, but —"

"They're not *that* small," Divina cut in. "You've killed people before, right? A teacher?"

My heart fell into my stomach as both Rocky and I turned horrified gazes on Divina. Rocky's mouth moved as though she wanted to speak, but her words didn't find purchase. My entire body went numb. "How did you know that?" I whispered.

"Angie told me," she said, brushing away the question. "But anyway, we'll take the risk. You're right; it's small. And we're both pretty sure we're immune, anyway."

I met their eyes with doubt in my own. "How can you be so sure?"

Rocky answered with a laugh, walking over to me and linking her arm in mine. "Nothing is sure," she said, guiding me to the door. "Sometimes, you just have to go on faith." She turned, calling over her shoulder. "Divina? You coming?"

The other woman answered with a grunt, and in a moment, we were on our way.

SAFE PLACE USED to be an old hotel but had been converted in recent years to a battered women's shelter. The place still smelled of flowers and furniture polish. It was the kind of building that, under different circumstances, some shyster might have tried to peddle around town as haunted so he could host $20-a-head tours of the place. The vaulted ceilings were ornately painted with scenes from Georgia's history, but ruined with water stains.

When I pointed this out to Rocky, she nodded with a sigh. "This place almost burned down a while ago. The city put the fire out, obviously, but then the hotel underwent extensive rebuilding. Some things like the ceilings are original, but pretty much everything else is reconstructed. Badly. The contractor cut corners," she explained with a shrug. "So Angie bought this place for a song."

My brows went up at that. "Evangeline owns this place? I thought —"

"She bought it," came a voice, "but make no mistake. *I* own it."

I spun around to be greeted by a small, wiry woman with freckled skin the color of pinecone. A nest of gray hair was halfheartedly tamed by a cotton headband. She hugged Divina and Rocky in turn, but to me, she offered a hand and a smile.

"I'm Claudia Buchanan," she said. "This is my shelter." Her voice crackled like firewood. "And you are...?"

"Kezia Bernard," I said, accepting her handshake. "Nice to meet you."

"Likewise," the woman said, folding her hands in front or her. "You're a friend of Angie's?"

"Angie's helping her out," Divina answered for me. "Not a friend. More like a project." She winked, hand on her hip. "This one's broken. Angie's trying to fix her."

I opened my mouth, offense rising in my throat like bile. "That's not — Divina, I'm not *broken*, I —"

But Claudia only laughed, taking my hand in hers as she led the three of us down a hallway. "Oh, don't take offense to that, sugar. We're all of us a little broken, present company included. And Angie? Well, she likes to fix things. That's how I ended up with this shelter. Angie thought it might fix me."

"Oh. Are you a necromancer, too?"

Claudia tittered as she patted my hand. "No, I'm no necromancer, but there's more than one way to be broken, you know. Come on now," she said, more to the others than to me. "Y'all ready to get to work? I swear the workload around here gets bigger every damn day."

"Sing it, Miss Claudia," Rocky called from behind. "The devil's always busy in Georgia."

I felt Claudia's hand tighten on mine. "The devil's always busy everywhere," I murmured.

The old woman sucked her teeth. "Ain't got to tell me."

Claudia led us down several flights of stairs toward a storage room packed to the gills with boxes, stray furniture, and heaps of clothes. Divina and Rocky immediately got to work, used to doing this chore. "We can take it from here, Miss Claudia," Divina assured her. "We'll check in with you when this is all sorted."

After the older woman left, I put my hands on my hips, turning in small circles as I summed up the mountain of work we had ahead of us. "We're really going to get all this done today?"

Rocky grunted. "Not if you just stand there like a jackass. There." She pointed to a large box overflowing with clothing. "Separate those out, would you? Anything torn, stained, or that you wouldn't wanna wear yourself, put over there to be recycled." She pointed to a far corner. "You'd be surprised the shit people donate. A lot of it is trash."

"I'm not sure I would be surprised," I said with a sigh. "We went through a rough patch when I was growing up. Spent a lot of times sifting through clothes at the Goodwill. Lots of shit to get through."

We worked in silence for a short while, but every so often a shiver ran down my spine, the hairs on my arm standing up. I wondered idly if maybe the old hotel *was* haunted after all. But I would have sensed any ghosts nearby; my hands would tingle, and the death current would move more than it was. It didn't take too long for me to figure out that the strange sensations were because I was being watched.

I focused hard on the baby romper I was folding and cocked my head to the side. "Seems like something's on your mind, Rocky," I said. "What's up?"

Rocky chewed her lips as she continued digging through a giant box of toiletries. "Well, I hope it's not too ghoulish of me to ask, but I've been thinking about the grave robbery. What do you think that was about? I heard they stole her *skull*," she said in a stage whisper.

I sucked in a breath and placed the romper aside. "I don't know exactly what they wanted to do with it, but there's a lot of potent magic you can do with human remains."

Rocky's eyes went wide. "Really? People use human remains in magic work?"

I shrugged. "Sure. All parts of the human form are very powerful, and people have used human remains in magical practice since the beginning of time. In hoodoo, for example, we use fingernails, hair, and blood. Some mages and shamans use bones and blood, and alchemists even transmute the human soul."

Rocky whistled, her eyes growing impossibly wider. "You can use a human soul in magic? How does that work? Do you, like, use your own or do you take one from somebody else?"

Divina sucked her teeth. "You're right, Rocky, this is ghoulish. Can you not?"

Rocky ignored the other woman, eyes trained on me. "Well?"

I tried to ignore the stink eye Divina was giving me. "I guess you could transmute your own," I drawled, "though it's also possible to steal one. Not easy, I don't think. But possible."

Divina grunted. "I've read about that," she said. "Soul stealing, I mean. But it seems like a bunch of bullshit if you ask me."

I raised an eyebrow. "You think so? I might've agreed with you a few months ago. But I recently met a woman who helps people integrate the parts of their soul that were stolen by others."

Rocky nodded, rubbing her hands together in excitement. "Yeah, Divina, you remember Andromeda Clark. That psychic Evangeline had over to the house a few years ago? She does that work. She says people can steal your soul in a lot of different ways. I mean, they can't just steal the whole thing. But they can take pieces. That's how you end up in toxic relationships with low self-esteem and stuff."

"Yep," I agreed. "That's actually who I'm talking about. I met Andromeda recently."

Divina stiffened, pressing her lips into a hard line. "Of course I remember Andromeda. I even bought her book, remember?" She rolled her eyes, blowing out her breath in a hot puff of air. "I just don't think it's as easy as all that," she said. "I think people who talk about soul-stealing are selling fear and hate to make a quick buck. I find it disgusting."

Rocky clucked her tongue as she dug through her box, pulling out expired aspirin and tossing it into a wastebasket. "Well, I don't know why you think that. Even in your culture, you guys have the same concept. People who lure the souls of others out of their bodies so they can possess them."

Divina froze as she stared daggers across the room at an oblivious Rocky. "When you say *my* culture...do you even know what Nation I belong to? You *do* know that not all Native tribes are the same, right?"

"I know Indian dreamwalkers trap your soul in another dimension and then take over your body and then —"

"That's *racist bullshit*, Rocky," Divina spat, "and you know it. There is absolutely nothing in *my culture* that calls for luring someone's soul away to possess their body." Divina's eyes flitted toward me, her expression exasperated. "*This* kind of racism is exactly why I'm trying to help Dominic get to know his tribe. Because if all he knows about his own people is shit like this, he'll grow up hating himself, and I wouldn't wish that on anyone."

Rocky howled. "How are you going to help him know his tribe? Your whole family is *White*."

I cleared my throat, throwing Rocky a dark gaze I hoped even she could read. "Maybe you should let it go," I said. "It *does* sound racist."

"How is that racist? You can't be racist against White folks," Rocky said. "I read that on Twitter. Plus —"

"My family is White," Divina said, seething, "but *I'm* Native. Don't use my being adopted as an excuse for your bigotry. Jesus, I thought you were better than that. Not by much, but still."

"Whatever," Rocky said, her attention back on her task. "It's not like I haven't experienced racism myself."

"It's not any of my business," I said, my voice measured, "but what ethnicity are you, exactly?"

Rocky looked up, the tension in her face replaced with a smile. I grinned to myself; I'd guessed right. Rocky was one of those people who loved talking about themselves. "Well, both my parents identify as Black, but technically, they're both half. My maternal grandmother is Irish, and my paternal grandfather is German. And I'm the resulting mutt."

"A mutt who happens to look completely White," Divina muttered.

"Genes are funny that way," I agreed, trying like hell to soothe the fires these two seemed hellbent on igniting. "Each parent donates half their genes to their child, but there's no telling what half you'll get or what traits will show up. Even siblings can inherit different DNA from the same parents."

"I just think it's *suspicious* that someone who presents like Rocky can claim herself Black," Divina opined with dull annoyance. "I bet your parents had actual *cookies* in those Royal Dansk tins instead of sewing supplies."

Even I had to choke down a laugh at that. Every Black person knew if you opened a blue cookie tin, it wasn't a damn chance in Hell you'd find actual cookies. Though I did think it was funny and sort of odd that Divina knew that.

"And yet," Rocky added, her voice deceptively sweet, "I

receive my necromantic gifts every month like clockwork. So, as Angie always says, the bones know."

"Have you always gotten your gifts from Evangeline? I mean, has she always been the only necromancer in Atlanta?" I asked.

"I don't think so," Rocky said. "When I was a kid, there were others for sure. But slowly over time, they just kind of dwindled until Angie was the only one left." She looked up. "Do you guys have lots in LA?"

"Too many," I said with a chuckle. "My friend Opal was lamenting just the other day that there's so many now that sometimes she doesn't do any business at all."

"That's a shame," Rocky said, "for your friend, I mean. But it's not good for Angie that there aren't any here. She works too much. She's exhausted all the time, and it takes its toll. On her, on Dom…We've tried to convince her to take a vacation, but she won't hear it. Making sure people have their gifts is the only thing she cares about."

"It's not the *only* thing she cares about," Divina put in, rolling her eyes.

"It might as well be. Look at her. Look at how miserable this curse is making her. It's because she's not out there doing her calling. But I get it. You can't *possibly* understand."

Divina opened her mouth to retort, her cheeks red, but I was saved from further argument when the door creaked open, and Claudia poked her gray head inside. "How's it going in here?" she asked.

"It's going good, Miss Claudia," Rocky called out cheerily. "You've got some badass stuff in here today."

Claudia shuffled into the room, wringing her hands and smiling brightly. "Oh, excellent, I'm glad to hear that. People don't realize how important it is for a woman to look and feel her best. Some women that come through here go on to get good jobs and help other people. I had a lady a couple years ago who now runs a low-cost nursery for at-risk mothers. She takes care of their children while they work or go to school — whatever they can do to make something of themselves. That's what we do. That's how we help each other. Don't even need necromantic gifts to do it, right, Divina?"

Divina looked up then, her eyes like ice. Cursing under her breath, she dropped the garment she was folding and stomped out of the room.

"Did I say something?" Claudia asked.

Rocky huffed, jabbing a thumb in my direction. "No, it was Kezia that pissed her off."

I blinked. "Me? What did I do?"

"Reminded her she doesn't have a lick of magic in her bones."

"Dominic said something similar," I said, ignoring the part where *I* initiated Divina's temper tantrum instead of Rocky. "But you don't have a magical bone in your body, either, and you don't act out about it."

Claudia and Rocky glanced at each other, and once again I felt I was on the outside, trying to decipher an inside joke. The corner of Rocky's mouth quirked into a half smile, and she brushed her hair from her eyes. "But that's not exactly true, is it?" she said. "I mean, I get my gifts, like I said. Not recently, since Angie hasn't been able, and I'm not driving out of my way to see anybody else. But the point is, even though I can't do magic on my own, our community can. And anything the community can do, the individual can do. That's why protecting the group is so important. It's symbiotic."

I hadn't ever thought of it that way, but Rocky's words made sense. Every person who got a gift had magic, whether or not they were born with it, whether or not they deserved it. The ancestors didn't judge. They simply gave.

"That's right," Claudia agreed. "And that's why y'all got to be kind to Miss Divina. It ain't about the magic, you know. It's about belonging. It's an unwelcoming world out there for someone ain't got her own family."

I shivered at those words, even my scalp pimpling over with goosebumps. I parroted Claudia's earlier words back to her, my expression stoic. "Ain't got to tell me."

IT WAS evening when we arrived home. We knew more moving trucks would arrive in the morning, so we parked on the street. I was the last to pull myself out of the car, slamming the door behind me and stretching the day's kinks out of my back and shoulders. But as I headed toward the house, my breathing became heavy, labored. On the sidewalk, I slowed my pace as my throat went dry, my mouth like cotton as I broke out into a cold sweat.

My vision swam, and I hesitated, swaying on my feet as I peered at the house through the mounting moonlight. Something wasn't right. Something...

I took a step. I tried to take another, but a wave of nausea and misgiving washed over me, telling me not to move, not to go any further. I sucked in a heavy breath and up ahead, Rocky paused, turning to watch me, her brow creased with worry.

"Kezia? You all right?"

Was I all right? No, I wasn't. Something was terribly wrong. An overwhelming desire to turn and run rushed through me, and I stumbled backward until I tripped and fell, landing hard on my ass.

The front door opened, and Angelo tumbled through, hurrying toward me wearing the twin expression to Rocky's. He got down on his haunches, peering into my face. "Kezia? What's wrong? You're white as a sheet. Metaphorically. Don't worry, you're still Black."

I shook my head, my teeth clattering. I was suddenly cold. Freezing cold. I tried to answer, but my tongue was thick and slow, and no words would come out.

"She's having some kind of panic attack," Angelo said. "Here, let's get her inside."

Angelo moved forward, wedged his hands underneath my armpits, pulling me to my feet. But as he guided me forward, something in my brain snapped.

"No!"

I whirled on him, throwing my weight against him and knocking him off balance. Before he could recover, I threw myself at him, punching him squarely across the face. Pain like lightning rippled through the bones of my hand — I could almost hear the micro breaks in my metacarpals. "Don't touch me!" I screamed. "Leave me alone!"

"Kezia!"

It was Rocky's voice, distant and fuzzy but coming nearer. When she was within range, I pivoted, sweeping my foot out to catch her in the ankles, knocking her to the ground. She cried out as she hit the pavement. I dimly noticed a trickle of blood seeping from the corner of her mouth.

My heart was an earthquake in my chest, sending tremors to all of my extremities. Angelo was already coming for me again, but this time, he wrapped his arms around me, pinning my limbs to my sides. I struggled against him, screaming and kicking and bucking like a wild bull. It was then that Rocky sidled up beside me and grabbed my head in her hands, pressing gently but firmly.

"Kezia," she whispered, "where are you, honey? Who are you fighting? You're safe here. Safe."

I heard her words, but they didn't register. I wasn't safe. My Terminator gift was plowing full steam ahead, revving my engines so I could fight and stay alive.

But something else was tugging at my brain, at the small, stubborn piece that hadn't turned completely to survival. A tiny voice spoke sharply in my ear, demanding my attention.

You have to fight, Mama Fat said. *But not these people. Think, Kezia! What do you have to fight? Mind over matter! What is it?*

My eyes flew wide as I willed my body to stop attacking, commanding my muscles to relax, to allow my logical mind to take control. These people were not my enemies. They would not hurt me. But something here *was* my enemy. Something had excited my Terminator gift. What was it? *What was it?*

Suddenly, I looked up at the house looming over me in the distance. The Terminator gift had flared to life as I walked toward it. As I tried to enter.

Don't go inside, something inside me screamed. *Turn around! Flee! Go home!*

My breath caught as I slowly came to understand. It wasn't Angelo or Rocky that I needed to fight. They hadn't triggered my survival response.

It was the *house*.

Fight, Mama Fat commanded, her voice stern in my ears. *The house don't want you to go inside, but you need to be there. It's life or death, and you know it. So fight, Kezia, baby. Goddammit, fight!*

In an instant, I let go. I surrendered my conscious thought and forced my body to go limp, letting my subconscious mind take over. I didn't know how to fight a house that didn't want me there, but my Terminator gift did. So I swallowed my pride and surrendered.

Psychic shields sprang up around me. One moment the world was terrible and threatening, and the next everything was quiet and calm. Dim. The shields locked everything out until I was inside a cocoon of my own making, where I heard nothing but the rush and gurgle of blood in my ears, feeling nothing but the thunder of my heartbeat rattling my ribs.

And in that haze where I was safe from the voices that screamed not to go inside, I passed out.

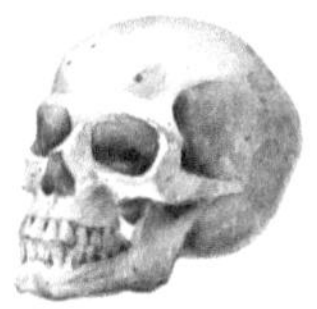

CHAPTER ELEVEN

THE NEXT MORNING, I awoke to find Evangeline snoring, slumped in the slipper chair at the foot of my bed. She had a book on her lap and a tea tray at her side. She must have heard about what happened and stayed with me all night.

I glanced at my phone to see the time. Not quite 8:00 a.m. More movers would be here soon. Carefully, as if testing the limits of my body, I climbed out of bed.

I was still wearing the same clothes as yesterday. Thank God for that; I couldn't stomach the idea of someone undressing me and tucking me in like a child. A terrible pain forced me to look down to my hand. The skin was black with bruises and tender to the touch. I recalled that I'd hit Angelo; this must be the price I paid. I winced; I'd need to find ice and ibuprofen before long.

Gingerly, I padded over to Evangeline and placed my good hand on her shoulder. She jolted awake with a start, eyes flying wide. When she saw me, she staggered to her feet, taking me by both shoulders and squeezing softly.

"You're awake," she said, pulling me in for a gentle hug. I relaxed against her, grateful for the human contact. When I pulled away, she was peering at me intently, her mouth pressed in a hard line.

"What's wrong?" I asked.

Evangeline shook her head. "You tell me."

"The house doesn't want me here," I said, my voice hushed like I was afraid the walls might hear. "It tried to keep me out last night, but I fought it. I fought so hard I passed out."

Evangeline fretted her lips, her eyes imploring. "How did you do it?" she whispered. "How did you go against the house's wishes?"

I dropped my eyes, the wind gone from my sails. I knew what she wanted. She wanted me to tell her I had the answer, that I knew how to tell her brain to tell her legs to just walk out the front door and keep going. And maybe that act of defiance would free her, returning everything to normal.

But I couldn't tell her any of that because none of it was true.

I'd had help.

"I've got Terminator on me," I said. "It told my body how to fight against the compulsion. But when the gift wears off..." I shrugged, letting my voice trail. But Evangeline understood.

Wearily, she dropped back into the chair, her face buried in her hands. "I shouldn't have done what I did," she said, so softly I had to strain to hear. "I should never have moved those folks' graves. I could have moved my family here without moving their family out." She looked up then, liquid eyes rimmed red. "Was it selfish, Kezia? Was I selfish?"

I didn't want to answer. Was it selfish? Perhaps. Yes. But

humans were like that, programmed by biology. Our DNA was coded to look out for ourselves and our families. Looking out for those not in our tribe wasn't necessarily natural; it was learned.

But it didn't matter. Even if she'd been selfish, the transgression didn't warrant this punishment.

When I didn't answer, Evangeline shrank again, hiding behind her hands. Her shoulders quaked softly, and I thought I should comfort her, but I didn't know what to say. I could still feel my spiritual body fighting against a desire to run, and my disposable emotional resources were depleted.

"The house knows you're trying to help me," she said. "That's why it wants you gone. The house wants me to suffer for my pride and selfishness. It wants me to suffer for my sins."

"I don't believe that."

Again, Evangeline looked up, surprised. "Don't you?"

"If the house is punishing you, then it's selfish, too. You can't repay blood with blood. If the spirits of those who lived here before —"

An idea struck me dumb. It was so obvious that I nearly laughed. How had I missed it? How had Evangeline?

"I'll ask them," I said.

"Who?"

"The Scarboroughs," I said. "I'll cross over and speak to them myself. Maybe this whole thing is just a misunderstanding."

Evangeline looked afraid to hope. "Can you do that? Can you work magic?"

"Yes, I still can," I said, smiling at the relief in Evangeline's face. "Listen. The movers will be here soon. Go get cleaned up and have some breakfast. Don't worry about this. I'm taking care of it. I promise."

Evangeline nodded, saying nothing more as she collected the tea set and book and slipped from the room.

After a quick shower and changing into shorts and a camisole, I got down to business. I curled up in my slipper chair with the file David Pope had given me. I read over the pertinent documents carefully, noting any personal information that might prove useful. According to a newspaper obituary included in the file, Joseph and Cordelia were childhood sweethearts, married when Cordelia was just 16. They had twin children, Rupert and Emilia, both of whom died in a car accident.

Born on the same day, died on the same day. I shivered, though the house was warm. It meant nothing. There was no magic or mystery in it — just dumb coincidence.

But I'd be lying if I said it didn't give me the willies.

It was strange to pore over the records of the dead. I was used to death, of course. As a hospice worker, I'd sat with countless dying patients, easing their fears, helping them transition from this plane to the next. I had death in my blood, but not like this. Usually, death was intimate and personal. I could feel it, smell it, see it sometimes. Death energy was active.

This felt distant and academic. Cold. As I looked through the records of the Scarboroughs' lives, I had to remember that these were real people: warm, human bodies who had lived in this house, tended its gardens, made love in its rooms, and been buried on its grounds.

Was that why this place was cursed? Because Evangeline hadn't properly honored the lives that once lived here? David assured me the graves had been properly transported. But there was propriety under the law, and propriety under God. And everyone knew those two were rarely the same.

I sighed, shutting my eyes. *Shouldn't have moved the graves,* I thought, despondent. *At least, not without a ritual. Gifts. Offerings. Shit, Evangeline. Maybe you shoulda let those people's bones be.*

I looked down again into the file, flipping past the legal stuff that I didn't care so much about to the faded photographs at the end. I let my fingers trace over their faces. They looked so serious, like life was a burden to endure rather than a gift to celebrate.

Well, maybe it had been. What did I know?

I had crossed through the veil almost before I realized I was doing it. Either I was getting better at riding the death current or the house magic that wanted me gone made the transition easier. That made sense, actually: the other side technically wasn't *in* the house. So of course the house would usher me along.

Once I crossed over, it took me a moment to realize where I was. The initial emergence was always disorienting because I never knew where I'd find myself, especially when I did necromancy for strangers. I might end up in a schoolhouse, a barn... hell, once I'd ended up in a bordello. That had been wild. Depressing, but wild. No one should have to suffer the indignity of being called back to work in the afterlife.

As I waited for my surroundings to come into view, I focused my mind on the image of Joseph and Cordelia Scarborough. I willed them to welcome me. I willed myself to be brave and accommodating and gentle like I was when I held the hand of a dying patient.

The environment finally pieced together. Everything was still hazy and ill-defined, but my whereabouts felt familiar. And after a moment, I realized why.

I was on the Scarborough property.

I was *here*. Well, not here. There?

Listen, sometimes this work is confusing.

In any case, I found myself on an earlier version of Evangeline's property. I was in the backyard before it was a cemetery. About halfway between where I stood and the house was a gazebo that didn't exist in the present day. Sitting in the gazebo were two people.

I walked toward them, hands clasped at the small of my back. The forms of Joseph and Cordelia Scarborough swam into view, appearing as they might have in their midlife years. Still vibrant. Beautiful. When they saw me, they lifted their hands in greeting as though they had known me for a long time. They beckoned me over, and I was happy to obey. They made room for me at the small iron table. Cordelia tossed her hair from her shoulders. "We haven't had visitors in such a long time," she said.

Joseph chuckled and patted his wife's hand. "Didn't think we'd ever have visitors again," he said. "Not much cause to, I guess. Our line has long run out. Well, almost."

"Are you Joseph and Cordelia Scarborough?" I asked.

"Well, yes, we're Joseph and Cordelia," answered the woman, all smiles. "And who might you be, sweetheart?"

"My name is Kezia Bernard. A friend of mine purchased this property a few years ago. I'd like to ask you some questions about that, if it's okay." I always asked the spirits for permission to interview them. Sometimes they were loquacious. Other times they were private. It was better to know what I was dealing with, especially since I might have to ask them to pretty please with sugar on top lift the fucking curse they'd put on this property.

I had to start out on the right foot.

Cordelia smiled. "Of course. We're happy to help."

"How many generations of Scarboroughs lived in this

house?" I wanted to get a feel for how many potential suspects I was looking at.

"Only three," Joseph said. "My parents bought this property after they wed, and I was born here. Cordelia and I inherited the house upon my father's death, and both our children were born in the house."

"Were your parents buried on the property?"

"They were not," Joseph said. "My father wanted to be laid to rest in his family plot back in Virginia, so we honored that request when he and Mama passed. Only Cordelia, the children, and I are buried here." He shifted then, eyes flitting momentarily away. "*Were* buried here."

That was my opening. I took a breath. "I understand the family was moved to another location a few years back. Is that right?

Joseph's lips lost a bit of their color. "That's right."

I hesitated before saying, "Please excuse me for saying so, but you don't seem so pleased about that."

"Pleased?" Joseph frowned, uncrossing and recrossing his legs. "No, I can't say I was pleased. I find it distasteful to move a final resting place. But I'm a man of God, and I also understand that our bodies are only a vehicle to move our spirits about the mortal coil."

"So you weren't...upset?"

Joseph's eyes widened. "Upset about graves? Of course not. What happened to our earthly bodies was unseemly, but we've moved on." Joseph must have noticed something in my body language because he rolled his eyes and snapped his fingers at me. "Quit beating around the bush, girl. I know you didn't come all this way to ask me how I *feel* about my bones being moved. If you have something you want to say, say it."

I nodded. "All right. It's been suggested to me that there

might be a curse on this property. Do you know anything about that?"

Cordelia's face blanched, her mouth going slack. She flicked her eyes to her husband, who had folded his arms over his chest. "What a ridiculous suggestion," he said in a voice that belied his words. "Neither I nor my wife and children would have the first *idea* how to cast a curse on a property. And even if we did, why would we? I just told you we have no need for the bodies that were moved."

I dithered, wringing my hands in my lap. "Well, it might not have been intentional. Sometimes, when magic runs in a family —"

"Magic does *not* run in our family!" Joseph interrupted, his face blooming red. Cordelia's jaw hardened; her eyes dropped low. "Ours are good Christian people, and we don't consort with that kind of thing!"

I shifted my gaze from Joseph to Cordelia, but when she caught me looking, she squared her shoulders and clenched her small fists in her lap. "Our family wouldn't have anything to do with curses," she managed to squeak out.

I returned my attention to Joseph. "And what about your children? Were they —"

Fire blazed behind Joseph's eyes. "I will not have you speak of the children," he said. "The children have nothing to do with any of this. I won't sit here and be accused of witchcraft by a stranger I've never laid eyes on in my life! Rupert and Emilia were good, faithful children. They feared the Lord and obeyed their parents. None of my offspring had anything to do with witchcraft or devilry, and I'll thank you to keep those words out of your mouth when speaking to us!"

I wanted to ask more questions, but the scenery was already beginning to fade. The other side had a way of protecting itself from the living, and strong emotions like anger often forced me back across the veil into my physical body. And just as I was opening my mouth to ask one more thing, I awoke back in the bedroom.

I rubbed my knuckles into my eyes, taking deep breaths to center and anchor myself in my body as phosphenes swam in and out of existence. When I opened my eyes, the world was blurry, and I waited for the sensation to pass. But then, in the corner of the room, I saw something flutter. A shadow. I couldn't be sure, but I felt like it had been watching me.

But when I turned to look at it, it was gone.

UNSURE WHETHER I had really learned anything useful, I drew to my feet and went downstairs. I picked my way through the movers and heaps of boxes to finally find Evangeline on the front porch, swinging in the swing. When she saw me, she patted the seat beside her, and I joined her.

"Where's Dominic?" I asked.

Evangeline waved vaguely. "Out riding his bike. He's around the neighborhood somewhere."

I nodded. "Free range. I like that. That's how I'd want to raise Lola."

Evangeline grunted a sound of agreement. "Kids need their freedom," was all she said.

After a while, I shifted and turned to face my host. "I crossed over. Talked to the Scarboroughs. They're still here," I said. "Well, not *here*. But when I crossed the veil, I met them in a place that looked like this property must have decades ago."

Evangeline blinked, surprised. She must have forgotten the plan. "You found them? The folks who used to live here?"

"Yes," I answered, my brow wrinkled. "Why?"

"I've tried to find them myself, but I couldn't," she said, folding her hands in her lap. "Before Rocky had the graves moved. I tried to contact them and let them know what we were doing. I didn't have any personal objects of theirs, but I thought the house would be enough." She cocked her head to the side. "What did you use?"

"Photographs," I said. "I got a file on the family from that archaeologist David Pope."

"You can use photographs?" Evangeline made a face like she was impressed. "I've always had to use an object close to the person. Something they held or wore or touched frequently. Photographs," she mused. "You have a talent I don't."

I felt strange hearing that. It was a mix of pride and embarrassment, though neither was warranted. It wasn't like I had done something extraordinary to earn the ability to find people on the other side with only a photograph. That was just dumb luck. But I blushed and looked away all the same.

"Do you think it was them? Who placed the curse?"

"I don't know," I admitted. "Well, no, I don't think they did it. They seemed very uncomfortable with magic — even disgusted. And what's more, I don't think we need to worry about moving the graves back here, either. They didn't seem to care one way or another what happened to their remains. So that's good news. But the wife seemed like she was holding something back. I'll have to figure out how to get her alone. Maybe she'll tell me more without her husband there."

"Well, we can hope. How are you holding up? You still feeling like you need to get out of here?"

I recognized the change in subject and let it slide. "Yes," I admitted, another shiver making my skin pimple over despite the heat. "Fighting it makes me tired. It's not too bad right now. I just feel like I had a glass of wine on an empty stomach. Not sure how much longer this can go on, though."

Evangeline ran a hand through her lavender hair, winding a lock around a finger. "No, I guess you can't fight it forever. Has Terrence turned up anything yet?"

I shook my head. "Not yet. I don't know if we should get our hopes up."

Evangeline's eyes looked sad when she said, "Too late for that."

I opened my mouth, then closed it again. I had so much I needed to say, but I felt selfish for asking. But I had to bring it up. "Evangeline, I'm doing the best I can for you. But I'm gonna need something *from* you. You said you were going to help me with my affliction. Do you think it's time for us to get started on that?"

Evangeline shooed away my concern with the gentle flick of her fingers, not even meeting my gaze. "We have plenty of time for all that," she said. "You just got to trust me on this. I haven't forgotten why you're here. I think about you and that baby girl of yours all the time."

I was sure Evangeline was telling the truth, that my situation weighed on her. But I didn't need assurances. I needed *action*, and in all the time I'd been at Evangeline's, I hadn't learned a single thing I didn't know before.

Well, that wasn't exactly true. But I still had more questions than answers.

It was suddenly too warm, and I didn't want to be outside anymore. Or maybe I just didn't want to be on the porch. Or maybe I didn't want to be with Evangeline. Or maybe it was the house.

Whatever the reason, I needed to leave.

I stood and pulled my phone from my pocket to call a rideshare. "I need a break," I said, tapping in a request for a ride to a coffee shop. I turned, heading toward the street to wait. But I had scarcely taken two steps when Evangeline's voice stopped me.

"Kezia," she said. Her voice was strained, and I stopped, turning around. The color had drained from her face, her lips quivering. "You don't have a tattoo on your back, do you?"

I frowned. "A tattoo? No, I don't. Why?"

Evangeline raised a hand to her mouth. "You need to have a look at your back."

She said these words with no urgency, but I felt it anyway. I darted into the house, taking the stairs two at a time, sprinting to my bedroom. I flung open the door and dug a cosmetic mirror out from my bag. I tugged the camisole over my head and turned my back to the large vanity mirror, lifting the compact so I could see.

There, etched on my skin, were markings similar to those I had seen on Evangeline's legs. Dark veins pulsed, the unmarked surrounding skin red and raised.

Jesus Christ, I breathed, fear clotting in my throat. *Jesus Christ, what is that?*

But I didn't really need to ask. I had known it all along, as soon as I'd thrown a punch at Angelo when he tried to bring me into the house. Whatever was wrong with Evangeline was happening to me, too.

Except that where Evangeline had vines etched down her calves, I had been marked, shoulder to shoulder, with a brand-new pair of bird's wings.

At the coffee shop, I chose a table in the back corner, as far away from other people as I could find. As I settled in, I realized I probably should've gone to a bar instead. Caffeine would only heighten my anxiety, and I was already shaking so badly, the silverware on my table clattered. But it felt too early to get plastered, even for an old pro like me. Instead, I ordered a cappuccino, then called the only person who I trusted to talk me down.

Marcus answered the phone immediately. "Dove! Lovely to hear from you. How are things down in Georgia?"

I sucked in a breath and fought back tears, refusing to babble in public, let alone on the phone to Marcus. "I think this whole thing might have been a giant mistake," I admitted.

Marcus was silent for a heartbeat. Two. Then, "What's going on?"

I told him everything. I told him about Evangeline's curse, the strange dreams I'd been having, the curse on the property, the bone theft. Everything. When I finally finished, I was trembling, my voice hoarse. I really wished I'd gone to a bar.

Marcus took it all in with aplomb. He murmured in all the right places, making surprised or sympathetic sounds where appropriate. But I needed more from Marcus than passive support. I needed advice.

"So," I said, gulping down my rising anxiety. "What do I do now?"

"Well," Marcus drawled, "what does your gut say? What are you looking into now?"

I dug my fingers into my thighs, trying to steady my nerves. "My gut feelings are all over the place. At first, I told myself I was doing this to help Evangeline, so she doesn't lose her son.

But these markings on my back...This isn't a coincidence. I'm in it now. It's just like when I got the fire in my eyes at the temple. How do I keep *doing* this to myself?"

"You've never been one to do anything half-ass," Marcus supplied. "You get into these situations because you fully invest. I've never known anyone to give as much as you do. You're the most giving person I know."

The words hit a tender spot. I thought of Divina telling me that I was a taker, and I hadn't realized until now how deeply her words wounded me. But Marcus was right — I let myself get into these tight spots because I never gave up. I was a fighter.

But I was growing tired of fighting.

"I have this strong feeling like as soon as I get out of here, everything will be fine. I just want to leave. As much as I hate to admit it, I don't want to be here anymore."

Marcus sighed on the other end. "Do what you have to do, you know? But a lot is riding on the outcome of this trip. I don't have to tell you that."

He was right. He didn't need to tell me. Humans had been staring down the barrel of a gun and acting in the face of that fear for hundreds if not thousands of years. If my ancestors could survive wild lions and hyenas on the plains of Africa, then I could face whatever was waiting for me at Evangeline's. That thought was hardly comforting, though.

"I'm not going anywhere," I said. "I've got a job to do, and I might never get another chance like this one. So now that we've got that out of the way, what do I do next? I feel like there's so much going on, and I don't know which leads to follow."

"I can help you with some research if you like," Marcus

said. "I have colleagues here who probably know more about bone magic rituals than I do. So you can leave that to me."

I sighed with relief. "Thank you. I appreciate that. But while we're on the subject, can I pick your brain about something else?"

"Of course."

"So I was talking to that osteurge I met the other day, right? He seems to think the reason there are no necromancers in Atlanta is because someone has put a spell on the city, intentionally thwarting necromancy from flourishing here. Is that even something that could happen?"

Marcus hrmmed on the other end. "It's possible to cast a spell with a crazy large area of effect, but it would be very difficult."

I nodded. "Okay, tell me more. How difficult? What would it involve?"

"Well, to start, you'd have to involve many people, each with a different magical specialty. That's the only way you'd draw enough power to cover a city the size of Atlanta. And then you'd have to feed the magic regularly — with Atlanta's population, that magic would get used up *quick*. So you're talking about a bunch of people working together regularly across magic disciplines."

"You sound skeptical."

"It just seems unlikely. It's not impossible, but what would be the point?"

"Well, I don't know," I said, "but my lack of imagination doesn't prove anything."

Marcus chuckled. "True enough! So what do you make of this rabbit you've been dreaming about? Roger, you called it. Do you think it has anything to do with this house-not-wanting-you-there business?"

"I don't know," I admitted, hating how often I said that. "Evangeline seems to think it's some kind of benevolent spirit guide, and everyone at the house has dreamed of Roger with nothing bad happening to them. But...it creeps me out the way it watches. It feels dirty. Like, I feel violated when I wake up."

"That doesn't sound pleasant," Marcus agreed, "but it hardly sounds malicious, either. Let's put a pin in the rabbit. You said you had a feeling the wife — Cordelia — had more she wanted to say to you. Maybe that's what we should focus on."

"I agree with that, I just haven't figured out how to find her without him. The only photograph I have is of them both. But I'll keep thinking about it."

Marcus was silent a moment, and I had a feeling he was struggling with what he wanted to say next. I kept silent until he cleared his throat. "Listen, Kezia, when you get back...I think it's time we move past video conferencing with your daughter. I think we need to —"

"Hey, Marcus, sorry, I have to go," I interrupted. "Thanks for looking into the bone ritual stuff for me, I appreciate it. Give Lola my love."

I hung up and put my phone on Do Not Disturb before Marcus could call me back. I had enough to deal with, and I couldn't even think about meeting up with Lola, which I was sure he was about to propose. I was irrationally angry at him for even bringing it up. *I* would decide when I was ready to meet my daughter. Me. No one else. He knew that.

But even though my mind fought against the idea, my heart was interested. And by the time I finished my coffee and left the coffee shop, I couldn't brush away all the tears that found their way down my cheeks.

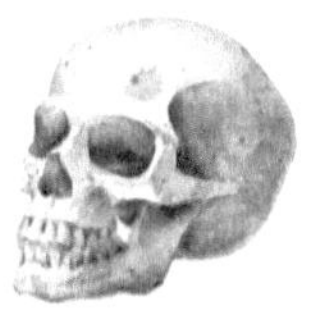

I STAYED GONE most of the day, partially out of magic-induced anxiety about going back to the house, and partly because I didn't want to deal with the chaos of moving. I had never been to Atlanta before, so I took myself sightseeing and to a nice dinner. I had hoped my little Necromancer's Day Out would rejuvenate me.

It mostly didn't.

By the time I got back to Evangeline's, it was dark. As soon as I crossed through the front gate, that now-familiar swell of anxiety tried to engulf me, but I fought it down, gritting my molars against the desire to flee. I let my Terminator gift do its thing, throwing up shields to guard me from the magic. When I felt sufficiently protected, I walked through the front door. As soon as I was inside, my adrenaline spiked, and a fresh wave of a new emotion washed over me.

Not fear this time, though. Fury.

A man stood across the room, his back to me, speaking on

the phone. I couldn't see his face, but I recognized the frame and that voice.

It was the same man I had tackled in Evangeline's cemetery.

I didn't stop to think. By the time I could ask myself what the hell I was doing, I was already on him, spinning him around and grabbing him by the throat, thrusting him into the bookshelf. He cried out and grabbed my face, but I was faster and, thanks to Terminator, stronger. I tackled him to the ground and straddled him, crushing his chest with my weight. I pinned his arms to the ground with my legs as my forearm pressed against his windpipe. I saw his eyes bulge with disbelief and pressure as he tried to rasp something out at me. He might've been asking what the hell I was doing, but I didn't hear his words clearly. The blood was rushing too loudly in my ears.

"What the fuck are you doing here?" I asked.

The man was bucking, trying to answer and get me off of him, but I was crushing his windpipe so he could barely speak. I relented just enough to let him wheeze out the words, "Get off me, you crazy bitch."

I was about to demand an answer when I heard scuffling followed by shouting. The next thing I knew, someone's hands were hooking under my armpits, yanking me off.

"Kezia! What the hell are you doing! Get off him!"

I allowed myself to be pulled off the man on the floor who now scrambled away from me, coughing and sputtering. At the same time, my Terminator gift ebbed, my adrenaline levels returning to normal, my muscles aching. I swooned, winded and exhausted.

I looked up to see that Evangeline was not alone. Standing next to her was Terrence Curtis.

Terrence stepped forward, lending his hands to the man on the ground and pulling him to his feet. The other man made a big show of dusting himself off, straightening his clothes and throwing me a murderous stare. I returned the glare, my hate levels still set to boiling. Everyone turned to me then, befuddled. "Kezia?" Evangeline repeated. "What are you doing? What's going on in here?"

I held up a shaking finger, pointing in the man's direction. "It was him," I said. "In the cemetery that night. He's one of the thieves who were summoning bones from the graveyard. He's the one who stole Delia Rae's skull!"

Both Evangeline and Terrence turned to the man, whose expression betrayed neither guilt nor shame. He just looked pissed off. "You need to put this crazy bitch on a leash," he said to Evangeline. "I don't know what the fuck she's talking about."

"Okay, okay," Terrence said, making patting motions with his hands, telling all of us to calm down. "I'm sure this is just a misunderstanding. Kezia, this is my brother, Devon. Devon, this is Evangeline's friend and fellow necromancer, Kezia Bernard."

My jaw fell open, and I gaped first at Terrence, then back at Devon. I wasn't sure what confused me more. The fact that I was absolutely, 100% certain that the man standing in front of me was the same man I had fought in the graveyard, or the fact that Evangeline and Terrence seemed absolutely unfazed by my conviction. "I know what I saw," I said, my voice trembling. "No, to hell with that, I know what I *felt*. I tackled him. I heard his voice. It was *him*."

Evangeline placed a hand on my shoulder, a gesture intended to calm me, but I shrugged away. "It was dark," she said. "Lots of people can favor each other in the dark."

Devon huffed and straightened himself out. "Not all bruthas look the same," he sneered at me.

"No, they don't," I agreed. "That's how I know it was you."

"Kezia, Devon and Terrence are longtime friends of mine," Evangeline was saying. "And as much as I want to believe your eyewitness testimony, my decades of friendship won't allow me to mistrust Devon. So, I'm sorry, Kezia, but you must be mistaken."

I wasn't mistaken, and as I watched Devon's frown turn into a smirk, half of me wanted to smash my knuckles against his nose. But I already knew I couldn't; my hormones were returning to normal, and my preternatural gift must not have believed I was in danger because it went back to defending me against the house's magic. If I tried to attack Devon now, it would be just me and my complete lack of both muscles and fighting prowess.

I didn't need the gift of premonition to know that wouldn't go well.

"I guess I must've made a mistake," I said finally, swallowing down my pride. It took every ounce of self-control I had to tell this bald-faced lie. "I'm sorry I attacked you just now. And kicked your ass."

The barest flush rose in Devon's cheeks even as Terrence and Evangeline swallowed down their chuckles, covering them with fake coughs. "You only took me down because I don't believe in hitting women," Devon said. "Plus, you took a potshot at me. Sucker punch. If you'd come at me like a man, we'd be having a very different conversation."

I donned a smile that didn't reach my eyes. "I'm sure."

Devon prepared his mouth to issue a retort, but Evangeline held up a hand, silencing us both. "I don't want to hear anything more about this," she said, her expression serious. "Now why don't we all have a seat and start over?" The two brothers and I followed Evangeline's lead, taking seats around the living room. When everyone was settled in, Evangeline turned her attention to Terrence. "You said you found out some information. What've you got?"

"Well, my people haven't turned up much about the curse per se, though I got some cats who owe me a favor working on that one." He rubbed his hands together and cocked an eyebrow. "I *did* find that other cat, though. Guy you bought the house from. Mister Garrett Milhouse." He said this as he checked notes from his phone. "Got a phone number, address, previous jobs, shit like that. He's retired now, but for the better part of his career, dude was a mail carrier."

I wrinkled my brow. "That doesn't sound right. I mean, I hate to make assumptions, but how does a mail carrier afford a house like this?"

"You right not to be making assumptions," Devon cut in, eyes blazing. "Ain't no tellin' how a man comes into his money. Folks got ways."

"You would know," I lobbed back.

"Enough!" Evangeline said. I'd never seen her angry before, but it looked like I was about to get a preview. The color was rising in her cheeks, and her nostrils flared. "I've about had it with the two of you. I swear to God, y'all workin' my last nerve." She calmed herself, redirecting her attention to Terrence. "Okay, so what are we supposed to do with Mr. Milhouse's information?"

Terrence licked his lips, his eyes flicking between me and his brother. "Well," he drawled, "I don't want to get in the middle of their little love spat, but Kezia might be onto something. I also question how Mr. Milhouse obtained this property. It's a little...ehhh." He wobbled his hand in front of him. "It's sus is all I'm sayin'." Now, Terrence turned to me, the slightest smile on his face. "I'm thinking *you* should talk to him." He shrugged, feigning innocence when he said, "Not everybody feels real comfortable opening up to me."

I sucked my teeth and rolled my eyes. "You mean some folks get shy around criminals?"

Evangeline shot me a look, and I dropped my gaze like a scolded child. "Okay, so y'all will talk to Mr. Milhouse. Anything else, Terry? This is slim," she said, her voice close to breaking.

Now, Terrence cleared his throat, his expression darkening. "Angie...I heard a couple of my guys talking. Seems folks is getting antsy waiting on you to get better. Nobody's been getting their gifts, and it's starting to make people nervous." He dropped his eyes then, searching the carpet like it might give him the courage to say what I already knew was coming. "They're talking about going to see that necro dude down in Albany."

Evangeline made a face. "Conrad? His place is a two-hour drive from here."

Terrence nodded. "I know. But there's been talk. He's not running his necromancy out his sister's hair salon anymore. He's got a real church. Like yours. And what I hear is he's advertising that he'll give gifts as well as other forms of magic."

Evangeline shrugged. "That's his prerogative. Conrad does good magic. I bought a glamour from him years ago. His work's nothing to sneeze at."

"That's not the point," Terrence said. "He's trying to lure your congregation away. Because this big house you got? Your fame? Your following? Word is, *he* wants that." Terrence sighed, sitting back into the couch cushions and crossing his arms over his chest. "Angie, we told you from jump you need to be offering people magic. They're gonna get it from somewhere."

"Sounds like they gonna get it from Conrad," Devon muttered.

"Then *let them*," Evangeline sighed, exasperated. "I have no interest in selling magic for a profit. None. I'm happy to lay hands and give gifts. You know that." When neither man responded, Evangeline grew despondent. "What do you want me to do, Terry? I *can't leave the house!* And even if I could, I don't *own* these people. They can go to whoever they want for their gifts. What does any of this have to do with the task I put you on?"

"He's suggesting that this Conrad guy may be the one who put words on you," I said, summarizing what I had already gleaned from Terrence's implications. "He saw an opening to attack and took it. Evangeline, look around you. You got this through necromancy. Other folks are gonna try to step in on your territory now that you —"

"*No.*" Her voice was hard, her stare so sharp it could have cut bone. "I won't do this. I hate this! Ain't no *territory!* What we got here is *community*, and I don't own that! And I will not speculate about *Conrad Tillison* putting words on me to pad his own bank account without evidence!"

"Angie —"

"*No!* Don't Angie me! I'm done with this! Bring me hard facts. Bring me something I can work with. But don't y'all bring me *Conrad Tillison is minding his damn business practicing necromancy and growing his community* like that's something I shouldn't want! Stop! I refuse to be a woman who turns on her own people! *Let* them go to Conrad and get blessed! *Let*

Conrad make a little money! I don't begrudge *anyone* their success. If it was up to me, I'd rain abundance on all my brothers and sisters. So stop this foolishness. I only want you to *find whoever did this to me* and make it right!"

Evangeline stormed out of the room and up the stairs, and after a few moments, I heard her slamming her bedroom door shut. Devon and Terrence winced at the sound, and I gave them both my best glare as I rose to my feet. I turned to Terrence, trying to keep my face neutral. "That night in the cemetery. Were you there with Devon? Were you the other guy I fought?" I asked.

He frowned and sucked in a breath. "Kezia, you don't know —"

"No, don't," I said, holding up a hand. "I can't prove it yet. But I know the two of you are up to something. For my life, I don't know what. But I do know that Evangeline trusts y'all too much. And if I find out you're responsible for this?" I clenched my fists by my sides. "I swear to God I will go to the ends of the Earth to make you pay."

Then I followed Evangeline's lead and went up to my bedroom.

To my surprise, I found Dominic there, sitting cross-legged on the floor with the comic book. He glanced up at me briefly as I entered the room. "Hey," he said, returning his attention to the comic. "Uncle Terry and Uncle Devon still downstairs?"

"Yeah, but I think they're leaving. I think they pissed off your mom."

He didn't lift his face, but I thought I detected a shadow of a smirk when he replied, "Yeah, they do that. Anyway, Mama's got a temper."

I edged around the boy, making my way to the other side of

the room before dropping into the slipper chair at the foot of my bed. "So what you doing in here?"

Dominic lifted his chin, indicating the door I had left slightly open. "Spying," he said. Now, his smile became more than a shadow. "I can't hear what they're talking about from my room. This room has better...What you call it? Coo sticks?"

I chuckled. "Acoustics. So you were listening in on grown folks' business? You best hope your mama don't find out."

Dominic just sucked his teeth and leaned back onto his hands. "You ain't gonna tell her," he said, calling my bluff. I grinned but made no reply.

"So what are you reading there?"

"Just superhero stuff," he said. "Do you like comics?"

I shook my head. "Never really read them as a kid."

Dominic shrugged. "It's not too late. Didn't you say you got a daughter? Maybe she'd like to read them."

"Well, maybe she would. What do you recommend? Which one's your favorite?"

Dominic grew thoughtful, so it surprised me when he said, "Can I ask you something?"

I folded my hands into my lap and crossed my ankles. "Of course."

The boy hesitated, worrying the inside of his cheek with his tongue. "If my mom gets better, will she go back to work?"

I puffed up my cheeks and blew out a little puff of air. "Well, I think so. There's a lot of people out there counting on her. And I think she likes helping people, so yes, I think she'll go back." I tilted my head. "Why?"

Dominic sighed. "I love hanging out with Divina because she's fun, and she doesn't care if I watch grownup movies, and she lets me play fight with her, but she's not my mom. And when Mom's working, I'm always with Divina."

I shrugged. "Well, maybe you could ask your mom if you could hang out with Angelo or Rocky. Or —"

"No, you don't get it," he interrupted. "I don't want to hang out with them, either. I want to hang out with my *mom*."

My throat tightened up, and I felt my shoulders slump. "I'm sorry you feel that way, Dominic. I understand what it's like to miss your mom, I do. But everybody has to work. She has to make money somehow, right?"

"No," Dominic disagreed. "We got enough money. She could sell this house if she needed more money! I just want her to be home with me more." He dropped his eyes, and I realized he didn't want me to see him crying. "Is that why you're helping her? Because she needs to make money?"

I shook my head as I worried my fingers against my palm. "I'm helping her because it's the right thing to do." It wasn't my place to tell him the real reason. That if she didn't get better, he'd be spending a lot less time with her than he was now. Just thinking about this left me nauseated. So much was on the line. But how could a boy his age understand?

How, indeed? And how about a girl just a few years younger? How could she understand why her mother refuses to see her? I shoved the thought away.

"I tell you what," I said, forcing fake cheerfulness into my voice. "Why don't you plan something really fun that you want to do when your mom is better? Do you have a favorite park you like to visit, or a movie theater you want to go to? Sometimes making plans for the future can help you deal with the present."

The boy gave a lame shrug as he clambered to his feet. "I guess," he said. "But the truth is, she won't have time for it, anyway. She always got time for everybody else. But not usually for me."

I watched him go with tears burning hot behind my eyes. I wanted to call him back and hug him, to promise him that everything was going to be okay. But as the door clicked shut behind him, I buried my face in my hands. Because for Dominic and Lola alike, it might just be that nothing was going to be okay ever again.

CHAPTER THIRTEEN

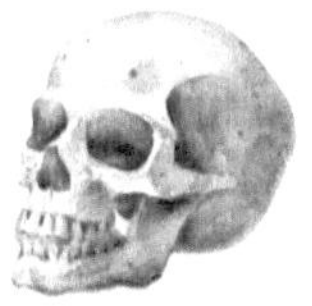

THINGS WERE QUIET over the next several days. Evangeline made herself scarce after the arguments with Devon and Terrence. She holed up in her room and only came downstairs for meals and to make sure Dominic ate, showered, and did his chores. But even though I didn't see much of her, I heard from her. She had taken to sending me text messages, telling me where to go and what work to do for the day. Even though Evangeline wasn't making personal appearances anymore, she was still very much running her church. At least, she was handling the community service side. Between me, Divina, and Rocky, I could've sworn we had performed some kind of charity work for nearly every resident of Atlanta. We delivered groceries, cleaned yards, weeded gardens, and sold vegetables at the local farmer's market. And while I swept floors, hauled boxes, and prepared meals, a small, selfish voice in my head kept asking, "When is it going to be my turn? When is Evangeline gonna help me with my affliction?"

Late one afternoon, after Rocky and I were finishing up our last Meals on Wheels delivery for the day, my phone buzzed with a number I didn't recognize.

"This is Kezia."

"This is Garrett Millhouse. I heard you wanted to talk to me."

It took me a second to place the name, but when I did, my heart skipped a beat. "Mr. Millhouse! I *have* been looking for you. My name is —"

"Kezia Bernard. I know who you are. What do you want me for?"

I cradled the phone against my ear as I indicated to Rocky I'd be along in just a minute. "Well, I'm doing some research on the old Scarborough property. I understand that you were the previous owner. Is that right?"

Garrett grunted on the other end. "County clerk's office coulda told you that. You don't need to bother me with property history, do you?"

He reminded me so powerfully of the old folks at the hospice that I had to bite back a chuckle. They could be ornery, too. Luckily, I had lots of experience dealing with ornery old people. I scurried to catch up with Rocky, covering the receiver with my hand as I mouthed, "I need a good ice cream place. Hurry." Into the phone, I said, "I know a nice place that sells gelato and coffee." Rocky's face lit up, and she mouthed back something I easily deciphered. I grinned and gave her the thumbs up. "If you're talking, I'm buying. I just have some questions I'd like to talk to you about, if you don't mind. Their strawberry is to die for."

Garrett Millhouse was silent for a moment, and I could almost hear him weighing his options on the other end. "Well, I *was* just about to have some dinner," he drawled. I smiled despite myself. Hook, line, and sinker. Old folks loved strawberry ice cream. "But I suppose I could have dessert first. Hell, at my age, it would be a sin not to."

Rocky mouthed the ice cream shop name at me again, and I nodded. "All right then. Amos's Dairy House on Forsythe in Castleberry Hill. I can meet you there in 30 minutes?"

Garrett Millhouse didn't even bother to reply. Just hung up.

Like I said. Ornery old people.

"Listen," I said to Rocky, sliding the phone into a pocket. "Can I get you to finish up without me? I might have a lead."

Rocky nodded. "Oh, sure, no problem. You want me to come with you?"

I waved the offer away. "No need, but thanks. I'll call a rideshare."

Rocky shrugged. "Ok, no worries. You'll like Amos's. It's one of my favorite spots in town. Bring me a pint of salted caramel, would you?" She blew me a kiss as she popped the trunk to dig out the last meals.

AMOS'S DAIRY House was everything Rocky promised it would be. They offered gelato in dozens of flavors, and an abundance of edible containers including cookie sandwiches, waffle cones, and even pancake wraps. I was browsing the menu when I heard a voice from behind me mutter, "Thought you said the strawberry was to die for. What you need to look at the menu for if they already got a flavor you would die for?"

I turned around to come face-to-face with the man I presumed to be Garrett Millhouse. He was about my height, slender, with a curve in his upper back. He must have been tall in his youth but was stooped with age. I wondered idly what

David Pope would see if he got his hands on Garrett's skeleton. His face was wan and deeply lined with wrinkles. Some quick mental math put him right around 90 years old. His black eyes sharp despite the gravel in his voice. Silver stubble gave him a gruff appearance, but an unruly crop of snowy white hair and bushy eyebrows tempered it.

"How'd you know it was me?" I asked.

He frowned. "You're the only person in here, and you said you'd meet me in 30 minutes. I took you at your word that you wouldn't be late."

Seemed reasonable. "Shall I order for both of us then? Strawberry?"

Garrett wrinkled his nose in disgust. "Hell no, I hate strawberry. I'll order for myself, thank you very much."

We retreated to a table where Garrett pored over the menu for another 10 minutes, refusing to talk until he had chosen a flavor. In the end, he chose butter pecan and I, because I didn't want to hear about it later, chose strawberry.

I clasped my hands on the table and put on my best smile. "So how long did you live in the Scarborough house?"

"A little over three years," he said.

I raised an eyebrow. "That's not very long."

"Well, I never expected to live there in the first place."

"What do you mean?"

Garrett gave me an irritated look. "I mean, I wasn't in the market for a new house when that one just fell into my lap. Living in a big house was an adjustment that I never quite made. But I had to try. I had to try for Cordelia."

My chair squeaked as I leaned back, settling in. "Were you and Cordelia friends?"

A waitress came over and brought us our ice creams. I pushed mine to one side, but Garrett immediately went to town. He took a few healthy bites before getting around to my question. "Can't really say we were friends," he began. "More like I was the only person she saw most days after her husband died."

"Is that right? What was the nature of your relationship? How did you know her?"

"Well, I carried the mail to the Scarborough place for about 30 years," he said, his voice and expression proud. "I was her mail carrier. Every holiday, she left me a package in the mailbox. Cookies and candies, mostly. She made a hell of a peanut brittle. And her fudge was an award-winner. Sometimes she'd leave toys for the grandchildren. After my wife died, Cordelia started sending me care packages in the mail. Cookies, mostly, and banana bread. Woman made excellent banana bread. It surprised the hell out of me because I hadn't thought of that woman once since I retired. But I guess you never know the effect you leave on people. I might not have thought of her, but it seemed she hadn't forgotten me. Finally, I thought, Oh, what the hell? I'll pay her a visit."

He grinned at a memory and took another bite of his gelato. "That's how I found out her husband had passed on. She said she'd seen my wife's obituary and wanted to express her condolences. I thought at first she might've had a crush on me." His cheeks blushed at the memory. "But after a while, I realized she was just lonely and needed someone to talk to. It was a good thing that I took the time to keep her company, too. That's how I ended up with the house."

My spoon was halfway to my mouth when Garrett dropped this piece of information. I stopped, lifting my eyes and staring. "What do you mean?"

Garrett pounded the table with a fist. "Can't you follow a story for nothing? I *mean*, when Cordelia died, she left the house to me in her will. Her lawyer said I was her only friend in the world, and she wanted me to be taken care of for the rest of my days."

I sat with that information for a moment. Something about it just didn't seem right. And then I remembered David Pope and his genealogy research. "She had a descendent though, didn't she? I believe it was a young woman named Erin Scarborough. Why didn't Erin inherit the house?"

"Well, that's some sorry business," Garrett lamented. He crossed his arms over his chest and stroked his chin as his eyes listed to one side, thinking. "The way I understand it, the family had a bit of a falling out. Of course, Cordelia and Joseph had every intention of leaving the property to Erin since both of their children had died already. Erin was the sole living descendent. Now, I'm not one to pry, so I didn't ask too many questions. But my understanding is, Cordelia didn't want to leave the house to a known devil worshiper."

Ah. There it was. When I'd met the Scarboroughs on the other side, they'd been repulsed by the idea of magic. I should've realized then the deceased had protested too much, but even I couldn't have seen devil worship coming. "A devil worshiper?"

Garrett nodded. "Understand that like most folks around here, Joseph and Cordelia were God-fearing people. Never missed a sermon on Sunday. But you never can tell with the younger generation. They just weren't raised like we were, no offense to present company. Not sure if it was poor parenting or just society gone wild, but the way I hear it, Erin was a bad seed from the beginning. By the time she got to college, she started practicing witchcraft and hanging out with them occult people. And Cordelia, well, she just couldn't abide that. So instead of leaving her husband's ancestral home to a Satanic, she left it to me."

I studied Garrett's face for some indication that he was lying, but he seemed sincere. And while I had heard crazier stories over the course of my life, this one just...didn't sit right. Something was still off. "Forgive me, but it seems like she would've contested the will. Erin, I mean."

Garrett whistled then, slapping a hand on the table and rolling his eyes toward the ceiling as he hooted. "Oh, she tried! Got herself a lawyer and everything. But the will was airtight, and even though Erin was a blood relation, she didn't have any rights to the property. She had never lived there or nothing, so she didn't even have squatter's rights. Now, I'd be lying if I said I didn't feel guilty for taking that property. At first. But that little lady gave me such a headache over the next couple of months that by the time I got fully moved into that house, any pity I had for Erin Scarborough had long since flown the coop."

"Okay. Did you ever hear from her again after that?"

Garrett shook his head. "Nope. Well, not until I contacted her a couple years later."

"And why did you contact her?"

"Because I was ready to sell her the house."

I took another bite of the ice cream and then bounced the spoon against my lips as I thought. "Okay. And you were selling the house because it was just too big for your liking? I can see how one person alone in that house would be lonely."

Garrett Millhouse looked at me like I had the word "Idiot" stamped across my forehead. "That's not why I sold it. First of all, I was having some trouble keeping up with the place financially. Costs a lot of money to care for a place that size. Plus, the property taxes were getting to be a pain in the ass, excuse my French. Even with those difficulties, I would've tried to muddle through because of the promise I made to Cordelia. But the final nail in the coffin, you see, was that the goddamn place was haunted."

Well, now we were getting somewhere. "Haunted," I repeated. "Tell me about that."

Garrett sighed as a cloud passed over his face, and he linked his hands before him on the table. "Well, at first it was little things. You know, items not where I left them. TV or radio coming on in the middle of the night. Things like that. For a while, I thought maybe I was just getting senile and forgetful. But then I started to see things. Reflections in windows and mirrors. At night, I would get the feeling like somebody was watching me. I heard whispering and sometimes giggling. It would even wake me up sometimes. Now, I know that doesn't sound like much, and believe me, I tried to talk myself out of my fantasies. But eventually, I couldn't pretend that nothing was happening. Closed doors would open on their own. Pillows and blankets would slide off my bed. Sometimes, I would reach for something, like my morning coffee, only to have it slide out of the way, just outside my reach. Even if you're old and forgetful, things don't move on their own right in front of your eyes."

I chewed my bottom lip. "Were you afraid?"

Garrett's head listed sideways as he considered the question. "Not at first. It was more of a curiosity in the beginning. Hell, I even called some friends over so they could see what I was seeing. But nobody else ever did. See stuff, I mean. Whenever I had company over, the disturbances stopped. But as time wore on, the antics weren't so funny anymore. I started to feel like I was in danger. Like the entity in the house didn't want me there. I felt like if I stayed, I'd be buried in the backyard along with them Scarboroughs."

My pulse quickened, and I felt excitement boiling in the pit of my stomach. Finally, it seemed my investigation was leading somewhere. "Garrett, did you have strange dreams when you lived there?"

The old man heaved a shrug. "What kind of dreams?"

I hesitated, knowing how stupid the words would sound. "Dreams of a...rabbit?"

Garrett went silent for almost a full minute before answering. "I had all kinds of strange hallucinations when I lived in that house, but I don't remember dreaming of a rabbit."

"But you did see things?"

Garrett nodded. "Already told you I saw reflections that weren't there. Sometimes I thought I caught a figure standing in the corner, watching me. But I could only see these things out of the corners of my eye. Whenever I looked directly at them, they'd disappear."

"Garrett, when you lived in that house, did you ever discover any strange markings on your body? Black marks or drawings that looked like tattoos?"

Garrett's brow wrinkled, and he scrunched up his nose. "No, hell, nothing like that. Mostly I just saw and heard things that weren't there. Objects moved around my house. Stuff like that."

"Did you ever feel trapped inside the house? Like you couldn't leave?" I searched his face, hoping for recognition, but I saw nothing. Pressing on, I asked, "Or maybe...did you ever feel like you had to get out of there?"

Garrett was shaking his head so hard I feared he might sprain a muscle. "You're not listening to a goddamn thing I'm telling you, girl! Nothing happened to me *physically*. It was just a standard haunting, but it was enough after three years that I couldn't take it anymore. That's when I called that Scarborough girl and asked if she wanted to buy her house back."

I sighed and settled back into my chair. "All right. So you asked Erin if she wanted to buy the house. Did she?"

Garrett clucked his tongue and rolled his eyes as he took another bite of his now-melting gelato. "She said she did, but the offer she made me was ridiculous. I laughed in her face, but she said that was all she could afford. So I told her, well, I'm very sorry, but I can't afford to take that kind of loss. I had already put quite a bit of money into that house, you see. I wasn't just gonna give it away."

I nodded encouragingly. "That makes sense. So you just decided to put a haunted house on the market?"

I felt mildly like an ass as I asked this question, and Garrett had the good sense to blush at his indiscretion. He stuck his spoon in his gelato so it stood like a plastic antenna. "Now, it wasn't exactly like that," he muttered. "I told my realtor I was gonna be real picky about who I sold to. Lucky for me, Evangeline Morris was one of the first people to put an offer in on the house. And I figured, well, she's already a necromancer, so if there's something funny at the house, she'd probably know how to deal with it."

I had to bite my tongue from saying something I would regret. It drove me crazy the way people misunderstood necromancy and what necromancers could do. We could cross to the other side and speak to the dead, but ghosts? Ghosts were not our cup of tea. Ghosts were not people, strictly speaking. They were imprints of people. Spiritual detritus left behind after death. We were no more comfortable with ghosts than your average person.

"I think you're supposed to disclose anything strange about

a house when you sell it," I said. "So did your realtor disclose to Evangeline that the house was haunted?"

"Yes. She bought it anyway."

I blinked in surprise. That was not the answer I expected. In all of our discussions, Evangeline had never mentioned that she knowingly bought a supposedly haunted house. What did that mean? Was she hiding something else from me?

We finished up our ice creams, and I thanked Garrett for his time. Just as we were parting ways, a question occurred to me. "Garrett," I said, stopping him in the parking lot, "just one more thing. On the phone, you said you heard I wanted to talk to you. Who'd you hear that from?"

The old man snorted. "Who else? I heard it from Cordelia."

LATER THAT NIGHT, after everyone else had gone to bed, I slipped out the back door and headed into the cemetery. I stood for a moment, trying to recall from David Pope's sketches where Cordelia and Joseph might have been buried. I made my way to the far back corner in the dark, careful not to lose my footing. When I found the approximate area, I reached into my pocket and pulled out a photo of Cordelia. Garrett had kept it all these years and had given it to me with some reluctance. But when I explained why I needed it, he agreed.

In the dim moonlight, I traced the image with my fingers, committing the face to memory. I knew she had information to give me, and I needed her alone to coax it from her. This had to work. It was the only thing keeping me going.

When I was ready, I sank my fingers into the damp earth,

letting the death current move through my body and carry my consciousness to the other side. I focused on Cordelia and willed myself toward her. When I arrived on the other side, I was once again on an earlier version of Evangeline's property with the gazebo in the distance. I approached the structure, and my heart skipped a beat to see that Cordelia was alone. She smiled when she saw me, lifting a hand in greeting. I returned the gesture.

I sat across from her under the gazebo, thin sunlight streaming through the latticework decorating the little building. Cordelia offered me tea, but I declined. I couldn't drink it, anyway. The other side has its limits.

After a moment, Cordelia cleared her throat and folded her hands on the table. "I guess you and I have some unfinished business, don't we?"

"I just have some questions about Garrett Millhouse. Well, I guess you could say I have questions about the house. And why you left it to him instead of keeping it in the family."

Cordelia heaved a heavy sigh and plopped her chin in her hand. The motion made her look young and helpless. Without her husband by her side, she seemed more herself. More casual. She blew out her cheeks in a puff of frustration before responding. "They don't tell you when you have a child that it isn't really your child. They don't belong to you; they are their own person. You can educate them and feed them and care for them and love them. But ultimately, they will make their own choices about how they live their lives. That's their prerogative. They're not supposed to be clones. But people, especially in the South, have expectations. And when a family doesn't meet those expectations, well, it can be embarrassing. And when a well-to-do man marries a lesser woman and then they have children that bring embarrassment upon his family…Well, I guess you can see where I'm going with this."

I had an inkling, but I needed Cordelia to explain. I made my expression as open as possible as I leaned forward onto my elbows. "Did something happen with the children? Did they end up embarrassing your husband?"

Cordelia ran her fingers through her white-blonde hair, her eyes growing soft and liquid as she thought. "Rupert was always a wild one," she said finally. "Maybe not wild by today's standards, but he never did what we expected of him. So when he got that young woman in a bad way out of wedlock, no one should have been surprised, but we were. Joseph was furious. I was disappointed, but mothers and sons have a special relationship. I tried to convince Rupert to marry the girl, but he wasn't interested. It took a long time just to convince the girl, her name was Catherine, to allow us a relationship with the child. She said we had treated her shabbily, which we had, and she wanted nothing to do with us. But eventually, she came around, and about the time she was thirteen, we invited Erin into our lives. Well, as much as we could. Erin took after her father. Headstrong. Defiant. She absolutely refused to adhere to the gentler protocols our family required. But even the fact that she refused to go to college and ran around calling herself a liberal and voting for Democrats could have been forgiven until…"

My heart and breathing sped up. Finally, Cordelia was going to give me something I could use. "Until what?"

Cordelia huffed, her expression turning cold and angry. "She started practicing witchcraft," she hissed, her voice barely above a whisper. Even as she spoke the words, she glanced around furtively, as though afraid some nosey neighbor might overhear her confession. "My family has…connections with

Salem," she explained, a fire of embarrassment growing in her cheeks. "It's one reason Joseph's family had such misgivings about our union. When Erin found out, she took full advantage. She even joined a coven. Changed her name. Refused to have anything to do with me or Joseph. At least until it was time to inherit the house." She laughed then, but the sound was bitter and utterly devoid of mirth. "To tell you the truth, if it had been completely up to me, I still would have left the girl the house. I wanted the property to stay in the Scarborough family. And even though she was a bastard, Rupert *was* her father. But I knew that if I left her the house, Joseph would never forgive me. And I had no intentions of spending my entire afterlife being snubbed by my own husband. So I did what any God-fearing Christian woman would do, and I willed the house to someone who could take care of it. Someone who wouldn't besmirch the family name with his witchcraft and satanic shenanigans."

I had to tread lightly because Cordelia was already getting agitated. She was tapping her fingers along her forearm and clicking her tongue against her teeth, her leg bouncing beneath the table. But there was something here. "Cordelia," I said, "did Erin's practice of witchcraft have anything to do with the ghosts that Garrett saw in the house?"

Cordelia's face crumbled. She buried her face in the palms of her hands, her shoulders shaking as she sobbed. The outburst was so sudden that it caught me utterly by surprise, and for a moment, all I could do was stare. Unsure what the proper protocol was, I reached out a tentative hand, placing it on her forearm. The gesture seemed to do the trick, and her sobs eased, declining into sniffles. She looked up, the rims of her eyes raw and red as a rivulet of snot dripped from her nose.

"This house was never haunted," she said. "The things that Garrett saw in our home were entirely in his imagination."

I hadn't realized I'd been holding my breath until I let it out in a whoosh, suddenly deflated. But the despair that tried to grip me quickly fled when Cordelia continued, "But his imagination was being manipulated by my granddaughter. She hoped that if she scared him good enough, he would sell her the house at a price she could afford. And so she and her little witchcraft friends put a hex on him. Made him see and hear things that scared him out of his wits." Cordelia wiped a tear and dropped her gaze. "I saw everything. Erin wanted me to know. She *wanted* me to know it was *my* blood, *my* family history that had brought this on the Scarborough family. There were times I tried to reach out to him, to let him know what was happening. But all the time Garrett lived in this house, Erin's will was strong on him. It wasn't until after he moved out that I could talk to him — to let him know that he had done nothing wrong, and I was grateful for the care and love he showed our home. It wasn't his fault that our granddaughter was a vindictive little bitch."

I swallowed around a lump of excitement that formed in my throat. "Cordelia, do you know if the hex extends to *anyone* that owns that house?"

Cordelia shook her head vigorously. "No. I'm sure it was specific to Garrett. Hexes can go wrong, can't they? If she hexed anyone that lived in that house, and assuming she ever got it back, the hex would apply to her, too. Plus, she wanted to hurt me by hurting my friend. No, the hex was just on Garrett. Nothing on the current owner." Cordelia sniffed. "Of course, I won't speak to *her*, either. Another witch, that one."

I stifled a sigh as I dropped my gaze. Necromancers had such a bad rap. "You know, Cordelia, Evangeline's not a witch.

She's a necromancer. She's just trying to bring justice and hope to a broken community. She's not worshiping the devil." Not that witches worshiped the devil, anyway. But that was neither here nor there.

But now, Cordelia snorted and her eyes narrowed as she leaned forward, her gaze boring into me. "Do you think I'm stupid? I'm not talking about Evangeline, the necromancer. I'm talking about Evangeline, the witch who *circled* in a *coven* with my *granddaughter*. They were witches together."

For a moment, I was certain that I had misheard. The world slanted beneath me and everything went blurry as my mind tried to make sense of what Cordelia had just said. Slowly, impossibly, the pieces came together, fitting like a puzzle as an image clarified in my mind. I recalled Evangeline laughingly telling me she had taken on a new name when she became Wiccan, calling herself Semele VioletMoon. "Cordelia, witches take on new names, don't they? When they join a coven?"

Again, that snort. "Yes. I believe I mentioned that Erin changed her name. Ludicrous practice, if you ask me. They take such stupid names, too. I almost could forgive the name change if Erin had chosen something sensible. But you can't talk any sense into a person who *legally* names herself Crystal Waters."

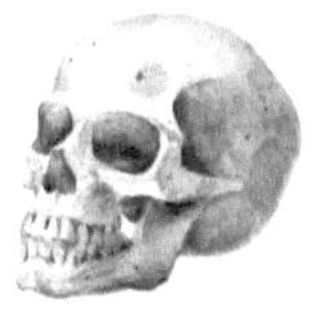

CHAPTER FOURTEEN

"I SWEAR TO *GOD* it's not as bad as you're making it sound."

We were sitting in Crystal's living room, I on the couch and she on a loveseat across from me, dabbing at her eyes with a tissue balled in her hand. I had brought Angelo along for appearances, but I had a feeling I wouldn't need his protection. Still, sometimes intimidation got to the truth faster than politeness.

"So, you're telling me you *didn't* hex Garrett Millhouse so you could steal the house out from underneath him? Because if you did, it's exactly as bad as I'm making it sound."

"I wasn't trying to steal it," Crystal objected, her lips pressed into a hard line. "By rights, that house was mine. Nana had *absolutely* no right to give it to Garrett Millhouse when she had a living relative who could have taken care of that place. I practically grew up in that house. She had no reason not to leave it to me."

I sighed, rolling my eyes. "Number one," I said, holding a

finger in the air, "you didn't grow up in that house. Maybe you've forgotten, but I'm a necromancer, and I spoke to your grandmother. She says she hardly got to see you growing up because your mom and dad's families didn't get along. You didn't have a relationship with your grandparents until you were a teenager, and from what I understand, that relationship was strained. To put it mildly."

Color bloomed in Crystal's cheeks, and her eyes grew damp once again. She dabbed at the corners of her eyes with a tissue paper, but luckily, I was immune to White lady tears. (Unless they or their loved one was dying. I wasn't heartless.) "Nana and Pop-Pop were devils to my mother because my father never married her. They acted like it was her fault. Like she was the Whore of Babylon for getting knocked up. But it takes two to tango, you know. Their son was the reason I existed. But you try telling them that. They were absolutely impossible to deal with. And then after my father and Aunt Emilia died in that car accident…Well, they just never got over it. They were hard people before, but the accident just broke them. There was no getting through to them after that."

Until now, Angelo had remained silent, but suddenly, he cleared his throat. "Kezia." When I looked over to him, his eyes were trained on a bookshelf on the other side of the room.

And sitting on that bookshelf was a human skull.

"Oh my God," I whispered, drawing to my feet. I crossed the room to stand next to the shelf, my eyes wide as I stared at Crystal. "Are you fucking kidding me? Is that Delia Rae? Did *you* steal that skull from Evangeline's property?"

Crystal leapt to her feet, discarding the wadded tissue from her hand. "Don't touch that!" she warned. "That's — you don't understand, I didn't *steal* anything! Angie *gave* me that skull!"

I stared at her, my disbelief mounting. "When? Recently?"

"Yes! Well, *she* didn't give it to me. Someone else gave it to me on her behalf."

"Who?"

Crystal huffed, her jaw hardening. "It's none of your business, Kezia. It really doesn't concern you, all right?"

"Yes, it does," Angelo said, rising to his feet. Great. Now we were all standing. I prayed this wouldn't end in more fisticuffs. I was tired of fighting. "If that skull is from Angie's cemetery, it involves us. So where'd you get it?"

"I don't know his name," Crystal whined. "He's a Black guy —" She stopped short, squeezing her eyes shut. "He asked me to hold on to it for Angie. He made it very clear I couldn't let her know I had it."

I took a step toward her. "Why?"

"*I don't know*," she groaned. "If you'd seen this guy, you wouldn't have asked questions, either. Okay? I just — I'm just keeping it safe."

"Well, not anymore you're not," I said, reaching out to lift the skull into my own hands. If it had dark magic on it, I couldn't sense it, but that didn't mean anything. There were plenty of things in the world that I couldn't sense. Didn't mean they weren't there.

Then something else caught my eye. On the same shelf was a small talisman, a bundle of what looked like hair, feathers, cloth and other bits and pieces I couldn't identify. The bundle was wrapped with leather cords and smeared with something dark and flaking. I recognized it immediately; it was dried blood.

I didn't need to get a closer look. I knew a binding spell when I saw one.

"Crystal," I sighed, my exasperation reaching mortal levels, "why do you have a gris-gris on your bookshelf right next to Delia Rae's skull?"

The woman was shaking her head, fresh tears seeping from her eyes. "Please, you *really* don't understand. I'm a *Wiccan*! I don't —"

I pointed to the bundle, unwilling to touch it. Even looking at it made me shudder with revulsion. "Do you even know what this is? Where'd you get it from?"

"The same man who gave me the skull! He makes me bless it," she whimpered, her shoulders quaking. "He said it would keep Evangeline in her place. Where she deserves to be."

"It's keeping her *trapped in her house!*" I hadn't meant to shout, but this woman's willful ignorance was getting to be too much. "And it's *brought back her affliction*. Did you know that? Did you bless that?"

"I don't know what you're talking about!" she sobbed. "He gave me that...that...*gris-gris* or whatever it is *years* ago. Way before she stopped leaving the house."

I paused, confused. "You've had this for years?"

"Yes," she sniveled. "Yes, it's been on the bookshelf for at least five years — maybe more like ten. He's been coming to my home every few weeks for *years*. He makes me enchant that thing — he calls it *feeding* it. I guess that's how he keeps the magic from getting stagnant. I don't know! But I *can't* refuse him. I have too much to lose. My family, my business — he's threatened all of it. And I believe him, Kezia. My *soul* believes him!"

The blood drained from my face. "Crystal, what does he look like?"

The woman swallowed. "Big. Dark skin. Tall, with short dreadlocks. He has markings on his face, like a tribal tattoo."

I closed my eyes as the world swam. Kwame, Terrence and Devon's Ghanaian wizard cousin.

"Does he pay you?" I asked, suddenly furious. "Does he pay you to work magic against Evangeline?"

Crystal's mouth twisted as her eyes darted from me to Angelo. If she hoped to find forgiveness with him, she was in for disappointment. "Well, yes, he pays me. But I *need* the money. I'm not like the others, who live in lavish homes and —"

She cut herself off, snapping her jaw shut.

"What others?" I asked, the floor dropping out of my stomach.

"Please, Kezia, you have to believe me. I've had it for ages. Whatever it's for, it's got nothing to do with her current situation."

Angelo gave me a baffled look. "Then what does it mean, keeping Evangeline in her place if not...?"

He was right; that made little sense. Or maybe Crystal was lying. But the bundle *did* look old.

"I swear I never did anything to hurt Angie — not on purpose," Crystal continued before I could answer. "That... that *man*...he gave me that charm! And yes, of course I did what he told me, but how could I know what it was?"

"You should have asked! You should have demanded answers!" I was shaking now, unable to keep my emotions in check. "You can't just be out here casting spells willy nilly for every gangster who asks! What's the matter with you? You could have really hurt her!"

But at this, Crystal threw her head back, issuing a little scream that made me jump from surprise. "*No I couldn't!* I couldn't hurt Angie even if I wanted to. We circled together as witches in the same coven, as you know. And as part of that bond of sisterhood, we took vows to never hurt or harm each other. Sacred vows. *Unbreakable* vows," she emphasized. "All I did — like, actually *did* — was tell *you* that the property was cursed. And yeah, I did that hoping Evangeline would sell to me. Is that really so awful?"

Angelo and I exchanged glances before I looked back at her, my mouth agape. "Yes. Yes, it is. It's a shitty thing to do to a friend. That was monstrous."

Crystal flashed furious eyes at me. "I didn't have any choice! It's *my family home!* I couldn't let Garrett sell it to some random person, so I convinced Angie to buy it. I *always* intended to buy it from her one day, when I could tell her the truth and I had enough money to make her an offer. But then I got divorced and business was bad —"

"So that's why you took the money," I interrupted. "To buy back your family home." I laughed then, a dry sound that felt like sandpaper in my throat. "Wow, that's rich. I mean that's fucking *poetic* is what that is."

Crystal cut her eyes at me. "You couldn't possibly understand."

"I'm sure I couldn't," I agreed. "I don't believe there's anything in me that could pull what you did to someone you call a friend."

"Believe what you want!" she said, throwing her hands in the air. "I don't owe you any explanations." Crystal looked away as she heaved a sigh, plopping back down into her chair and folding her arms across her chest. "I'm sorry for what I did to Garrett. That wasn't right. But I didn't do anything to Angie except start a little rumor. Which, I might add, didn't pan out anyway, since here you are."

"You're not absolved of responsibility just because things didn't turn out as badly as you hoped."

Crystal refused to meet my eyes when she said, "Good thing for me, then, that you're not the one parceling out forgiveness, isn't it? This is between me and Angie. It's got nothing to do with you."

In a way, she was right, and hearing her say those words released a knot of tension that had formed between my shoulder blades. She didn't owe me anything, and her betrayal was for Evangeline and Crystal to figure out. I'd done what I told Evangeline I would do — I'd found the source of the curse. All that was left to do now was clean up the last of the mess.

"I think this conversation is done. But before I go," I said, almost as an afterthought, "I need to break any magic you have over Evangeline now."

Crystal's head snapped toward me, her eyes narrowing in suspicion. "What do you mean?"

I reached into my pocket and pulled out a glittering red cord. As soon as Crystal's eyes landed on it, they went wide in recognition. Her mouth dropped into a little *o*. "You're going to bind me? Is that *Kismet's* binding spell? I *taught* her that spell!"

"Then you should already know how effective it is," I said, my voice even.

"The effectiveness of that spell is above debate, but I already *told* you I haven't done anything to Evangeline! I certainly haven't cursed her! If you put that binding spell on me, it won't do any good. It'll only come back on you times three."

I shrugged. "I'll take that chance. Now hold out your hands."

Anger flashed over Crystal's face, but she did as she was told. She huffed as she held out her hands pressed together at the wrists. I took the cord as Kismet had shown me, wrapping it figure-eight style around her wrists. "This is a waste of time and magic," Crystal grumbled. "I'm telling you, whatever's going on with Angie has nothing to do with me."

I studied Crystal's face. In grad school, I'd taken an elective on the physiology of human emotion. Some studies had suggested that a lie might be revealed through dilated pupils, the pressing together of lips, the slight list of the eyes upward and to left. I didn't put much stock in such pseudo-biology then, and I didn't now. Still, I looked. Crystal's face was stoic, her eyes blazing with fury. But the pupils did not dilate. Her gaze never wavered from mine. If I didn't know better, I might almost believe her. Almost.

But I was already bored with the confrontation. I held the cord between my fingers, a blush of embarrassment rising in my cheeks as I tied the knots. "Three knots to find her, three more to bind her, three knots to sever her spell. One spell behind her, two spells remind her, three and her magic is quelled." I squeezed my fingers around her wrists. "By the power of three times three, as I will it, so shall it be."

Wiccan magic still felt ridiculous to me, but silly rhyming chants aside, I couldn't deny that it was just as real as my own. The moment I released her hands, the thread pulsed with a neon red glow. For a moment, the light filled the room, but just as quickly as it had pulsed, it disappeared. When I looked back down, the cord was gone.

"There. You did it. Congratulations, you bound someone who didn't need binding. I hope Kismet gave you a good price on that binding cord because you'll need to buy another one when you find out who *actually* put the curse on Angie." Crystal turned her face away from me, but not before I saw her eyes at once again gone hazy with tears.

I turned to Angelo. "Let's get out of here," I said. We gathered the skull and even the disgusting gris-gris, which Angelo kindly slipped into a pocket so I didn't have to handle it. "Let's go give your boss the good news."

As it turned out, Evangeline and I had different definitions of good news.

"Crystal did this to me?" she asked, her brown eyes wide with astonishment and grief. "But she's my friend."

"People are complicated," I said, keeping my voice soft. "She wanted the house back. She hoped she could frighten you into selling." I didn't tell her about the skull or the gris-gris I'd found; I was keeping that under wraps until I'd confronted the assholes I believed were responsible.

Evangeline seriously needed to become more discerning in her friendships.

"Well, thank you," she said finally, her eyes liquid. "I could never have done this without you. You said you bound her? So I'll be able to leave the house? Go back to my work?"

"I imagine so, yes," I said. "But Kismet told me the spell takes three days to reach its full effect."

Evangeline seemed to agree, though there was little joy in it. "Well, I guess we'll see where we land in three days, then."

I nodded. "Try not to think about it," I said, knowing how ridiculous my words sounded. "One way or another, this is all going to be over soon."

For the next three days, Evangeline and I walked on eggshells around each other as we waited for the results of the binding spell I had worked on Crystal. We fell into an easy rhythm, sharing meals together and dividing up household work in between the charity runs I was still making with Divina and Rocky. On several occasions, I'd gone to the Blue Oyster Bar to confront the Curtis brothers, but I'd been unable to find them.

Now and then, I caught Evangeline stealing furtive glances at the vines wrapped around her legs, and I saw the hopefulness and anxiety that colored the lines of her face. I saw the way she glanced at me when she thought I wasn't looking, the hope in her eyes and the set of her mouth saying everything her words didn't. Could she trust my magic? Had I performed the ritual correctly? Was her life finally about to get back to normal?

If I could have, I would've taken these worries from her, but I was on pins and needles myself. Wiccan spellcraft wasn't exactly my forte, and I had never worked with Kismet's spells before. If the spell had come from Opal, I wouldn't be worried. But working someone else's magic was like cooking somebody else's recipe: you didn't know what they left out, changed, or added by sixth sense. Just because you follow a recipe don't mean you can *cook*.

Finally, the three days passed, and I woke the fourth morning with my heart pounding in my throat. I sat on the edge of my bed, head bowed as I chewed my lips to force myself to calm down. *Everything is going to be okay*.

Finally, I pulled myself to my feet and padded down the hallway to Evangeline's door. I knocked lightly but didn't wait for an invitation to enter. I turned the doorknob and pushed the door open, taking a tentative step inside. But when no light met me, and Evangeline didn't greet me, my heart seized, and my blood ran cold.

Oh, no.

Evangeline was curled up on the edge of her bed, her face

buried in her hands. She was dressed in a light cotton shift that reached only to her mid thighs, leaving her bare legs exposed. I looked down at her calves to the dark, twisting vines weaving around her limbs. The grotesque marks pulsed and writhed as Evangeline cried, her shoulders shaking with her sobs.

"It didn't work," she sputtered. "The curse isn't broken. It didn't work."

I bit hard on my bottom lip, my hands clenching at my sides. "I followed Kismet's instructions *precisely*," I said, my voice thinner and weaker than I wanted it to be. "I'm no expert in witchcraft, but I *saw* the spell take effect. I don't think I fucked it up."

"The failure isn't yours," Evangeline said. "It's mine. I've always known this is my punishment. This is —"

"Stop it," I interrupted. I couldn't stomach any self-flagellation, not on top of everything else. "This is a curse, plain and simple. Cast on you by a *person*, not by God."

I sank down onto my knees next to Evangeline's bed, pressing my forehead against the mattress. It was a prayerful position, and I meant to lift my hands to heaven and beg God for help. But as I lifted my hands, my fingers found Evangeline's ankle, then her calf. And the next thing I knew, I wrapped my hands around her lower leg, my fingers pressing into her flesh. I felt the writhing vines beneath my palms. I felt their heat and strength. And suddenly, a wave of nausea hit me so hard I nearly retched. But I didn't let go. Images flashed before my eyes: Evangeline holding her son, cooking beans, brushing her hair, getting ready for bed. With each image, a fresh emotion tore through me: pain, longing, sorrow, grief, fury. And at once, I knew this curse wanted Evangeline all to itself.

And it wanted absolutely nothing to do with me.

I snatched my hands away, curling them into fists that I pressed against my chest. "Evangeline, I don't think I can stay here much longer."

Now, my benefactor looked up, her eyes red and swollen with crying. "You're not thinking about leaving, are you?"

I struggled to keep my voice even amid the desperation rising in my chest. "I have to. I feel it. I've felt it for a long time, but I was so convinced that I could help you with this that I swallowed it down. And my Terminator gift helped. But now I think we both have to admit that this is far beyond my knowledge. I don't know how to help you. And it's obvious that I'm not doing any good, and in fact, may be harming you. I just feel it in my bones. I have to leave."

Evangeline didn't answer but gave a brief nod. I climbed to my feet, my legs heavy as lead. It was a horrible feeling to know that you did your best and still failed. Especially when so much was on the line. But even I had my limitations. Even I knew when I had reached a breaking point.

I trudged back down to my room, getting ready for the day. I showered, made coffee, and was contemplating the best way to fill my time when my phone buzzed.

It was a message from Marcus that just said, "Call me."

It was still early in the morning for California, so if Marcus was already awake and messaging me, it was probably important. I dialed him back immediately. "Got your message. What's up?"

Marcus cleared his throat, and I could almost feel him stroking his chin. "Well, it might be nothing, but I've been thinking about our last conversation. About the bone summoning ritual. Indulge me a moment. Tell me about the woman whose bones were disturbed," he said. "This Delia Rae. What was her status on the property?"

I wrinkled my brow. "Status?"

"Yes. Hierarchically speaking. Where does she sit with the other people buried on that property?"

I wasn't exactly sure, given that I wasn't privy to Evangeline's family tree, but I did remember her pointing out the grave when she had given me a tour of her home. "If I recall correctly, Delia Rae could be considered the matriarch. At least, I'm pretty sure hers is the oldest grave of all of them."

A tinge of excitement entered Marcus's voice. "I thought you might say that. You know, Kezia, this whole grave robbery thing...It might not be what we previously thought."

I switched my phone to the other ear, confusion drawing my mouth into a frown. "What do you mean?"

"You seem sure that whoever summoned those bones from the ground did so with malicious purpose. But after our conversation, I mentioned the incident to a colleague. Don't worry," he crooned, "I kept the details on the DL. But she mentioned there are some African tribes that use bone magic in protection rituals. Let's just say, for sake of argument, that an ally of yours suspected you were under attack. Or not you, specifically, but Evangeline and her property. The most effective form of magic would be to use the strength of the head of the household to repel any hexes or negative energies. And in this case, the head of the property would be Delia Rae Brown. And as you know, some of the most effective magic is sympathetic magic. Meaning —"

"Someone might've wanted to use Delia Rae's *literal* head to harness her power as the head of the household," I breathed, understanding washing over me. "So you're suggesting that whoever summoned Delia Rae's bones might not be Evangeline's enemy, but her friend?"

I heard the shrug in Marcus's voice when he said, "I'm just saying it's a possibility."

"But if so, why wouldn't that person just come forward and admit what they'd done?"

"Because it's still unethical and illegal," Marcus said. "That, plus, from everything you've told me about Evangeline, she's chosen *you* to help. Now, I don't know if there's jealousy involved here or just run-of-the-mill overprotectiveness, but maybe your ally doesn't want to admit that they don't trust you. And by extension, they don't trust Evangeline's judgment. There's lots of reasons people don't want to admit what they've done, even when they do it for a good purpose."

Never in a million years would I have considered that a friend performed the bone summoning spell. And while I still wasn't convinced Marcus was right, it was certainly a new possibility.

"Crystal said the same person who gave her the skull has been visiting her for years. She had a gris-gris on her shelf. She said the spell keeps Evangeline in her place where she belongs. What do you think that means?"

"Sounds like a curse to me," Marcus said. "Racists been trying to keep us in our place since Jim Crow."

"At least that long," I agreed. "Somebody's always trying to keep our people down."

I blinked, aware of what I had just said. Somebody was trying to keep our people down. And little by little, I realized I knew who.

Who had warned me that magic might be the cause for Atlanta's necromancer problem? Who had flicked his eyes to his bones where he had a bundle just like Crystal's jammed into the socket of a skull?

David Pope. An osteurge.

And who had told me that she didn't live in a lavish home like the others?

Crystal Waters. A Wiccan witch. And though at the time I hadn't known what others she was talking about, it was becoming clear.

How did you put a hex on an entire city?

With *different kinds of magic* distributed throughout and around the area.

A Wiccan witch. A bone mage. That was only two, but in my heart, I knew there was a third.

A Ghanaian wizard. I recalled the first time I'd met Kwame in the Blue Oyster Bar. He'd told Terrence that he'd make fifteen stops, including a visit to a Strega in a wealthy part of town. I had assumed he was bragging about sexual exploits.

But when he'd said the bitches were hungry, he wasn't talking about women. He was talking about the gris-gris — the magic sachets he needed to feed to keep alive.

An idea began to form in my mind, the enormity of it rendering me momentarily speechless. If Marcus was right — and if *I* was right — everything was about to change forever.

"Jesus," I said, "This is all starting to make sense. And it answers a question Opal asked before I left about why Evangeline is the only necromancer in Atlanta."

"It does?"

"Thanks, Marcus," I said. "This changes things. I think I know exactly what I need to do next."

<hr>

"I thought I told you if you ever came for my neck again, you was gonna regret it."

Devon Curtis hardly looked up from the pool table, lining

up his shot as I stood with my arms crossed, my expression blank. "Good thing I just came here to talk," I said. "Listen. I'm sorry about the other day. Is there somewhere private we can talk?"

Devon gestured with his chin toward the pool table. "I'm kinda busy here," he said.

But I wasn't going to be dissuaded, nor was I in the mood to be intimidated. "It's important. I know why you took the skull. And I know why there are no necromancers in Atlanta."

Devon heaved a sigh and stood upright, holding out his cue stick for his partner to retrieve. Empty-handed, he brushed his hands together and jerked his head to the side. "Let's get us a table over here."

We picked our way through the crowd to a table occupied by a group of three women. But when they saw Devon approaching, they quickly collected their things and scurried away, leaving their table to us. It still needed bussing, but at least it was private. I couldn't help but be impressed that Devon had that much influence. Impressed or unnerved, I wasn't sure which.

"Last we met, you tried to take my head off my shoulders. Now you out here actin' like you want my help. What gives?"

I folded my hands atop the table and made myself look as contrite as possible. "I know I saw you in the cemetery that night," I began. "What I didn't realize at the time was that you didn't take the skull to put a curse on Evangeline. It occurs to me that you might have taken the skull thinking you were helping her."

Across from me, Devon's expression didn't change, but he dropped his gaze just for a second before answering. "What gives you that idea?"

I let a light smile flit over my lips. "Well, it started with something a friend of mine said before I left home. She's another necromancer in Los Angeles. Lives about twenty minutes away from me. And I know several more beside her, everybody within thirty minutes of the house. Which got me thinking: why is Evangeline the *only* necromancer in *all* of Atlanta?"

Devon shifted. "What's that got to do with me?"

"Stay awhile," I grinned. "I will be faithful." I pushed several glasses out of the way and leaned forward onto my elbows. "I knew I saw you in the cemetery with your brother. I was certain it was y'all, even though Evangeline said it couldn't be. But I knew. And when I found the skull at Crystal's, she confirmed it."

Now, Devon stiffened. "You were at Crystal's?"

"I was. And that's where I also found the gris-gris Kwame gave her for safekeeping." I watched as Devon squirmed, a thin film of sweat forming on his brow. "I was convinced at first that y'all had put a binding on Evangeline. But Crystal swore up and down that she'd had it for years — long before this curse business ever started. And that got me thinking. If the bundle *had* been a curse on Evangeline, it would have had her hair and whatnot in it. It had hairs all right...but none of them purple."

Devon rubbed his face, narrowing his eyes. "So?"

"My ex-husband is a mage. Can't do magic for shit, but he knows all about it. He told me it was possible to put an entire city under a spell, but it would take a concerted effort among different kinds of magic workers. You put Rocky in touch with David Pope when she needed to have the graves moved. Dr. Pope *also* happens to be a bone mage. And when I was at his house getting him to create an interment spell to undo the shit you pulled at Evangeline's place, I noticed he had a gris-gris jammed into a skull just like the one Crystal has. It didn't register at first. But in retrospect, it makes sense." I lowered my voice, letting a smile creep over my lips. "Kwame's got gris-gris all over the city stashed away with different types of magic users, and each of them feeds the gris-gris with their own brand of magic. Crystal's a Wiccan. David Pope is an osteurge. I'm guessing Kwame's got more gris-gris stashed with Conjure workers, druids, shamans, you name it. All working togeth-er — albeit unknowingly — to keep necromancers down."

"If that were the case," Devon drawled, "wouldn't Angie also be affected?"

"Not if Kwame laid a blessing on her household," I supplied. "Which we both know he did. Which is interesting because it means y'all intentionally thwarted all the necros *except* Evangeline. At first I didn't really know why. But then I remembered something Crystal said: the bundle was supposed to keep Evangeline in her place. Y'all put binding juju on the *other* necromancers in the city, stopping them from working their gifts so that Evangeline could rise high — becoming the only necromancer in the area."

Devon dropped his gaze, offering a self-conscious chuckle. "You got some imagination."

"Oh, there's more!" I leaned away now, crossing my arms over my chest. "The summoned skull was really bothering me until my ex-husband told me that some African tribes use skulls in head-of-household magic. It's protection juju. When I told Terrence about Evangeline's curse, he must've thought Kwame's blessing was no longer strong enough to keep her safe. So y'all got the skull to beef up the protection on the household."

When Devon didn't respond, I knew I was right. I narrowed my eyes. "Was Evangeline in on it?"

"*No!*" Devon slammed the flat of his hand on the table, suddenly meeting my eyes — and there was fire in that gaze. "Hell naw she doesn't know! She ain't like that. She ain't in it for herself."

Of course, I'd already known that. I'd seen how angry she'd gotten when the brothers suggested she try to shut down another necromancer. But I'd wanted to see his reaction. "Then *why did you do it?*"

Devon laughed then, a sound that made my skin crawl. He licked his lips as he leaned forward. "I thought you was supposed to be smart. It ain't that difficult to comprehend, baby. We did it because Angie is too sweet for her own good. You think she'd have everything she has — money, fame, alla that — if we didn't intervene? She was never gonna take money from us. She wasn't gonna be involved in our business. But that ain't mean we wasn't finna look out for her. So we did what we had to do to make sure she got everything she needed."

"What a load of shit," I spat. "You did it for yourself. The first time we met, Terrence said people don't go looking for drugs or prostitution or gambling when they've got magic. Necromancy is bad for *business*. You spared Evangeline because, in your own twisted sense of the word, she's your friend. But don't pretend you did it for her. You kept your own people down so you could stand on their backs — just like folks have done to our people for *centuries*. You're a disgusting excuse for a human."

Devon rolled his eyes, and I saw not a speck of guilt flit across his face. How people like him could live with themselves was beyond me. I was sick to my stomach just sitting here thinking about all the people he'd hurt. "Where are the rest of the gris-gris?"

"With people I trust. And that's all you need to know."

"And you trusted Crystal Waters and David Pope? Why?"

"Because they're nice, respectable White people, and if the cops ever started sniffing around my business, they'd never find them and fuck up what I had going on. Last thing I want is for some FBI assholes to raid somebody's house and accidentally destroy all the magic I invested a lot of money in."

Well, that made sense, at least. "Why did they agree? Had to be more than money. How did you convince the milquetoast likes of David Pope and Crystal Waters and whatever other *respectable White people* to do your bidding?"

Devon smirked, cocking an eyebrow. "Do you really want to know?"

I opened my mouth to say yes when I realized that no, I really didn't. The ways an unscrupulous person with sufficient intimidation, magic, or money could coerce a victim into silent acceptance of a stranger's destruction were myriad. I put nothing past Devon Curtis, so I didn't need him to recount his methods. Selfishly, I wanted to sleep at night.

I clamped my mouth shut.

Devon sneered. "No? Well, let me put it like this: bitches was afraid of me. Like you should be."

I was too annoyed to fear Devon Curtis, but more than that, I was tired. Tired of seeing people keep others from finding success. Tired of jealousy and greed and everything that came with being part of the human rat race. I wanted to shake Devon Curtis, explain that when we rise as a community, everyone benefits.

But I guess there are some people who just don't want to see reason.

Devon sighed and leaned back, scrubbing his chin with his fingers. "We never meant to summon all them bones from the property. We was only supposed to summon the skull, leaving the rest behind. But we ain't know what the fuck we was doing, and that asshole who gave us the spell ain't specify. We didn't mean to upset Angie. If everything had gone off the way we expected, she'd never even had known that we had the skull. We was just trying to protect her. That's what we've always done."

He angled his body away from the booth, getting ready to leave. But something about those words just pissed me off. I reached out, grabbed him around the wrist. He looked surprised at the gesture but sat back down. "She wouldn't need protection if you weren't out here fucking with evolution," I said sharply. "The universe will protect her. Since I've been staying with her, I've run myself ragged running errands for various charities around town. And I've heard stories about the people she's helped. There are so many, Devon. So many people whose lives improved because of Evangeline Morris and her church. So if there is a God, which I think there is, He'd have to be some kind of vindictive asshole not to protect a woman like that."

I didn't realize I was still holding onto Devon's wrist until I saw his eyes travel down to my fingers and linger there a moment too long. I released my grasp, and Devon looked up, meeting my eyes. "Ain't you been paying attention? If there is a God? He *is* a vindictive asshole, and He's got a lot of explaining to do."

And with that, he stood and walked away.

CHAPTER FIFTEEN

WHEN I ARRIVED back at the house, I had to push past the magic that tried to keep me out. It was getting harder, and I knew I couldn't hold out much longer. I walked to the front door and locked it behind me as I entered. "Evangeline? I need to talk to you." She wasn't in the living room, but I continued calling out as I searched for her. "I just met with Devon. It turns out —"

I found her sitting on the stairs, elbows on her knees, cheeks wet with tears. She was holding her phone between her hands, and when she looked up at me, her expression was full of sorrow.

"What's wrong?" I asked, going to her.

Evangeline's eyes dropped to the phone. "I just got a call from Child Protective Services," she said, her voice breaking. "They're on their way. And they're bringing in an aura reader. He's going to use his abilities to see if I still have my affliction."

Her hand drifted to her calf, absently caressing the marks

that I knew still scarred her legs. As long as those marks were there, we had no reason to believe that we had lifted the curse. Evangeline still had her affliction. And if she still had it, social services would take Dominic away.

I tried to think of something helpful to say, but my mouth was dry and my mind blank. There were no words of comfort I could offer. We saw the crisis on the horizon but were powerless to stop it. We were marching headlong toward disaster and heartbreak. My tongue was thick with grief, and my eyes burned with tears. If I could, I would have stopped time. I would have torn the fabric of the universe apart for Evangeline, doing everything in my power to save her from the fate I'd already suffered.

But the universe didn't have that gift on offer.

"I'm so sorry," I said, knowing it wasn't enough. "We did everything we could." I took a few tentative steps toward her, weighing the words before letting them out into the wild. "Whatever happens, it's not the end. We might lose Dominic tomorrow, but we will keep fighting. We'll keep —"

But now, Evangeline's expression turned hard, and when I saw her eyes, the words dried up in my mouth. "We?" she whispered. "Check your heart, Kezia. You're still leaving. Ain't no we."

I tried to swallow around the lump in my throat, feeling more and more like a traitor. She needed me now more than ever, and what was I about to do? Turn tail. Run home. But it wasn't because I wanted to. I was being chased out. Worn down. Whatever energies were in this house, I couldn't weather them anymore. My time was up.

But how could I say these things to someone who was about to lose everything that mattered?

"I'm sorry," I said again. "You're right; there's no we. It'll be you and your family. But you'll have them. I've never known more loyal people in my life. What you've done here is a miracle. These people love you more than life itself."

But I could see that my words weren't getting to Evangeline. And how could they? They were just words. She was facing a fate worse than death.

No one knew that better than me.

Evangeline set her phone aside, wiping away the tears and scrubbing vitality back into her skin. "They'll be here in about an hour," she said, though the words were almost not meant for me. "I've been trying to call Divina to ask her to bring Dominic home. But she's not picking up the phone. I don't suppose I could lean on you one more time for a favor? I know you already made up your mind to go, but —"

"Of course I'll go get them for you," I interrupted. "Is that all you need me to do? Gather up Dominic?"

Evangeline took a shuddering sniffle and closed her eyes, her head bent low. She looked like a woman about to break in two. "It would mean a lot to me," she said, opening her eyes. "They'll want to talk to him, get his version of everything. Doesn't really matter what he says though." She chuckled then, a dry, crackling sound in the base of her throat. "Once they see that I've still got the devil's breath on me, they'll take him away. All I can do is hope though they let him stay with Divina so at least I can see him sometimes. If they give him to some other family, I might never see him again."

This was too much. Even though I had lost Lola similarly, I knew exactly where she was and who she was with. I didn't see Lola, but it wasn't because I wasn't allowed to. It was a choice I'd made — maybe a selfish one, but at least I had the autonomy to make that decision. Evangeline was right. If they gave Dominic to some random family, who knew what their opinions on necromancy and magic would be? She might lose her boy forever. Or at least until he was old enough to make that choice for himself, and by then, it might be too late, anyway.

"I'll call a rideshare for you and give them directions to Divina's house," Evangeline was saying when I snapped back to attention. "She doesn't live far, so there's that. I'll try to let her know that you're coming. I can't imagine Divina will just give him up to you without my say-so. She's protective of that boy, and she knows better. I'm sorry to have to ask this of you."

I waved a hand, brushing off the remark. "It's the least I can do for everything you've done for me," I said.

Evangeline shrugged, a frown tugging at the corners of her mouth. "You don't even know what I've done for you," she said.

I wasn't sure what that meant, but then, I could tell from the look on her face that now wasn't the time to ask; she was deep in her grief. "Is there anything else you need while I'm out?" I asked.

Evangeline didn't answer. She returned her attention to her phone, presumably calling me a rideshare. Suddenly, the grief in that house was too heavy for me to bear. I stepped away, slipping out the front door, taking refuge in the shade of the eaves as I waited for a stranger to arrive and drive me to Divina's, to usher in the worst moment of Evangeline's life.

DIVINA LIVED in a tiny house at the end of a quiet cul-de-sac. I thanked the rideshare driver as I stepped from the car, slamming the door behind me.

I knocked on the front door, casually looking through the

windows for signs of movement. When I didn't see any, I rang the doorbell a few times, impatiently waiting. It had taken 20 minutes to get here, and I wanted to make it home in time for Evangeline to explain to Dominic what was happening. Thinking about the upcoming encounter made my heart pound and my palms sweat.

When still no one answered the door, I took a deep breath and tried the doorknob. The door swung open quietly, and I stepped inside, knowing full well that I should never step my black ass into someone else's house without being invited. *Shit,* I thought, chewing my lips. *Please don't let Divina be one of those antsy 2A types. That's all I need right now is somebody to pull a gun on me.* I closed the door and looked around as I called out. "Divina? Dominic? Y'all here?"

Only silence met me. Blowing out a sigh, I stepped into the middle of the room, taking in the decor. Dominic wasn't kidding; Divina must've been a pretty badass MMA fighter. Plaques, certificates, and trophies lined the walls, commemorating her achievements. It seemed she had been doing mixed martial arts for a long time. Among her awards was an assortment of art, some of it traditional Native American and some of it was the mass-marketed variety. But it all worked well together. Large paintings of leporidae covered two of the walls, and on the others, she'd hung beautiful tapestries to match. It felt cozy and homey and strangely familiar. I padded into the next room, keeping my ears open for signs that someone was home. "Divina? It's Kezia. Are you asleep?"

I strained to listen but still didn't hear a response. Luckily, most of the doors lining the hallway were open, allowing me to peek into the rooms. She wasn't in the bathroom or the kitchen. I didn't see her in the laundry room, either. When I came to the end of the hall, the last door was closed. It was probably her bedroom.

I tapped lightly at the door. "Divina? Are you in there?"

Still no response. Sucking in a deep breath and steeling my nerves, I turned the doorknob and pressed the door open. On the other side, the room was dark. The only light was the flickering of candles set along the far wall. My eyes caught the flames, and I was drawn to them, taking slow, careful steps toward the dancing light.

I was not at all prepared for what I saw there.

Along the wall was a low table, seated height. It was bedecked with a series of framed photographs all in a row, sitting flush against the wall: one each of Rocky, Angelo, Dominic, Evangeline, and...me. I stared at the last one, my mouth falling open. I didn't even recognize when the photo had been taken, but it was clearly a recent candid of me. In front of each photograph was a single black candle, and next to each candle was a cone of incense. I didn't recognize the scent, but it wasn't unpleasant. Herbal. Comforting, even.

Something niggled at the back of my mind, and I broke out in goosebumps. I didn't want to see more, but my curiosity and sense of self-preservation caused me to keep looking. Taped to the wall above each photograph was a translucent piece of vellum bearing a complex glyph made up of several alchemical symbols. I wasn't sure what the symbols meant. Alchemy had never been my strong suit. I cursed myself, wishing not for the first time that I had Marcus with me. He'd know exactly what we were looking at.

Instinctively, I reached out and touched the first glyph, letting my fingers trace over the strange lines. A trill went down my spine, and I stood straight, my hair standing on end as realization and memory dawned on me. In the center of each glyph was an alchemical symbol I recognized. I'd seen it before on a scroll used to summon a jinni. It was the alchemical symbol for soul.

It was then that the other objects on the table registered. At first, I had dismissed them, thinking they were just junk that Divina had left. But now I saw that it wasn't junk at all. Next to Dominic's photograph was a toy truck. Next to Evangeline's was a silver bracelet. Next to Angelo's, a money clip, and next to Rocky's photograph a compact mirror. And next to mine? A single earring — the match to the one I'd found in my suitcase. I hadn't even worn them before I'd misplaced this one. Which meant that Divina had gone into my room and stolen it. Intentionally.

Cold dread welled in my stomach. I didn't know exactly what I was looking at, but I understood the purpose. Divina was working magic here.

Magic. Which she supposedly didn't believe in.

I heard Dominic's voice ringing softly in my mind. "Divina lies sometimes," he had said.

Lost in my own thoughts, I didn't hear the footsteps behind me until a voice spoke into the darkness. "What the fuck are you doing in my bedroom?"

I spun around with a gasp, clutching my throat. My eyes grew wide; my heart was a jackhammer behind my ribs, rendering me momentarily numb and silent. A voice inside my mind screamed, *Get out!* But I was rooted to the spot, caught red-handed.

"You had better have a really good explanation for all this," I said, pointing to the altar. "And don't try to fucking tell me this is protection magic. You'll have to lie better than that, Divina."

Divina made no motion to answer me and didn't make a

move. She merely watched me, her eyes narrowed in the darkness as she shifted her weight from foot to foot, her arms crossed over her chest. "I don't owe you a goddamn thing, and if you don't get the fuck out of here right now, I'm calling the police."

"You do what you have to do," I said with every ounce of the bitterness I felt, "but I will make goddamn sure Evangeline hears about whatever the fuck this is."

We were at a stalemate. We stared at each other from across the room, each of us poised to attack. The tension grew thick between us as my Terminator gift roared to life, and I watched Divina, her own inclination to fight settling deep into her muscles. She was coiled tight as a spring.

"What is all this about? Huh? And don't lie to me, please. I know these are sigils for some kind of soul magic. I'm not stupid, Divina. But please make it make sense. Explain to me why you're working magic on these people who love you." I left out the part where she was also working magic on *me*. "What are you trying to do with their souls?"

"It's not what you think."

I sucked in a sharp breath. "Then you best *tell me* what to think."

The woman went quiet and thoughtful. After a while, she ran a hand through her hair and tilted her head back, closing her eyes to embrace a memory. "As you know, I was adopted. My parents were — *are* — amazing people who loved me very much. Even so, I never fully felt like I fit in the family. That happens a lot with Native children raised by White parents. It was part of why I wanted to make sure Dominic had a connection to his tribe. Anyway, one day in elementary school we read a poem about a poor woman who could travel to other people's dreams. She could only dream in black and white, but other people dreamed in *color*. Other people dreamed of places she'd never seen in real life or her imagination — London, Paris, the pyramids. So she started traveling at night, to live in other people's dreams, hoping she'd learn how to have dreams like that. Because if she could *dream* big, maybe she could *manifest* something big. And what poor girl doesn't dream of becoming rich? And what adoptee doesn't dream of finding her parents, her culture, her people? So I decided to try it."

Divina frowned then, her face clouding with the reverie. "My closest friend was a girl named Nora, who was Chinese. We grew up together like sisters. She was always spending the night at my house, or I at hers. One night when Nora was sleeping over, I tried to see if I could visit her dreams. Of course, it didn't work. I tried again and again, but I never saw Nora in my dreams. Just...random visions, I guess. Images and scenes that didn't make sense. But at the same time, I began *knowing* things that Nora knew. I knew how to write the Chinese character for *mother.* I knew if I got sick, I needed to eat congee. I knew we were born in the year of the rabbit. She'd never told me that, but I *knew*. And I could do things that Nora was good at. For example, Nora was an amazing painter. And one day, I just knew how to paint. I guess you saw the rabbits and hares in my living room. I painted those. But the *better* I got at painting, the *worse* Nora got."

I could almost see where she was going with all this, but the picture wasn't clear yet. So even though my brain was screaming at me to find Dominic and get the hell out, I couldn't move. I was transfixed by her tale.

"Well, eventually, Nora stopped coming over, claiming that every time she slept at my house, she had bad dreams. At first, she didn't want to talk about it. But finally, I got her to explain that she was seeing *me* in her dreams, and I was eating her body. She said she saw me sucking marrow from her bones and licking bits of her brain from my fingers." I felt the color drain from my face as bile rose into my throat. "One night, a bunch of us girls had a sleepover, and everybody woke up crying, saying they'd seen me in their dreams, and I was trying to *eat* them. And, of course, all it took was one little girl to claim that I had done *Indian magic* on her, and *bam*, no one wanted me to sleep over anymore."

I clenched my hands into fists at my sides. Did she want me to feel sorry for her? I didn't. I wouldn't. Childhood was full of rotten shit. That didn't make her special.

But I felt my Terminator gift slipping into silence. Shit.

"Little by little, Nora stopped wanting to see me at all. By then, I was entering art competitions and Nora couldn't even sketch anymore. It was like I absorbed her talent. Once I realized what I had done — that I had traveled to her dreams and stolen her ability to draw — I tried to undo it. But not everything can be undone." She shrugged, her lips pressed into a hard line. "But I also realized something else. That even though I couldn't see the people whose dreams I visited, they could see me. And if I wanted to keep visiting people, I needed to disguise myself. So I practiced making myself small and harmless. I relied on my zodiac sign — I became the rabbit."

"*You're Roger?!*" I screeched, disgust roiling in my stomach. "It's been you all this time?" I thought of the dreams I'd had, the unease I'd felt when that creature's beady eyes had turned on me. I shivered violently at the implication. "Even after you realized what you were doing, you *kept doing it?*"

"I had no interest in stealing other people's talents. Doing that had lost me Nora, and I still feel that loss like a hole in my head. What I did want, however, was to belong. And I learned quickly that talent, culture, soul, dreams — they're all connected. You can't borrow one without borrowing all. Going into Nora's dreams taught me things about her heritage and culture. And since I hadn't been born into a culture that wanted me, I thought...what if I can adopt one?"

My nostrils flared as my heart rate picked up. I was running short on time. "What does this have to do with the altar?" I demanded.

"When I met Evangeline and Dominic, they changed my life. For the first time, I felt like I truly belonged. I didn't look like Evangeline or Dominic, but we made sense. Evangeline's Black; I'm Creek. Dominic is both. Plus, they're outsiders, too. All of us brown people in a White world. I felt like we shared an understanding and experience. I felt finally like I was part of something bigger than myself." I saw the anger flash in her eyes then. "Except I wasn't. Not really. Because the one thing they shared above all else was their ability to receive gifts from necromancers. New magic that coursed through their veins once a month. They all had that. But I didn't."

Divina shuddered then, a red flush of anger rising in her cheeks. "I thought at first it was no big deal. I could just find a Native necromancer that I could get gifts from. Did you know there are *no Native necromancers* in the whole country? Probably the whole world? Because technically, Native people aren't in diaspora." She said these words with a biting coldness that sent shivers down my spine. "How ridiculous is that? Sure, maybe we weren't kidnapped and taken to the other side of the world and sold into slavery, but we were injured just as much. They came to *our* home and snatched *our* land right out from underneath our feet. They threw us a few crumbs and called it a reservation, and we were supposed to be *happy* about it. But

I'm just as disconnected from my people as Evangeline and you are. So why can't I have gifts? Why can't I receive blessings from my ancestors? Don't I deserve that, too? How is it fair that I don't have that connection and you do?"

I didn't bother to correct on that last point, that I myself hadn't made a direct connection to my ancestors, either. That was neither here nor there. "I get what you're saying, Divina. Evolution is rarely a perfect process. I don't think anyone understands exactly how necromancy evolved into what it is today. But that doesn't mean —"

"I'm not interested in your biological bullshit," Divina interrupted. "I figured out a way to be eligible to receive my own gifts. It just meant borrowing from the people closest to me. Borrowing some of their culture and heritage like I had done with Nora. Borrowing some of their...spirit."

It took a moment for the words to sink in. But I caught a glimpse of the altar from the corner of my eye, and suddenly Divina's narrative and what I had seen with my own eyes coalesced, and I understood. "So you've been going into our dreams to try to steal our *souls* to absorb our culture and heritage? All so you can receive necromantic gifts? That's *exactly* what Rocky said the other day at Claudia's! And you called Rocky a racist liar!"

"I wasn't trying to steal your soul," Divina snapped. "I mean, that wasn't the point. That was...a side effect. And anyway, I definitely wasn't trying to steal your soul to possess your body. Rocky, as usual, doesn't know what the fuck she's talking about."

I remembered the first night I'd seen Roger — well, Divina. I recalled that rabbit watching my memory of getting ready for church with Big Ginny. She'd seen my grandmother rubbing oil into my hair, braiding it. She'd seen me rubbing lotion into my skin. These were intimate memories of mine, but they were more than memories. They were memories that united Black people. We were church-going, kinky-hair-braiding, ashy-knee-having people who bonded over our faith, hair the dominant culture didn't understand, and dry skin you could actually see. These things were minor, yes, but they were communal experiences. They were part of what made me a Black woman in a community of Black people. They were part of what made *me*.

Divina had tried to crib that. It was stolen valor, and I was suddenly irate.

"That's how you knew that I'd killed people. I knew Evangeline didn't tell you that. You learned it by coming into my dreams." When she didn't deny it, my blood caught fire. "Divina, that is *hella* fucked up! Do you know the consequences of stealing souls? You must know, you've seen it firsthand! You've seen what you've done to Evangeline. You've completely destroyed her. You brought back her affliction, and now CPS is coming to take her son away from her. Do you understand what you've done? How could you do that to someone you supposedly love?"

But Divina was trembling, shaking her head in denial, and I knew she wasn't really listening. She had convinced herself long ago that what she was doing was morally acceptable. There was nothing I could say now that would convince her otherwise. "I just need more time," Divina said almost to herself. "I feel so close."

"Jesus Christ," I spat. "There is no *close*. You're a Native woman, and there are no Native necromancers. No matter how much soul you steal from Black people, you'll never be Black. You'll never be able to receive gifts from Black necromancers. I'm sorry about that. I didn't design the system, and I agree it's not fair, but that's the way it is. So you need to stop. We know what you've done to Evangeline, but we don't know the effects of what your magic has done to Dominic. Or Angelo?" Suddenly, an idea struck me like lightning. "You've marked me with *wings* on my back," I said. "You've made me feel like I can't spend another minute in that house with the *only person in the world* who can help me. Do you know what that cost me? Do you care?"

I should've been paying Divina's body language closer attention because all the signs were there if I had bothered to look. But the next thing I knew, Divina was screaming, hurling her body at me as she grabbed me by the collar and threw me against the wall.

A split second before her fist crashed into my face, my Terminator gift roared to life, and I dodged to the side, narrowly avoiding her attack. I ducked low, spinning on my heel and finding her stomach with a sharp uppercut. She doubled over and grunted but recovered quickly. Her next attack was a left hook that glanced off my shoulder, spinning me in a quarter circle.

I swept my foot behind me, catching Divina in the ankle, and she toppled over as she lost her balance. "It doesn't have to be like this," I panted. "I don't want to fight you. I just want you to end this nonsense."

If Divina heard my words, she didn't show it. She screeched again and tried to elbow me in the face. Once again I ducked, spinning around. I tried a backward kick, but she careered out of the way. We circled around each other, throwing punches and dodging attacks. If I let myself think too long about being in a fist fight with a mixed martial artist, I was going to lose my nerve. I just had to let my body do what my Terminator gift had taught it.

I'm not gonna lie, I was going to miss this gift when it was gone.

Finally, I got in a good right hook that connected right across Divina's face. She spun and fell to the floor, her hair spilling over her face. I hovered over her, hands clenched at my sides, waiting for her to stand or to kick my feet out from under me, but she did neither. Her shoulders shook as she sobbed silently.

"Are you gonna stay down?" I asked. "It didn't have to be like this, Divina."

She didn't answer, so I fumbled around in my purse until I found the binding cord I'd bought from Kismet. I dropped to my knees and grabbed Divina's hands in my own. She didn't resist.

I wound the binding around her wrists and tied knots in the end, just as I had done with Crystal. "Three knots to find her, three more to bind her, three knots to sever her spell. One spell behind her, two spells remind her, three and her magic is quelled." I sighed, suddenly exhausted. "By the power of three times three, as I will it, so shall it be."

Just as it had done last time, the cord blazed to life, emitting a bright, crimson light that filled the room. Then, the light faded away and a moment later, the cord disappeared, too.

"I have to tell Evangeline what you've done," I said. "I wish there were some other way. It's going to break her heart."

Divina said nothing, refusing even to look up at me. When I was sure she wouldn't renew her attack on me, I returned my attention to the altar, collecting the personal artifacts and smashing everything else to bits. I knew the binding spell had taken effect, but I didn't want to leave anything to chance. Plus, I was feeling vindictive. This bitch had been trying to steal my soul right out from underneath me. She owed me.

I found Dominic in the backyard playing on a tire swing. "Dominic!" I called out. "Let's go. Your mama sent me to come get you."

Dominic groaned, dropping his head backward and rolling his eyes. "But I don't want to go back right now. Divina said she'd take me to the gym and let me watch one of her matches."

I shook my head. "Change of plans, kid. You got everything you need?"

Dominic jumped down from the swing and gave me a dirty look. "I guess so. I guess I can see one of Divina's fights another time."

I bit back a reply. I suspected Divina's fighting days would be on hold for at least a little while.

When we arrived back at Evangeline's, Dominic ran upstairs. I found Evangeline in the kitchen, staring at a recipe but making no move to prepare whatever she was looking up.

"He's upstairs," I said. "But there's something I need to tell you. About Divina."

Evangeline still didn't look up, but I sucked in a breath anyway to tell her everything. It really wasn't the time, but if she was considering asking for Divina's guardianship, she needed to know. I laid it all out: the dream walking, the altar, the soul stealing. When I was done, Evangeline still hadn't moved, and part of me wondered whether she had heard anything I'd said. Finally, she looked up, the sadness in her eyes so deep I could have fallen in and drowned.

"I don't know why she had to do that," Evangeline said, her voice barely above a whisper. "All that child had to do was ask me, and I would've given her pieces of my soul for free."

I was so flabbergasted by that answer, the selflessness of what Evangeline had just said that for a moment, I could only stare. But eventually I composed myself, giving a little nod. On some level, I guess I understood. I knew how much Evangeline loved Divina, how she thought of her as her own daughter. I suppose no matter how much a child disappoints you, you'd still do anything for them. That's what it means to be a mother.

"Well, in three days, the curse should be lifted," I said, choosing to focus on the positive. "When the agency people arrive, we'll just explain —"

"I love your innocence," she cut in. "No, I really do. But do you believe for a minute that those people are gonna come in here and listen to this story, and give me three days to prove it's true? You think that's how the government works? You think these people gonna give folks like you and me the benefit of the doubt?" She sighed, shaking her head. "Ain't no three days, Kezia. We're out of time."

Evangeline said nothing more. She merely shuffled out of the kitchen and into the living room, where she shouted up the stairs for Dominic to come down. He appeared a moment later, a scowl coloring his face. "I don't have any chores today," he said. "I thought —"

"I need you to sit down a minute, son," Evangeline said, gesturing toward the couch. The boy did as he was told, folding his hands in his lap as he waited for his mother to speak. Evangeline stuttered a bit, dabbing at the corners of her eyes and clearing her throat repeatedly. Watching her was so painful, I felt my own heart would break into pieces. But eventually, she found the strength.

"Baby, there's some people coming to the house. They'll be here any minute now. They're gonna ask me some questions, and they're going to ask you some, too. And I need you to be honest. But what I need you to know is that your mama's sick, baby. And my sickness makes other people sick, too. So it's not safe for you here anymore. So these folks are coming to the house because it's their job to find you somewhere safe to live."

The boy frowned, uncomprehending. "Someplace safe to live?"

I saw the effort it took for Evangeline to hold back her tears. "They just want to keep you safe, baby," she said, her voice breaking. "That was supposed to be my job. But I can't do it anymore. You know that magic I got on me? The magic that makes it so I can't leave the house? It's also making you sick. Or it might, one day. But these people, they can't take any chances. And neither can I."

Slowly, I saw understanding dawn over Dominic's face as his expression crumbled, and he burst into tears. "But I don't want to go anywhere! I want to stay with you! I don't want to go live with some other family!"

Dominic's outburst was a sledgehammer against the fragile dam that had kept Evangeline's emotions in check. The woman cried out, throwing her arms around her son, pulling his head to her chest as they sobbed, collapsed against each other. "I love you so much, Dominic. Don't you ever forget that. No matter what happens, I love you so much."

The boy pulled free of his mother's embrace, his little face upturned as he stared into Evangeline's eyes. "Mama," he whispered, "if I take the magic off you, can I stay?"

Evangeline sniffled, swallowing hard and trying to calm her nerves. "Oh, my sweet baby. Thank you. But you can't take this magic off me. Nobody —"

"Mama," Dominic interrupted, "I got to tell you something. That magic so you can't leave the house?" The boy dropped his chin, and I saw a tear fall from his cheek and land on the hands in his lap. "I put it there because I didn't want you giving gifts to people no more. I put that magic on you because I wanted you to stay home and be with me." His head snapped up then, his eyes wide and pleading. "But I didn't know it was gonna hurt you, I swear! I just wanted you to stay here with me!"

For a moment, neither Evangeline nor I spoke. But I saw something in Dominic's face that caused me to break my silence. "Dominic," I said, "quit playing. You can't do magic, right? This is serious. You can't, can you?"

The boy's expression hardened, his eyes turning to stone. I saw him clench his small fists in his lap as determination lifted his chin and arched his back. "I dreamed it down," he said, a glint of pride making the words shine. "I didn't used to be any good, but I am now. The first time I put those roots on Mama, they didn't work. But I kept practicing until I got better. And now those roots are strong and she can't leave." He dropped his head again, his body trembling. "But they said I can take the roots off anytime I want. So I think I can do it. If I do it, will the people let me stay?"

It was Evangeline who spoke. "Dominic, who's *they*? *Who* said?"

The little boy's lower lip trembled as he said, "The ancestors."

Evangeline and I exchanged astonished looks, both of us so surprised by Dominic's revelation that for a moment neither of us could breathe. But then we turned our attention to him, our hands pressed against our mouths in a cautious but growing wonderment. "Baby? Have you been talking to the ancestors? Can you —"

The doorbell rang.

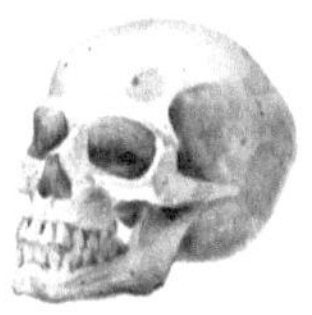

DOMINIC DARTED up the stairs, leaving Evangeline to stare after him, her mouth agape. So instead of waiting for her to come to her senses, I went to the front door, flinging it open.

Standing on the porch were a man and a woman. The woman was tall and slim, her red hair trying to escape its ponytail. Her smile was fake and uncertain; her gray eyes blinked too much. She carried a satchel on one shoulder and pressed a clipboard to her chest. She extended a hand, her smile widening. "Hi. I'm Sarah Paulino from Child Protective Services. I believe we spoke on the phone earlier? Are you Miss Evangeline Morris?"

I shook my head and stepped aside, bidding the duo enter. "She's inside. Please, come in."

The two came through the door, and I closed it behind them, waiting for Evangeline to join us. When she still didn't move, I went to her, placing my hand at the small of her back and gently prodding her forward. Finally, she emerged from her trance, blinking herself into wakefulness as she tried on a smile that didn't quite fit. "I'm Evangeline Morris," she said. She turned her gaze to the woman. "You're from the agency?"

The woman nodded. "My name is Sarah Paulino, and I'll be the caseworker today. I've brought with me our aura reader, Max Fishburne."

Max cleared his throat and extended a hand, and I had to bite back a smile. You almost couldn't call him a man, he was so young. I couldn't imagine that he had even graduated college, not with a face like that. Shaggy hair hung in front of eyes that turned down at their corners, giving him a sweet, innocent look. When he smiled, a real dimple formed in his left cheek. "Nice to meet you, ma'am," he said, pumping Evangeline's hand in earnest. "I've been wanting to meet you for a long time. I'm a big fan."

Evangeline nodded, accepting the compliment even though it was clear she didn't know what to do with it. "Please have a seat," she said, directing the three of us to the couches.

Sarah and Max got comfortable, and I wondered whether I should excuse myself and leave them to talk in private. But when Evangeline turned her gaze to me, I saw the need in her face. She looked like a lamb among wolves, and I couldn't leave her. So I sat down in an armchair and tried to make myself small. Small, but available.

"I understand that you've had some trouble with your necromantic affliction," Sarah began, choosing her words carefully. "I have it here in my notes that the adoption of Dominic was contingent upon the fact that you had cured your affliction, therefore not putting the boy in danger. Is that right?"

Evangeline nodded. "That's right. When I adopted Dominic, I didn't have the grave calling. It came back recently. I've been trying to cure it, but so far, nothing has panned out."

The woman nodded, glancing down at her notes. "I understand that at least one person has contracted necromantic exposure sickness, dying as a result? Is that right?"

Evangeline fretted, wringing her hands in her lap. "That's right. Celia Parker. She worked for me for several years before showing any signs of the blues. But, of course, we had no reason to recognize it at the time. I've been on record as being cured for a long time," she repeated. I could see that she was nervous. I could practically hear her nerves jangling. "By the time we realized Celia had the blues, it was too late. That's when we realized that my grave calling — sorry, my affliction — had returned."

I knew she was calling her affliction the "grave calling" on purpose — relying on the colloquial over the clinical in the hopes it would humanize her. It was a good strategy, but I didn't think it was working. Sarah's mouth drew down into a little frown, and her eyes narrowed as she studied the notes before her. "I see. And did you plan for the boy to stay somewhere else while you convalesced? Or has he been in the house this whole time?"

I didn't like the accusatory sound of the woman's voice, and I cleared my throat, leaning forward onto my elbows, catching her gaze. "Dominic has always spent a lot of time with other people," I said, my voice sharp. "You should have it in your notes that he has a Big Sister? Divina Perrault? Ever since Evangeline got sick, he's been spending more time with her. Evangeline is doing everything she can to make sure the boy doesn't get sick."

Sarah crossed her legs primly, tilting her head to one side. "Well, not *everything*, surely? Otherwise, she would have called us in earlier, wouldn't she?"

Indignation squeezed my throat, and for a moment I was

beside myself with anger. This woman had the *nerve* to come into this house and make such a cutting accusation? I wasn't ready to let that fly. I opened my mouth to lob a retort, but Evangeline beat me to the punch. "Don't speak about me as though I'm not here," she said, her voice low and even. "If you're suggesting that I'm a bad mother because I didn't give up my son to strangers before I had to, then you're right, I'm a bad mother. I held onto him for as long as I could. And he's healthy, he's strong, he's good-hearted. There's not a person in this world perfect enough to be worthy of the gift of raising a child like him. Not me; not you. But we all do the best with what we got. We all got our struggles. I did my best."

Chagrined, Sarah dropped her chin to her chest. The room was silent for a moment but for a clock ticking somewhere in the background. Finally, Sarah cleared her throat and looked up. She turned her attention to Max, who had been silent during this exchange. "I suppose we might as well just get on with it," Sarah said. "Max?"

Max squirmed in his seat, running a hand through his hair and offering Evangeline a smile. "Well, like Sarah said, I'm an aura reader. So, I'm just here to verify that your affliction has returned." He sighed, and his face softened, real sympathy in his eyes. "Ms. Morris, is it alright if I look upon your aura?"

Evangeline said nothing but gave her head a little nod.

Sarah reached into her satchel and retrieved a pair of glasses, which she then handed to Max. I frowned, indicating the glasses with a lift of my chin. "What are those for? I didn't think aura readers needed special glasses."

Max shook his head. "I don't *need* them. They're more like a trigger. I don't like to look at people's auras without their permission. I find it unethical. The glasses help me turn on my ability. Plus, they let other people know what I'm doing. Well, people who know me. If they see me with my glasses on, they know I'm reading. It's just a courtesy." He cleared his throat and bit down on his lip, turning to Evangeline. "I'm going to have a look now."

The room was still. I didn't even dare breathe. A few moments seemed to stretch into eternity as Max peered at Evangeline, presumably looking at the space around her, summing up her aura. After a few moments, he sucked in a breath, blinking and removing the glasses. He stared in wide-eyed astonishment, his head slowly shaking from side to side. "You don't have anything," he drawled.

Evangeline swallowed. "What do you mean, nothing? Do I —"

A smile broke onto Max's face, lighting him up like a light-bulb. "You don't have the necromancer's affliction," he said. He gestured towards me almost dismissively. "She does. But you?" His smile grew impossibly wider. "You don't have anything on you at all. In fact, you don't have any tarnish whatsoever. What I'm saying is, your affliction has been absent for a long time. Your aura is completely clean."

Evangeline's face crumpled with a relief and confusion so great I felt it in my heart. She was trembling, her hands pressed against her cheeks. "But I don't understand," she was saying. "What about Celia? How..."

I wiped tears from my cheeks and cleared my throat, chewing my lips. "Evangeline." I flicked my eyes toward the staircase. "I think I know what happened. It's not you. It was never you. It's Dominic."

Evangeline's hand moved to the base of her throat as confusion continued to color her face. "Dominic?"

I nodded. "Get him down here. I bet Max can confirm it."

Evangeline leapt to her feet and moved to the bottom of

the stairs, resting a hand on the balustrade as she shouted. "Dominic! Get down here, please. Hurry!"

Moments later, Dominic appeared, descending glumly down the stairs. His eyes traveled over the guests sitting on the couch. He looked nervous, like he had done something wrong. He looked so sweet and innocent and afraid, and all I wanted to do was hug him and stroke his back and tell him everything was going to be okay. It's what I would've wanted someone to do if Lola were in his position. But it wasn't my place to do any of those things, and so I just stood there, watching. Waiting.

"I don't want to go with them," Dominic said. "I promise I'll be good. Please don't make me go with them."

"Nobody's gonna make you go anywhere," Sarah said, startling me with her voice. Somehow, I'd forgotten she was even there. "My friend Max just wants to look at you. That's all. Won't you come here?"

The boy crossed his arms, hooking his thumbs underneath his armpits as he ambled over to Max, who was still smiling like a drunk idiot. He inspected Dominic and then laughed, removing the glasses from his face. "He's got it, all right. Even worse than this one," he said, indicating me with a jerk of his head. "Never seen a house full of necromancers before. Thought you guys were supposed to be pretty rare!"

"Dominic is a necromancer?" Evangeline's voice dripped with disbelief.

"Well, if he's not, he's the only non-necro in the world with the grave calling. So you know where I'd put my money," Max said.

It seemed none of us knew exactly where to look. My eyes went first to Dominic, then Evangeline, then Max, then back to the boy. If Dominic was surprised at hearing that he was a necromancer, he hid it well. He just stood there, staring, waiting for someone to tell him what to do.

"You can go sit with your mama, Dominic," I said. The boy looked relieved, hurrying to Evangeline's side as she pulled him down to the couch next to her, draping her arms around his shoulders, squeezing him close.

"Y'all, I think this has all been a misunderstanding," I said. "We thought...well, everyone thought Evangeline's affliction had come back because of what happened with Celia," I said, leaving out the details in front of small ears. "Nobody ever could've guessed that it was *Dominic's* affliction we were experiencing. Because nobody knew he was a necromancer."

Max turned to me, a quizzical expression on his face. "But *you* did. You said so just a minute ago. So how did you know?"

I chuckled, giving a little shake of my head. "Literally seconds before you arrived, Dominic mentioned that he'd been speaking to his ancestors. And then everything just sort of clicked into place."

"Well, it looks like everything is in order here." Sarah offered another one of her stiff smiles before drawing to her feet with Max quickly following suit. "I'm very glad to see that everything has worked out for the best. In our line of work, we're not always so lucky." She sucked in a breath, and I suddenly noticed her tightness, the plastic rigidity in her face and shoulders. She was shielded to the gills. I guess she had to be, otherwise the nature of her work might tear her apart. I understood that, at least. In a lot of ways, it was the same in hospice care. Working with vulnerable people often meant fending off evil people ready to take advantage.

"I'll send you a copy of my official findings, Ms. Morris. We're sorry to have disturbed you. We can see ourselves out."

Once Sarah and Max had gone, Dominic scooted to the

edge of the couch, hands folded at his chest in a pleading gesture. "Can we play Mario Kart now? I just unlocked a new level."

"Dominic," Evangeline said, her voice firm but flowing with love, "we got to talk about this."

The boy dropped his head, little shoulders sagging with guilt. "I know what I did was wrong," he said. "I shoulda never put that spell on you."

His mother sighed, gathering his hands in her own. "It was wrong, but I understand why you did it. It's *hard* to share the attention of someone you love. You want them all to yourself. I get that. And I know that when I was working hard to give folks their blessings, I wasn't always here for you the way I could have been." She kissed his forehead then, squeezing his fingers tighter. "But you got to trust that the work I'm doing is important. It's not more important than you," she added quickly, "but it is important. And there might still be days when I get home late and I'm tired and I can't play with you. But let's make us a deal, you and me." She smiled then, and I saw the hope that welled up in Dominic's eyes. "You're getting big now. So I want you to come with me more. One day, you're gonna have to do work like mine, so you might as well learn it now. Deal?"

Dominic's relief was practically tangible as his head bobbed vigorously up and down. "Yes, Mama. It's a deal." He threw himself into her arms, and they stood that way, holding onto each other as if for dear life, for a long time.

Finally, Dominic pulled himself out of Evangeline's embrace. "Okay, *now* can we play Mario Kart?"

Before Evangeline could answer, I held up a finger. "Before you do anything else," I said, "you need to remove the magic that you put on your mom. *And* me."

Dominic's eyes widened in surprise as his mouth dropped into a chagrined *o*, and I couldn't help but snicker. "Yeah, I know you put this magic on me. What I don't know is why."

Dominic sucked in a breath, dropping his eyes in shame. "I gave you wings so you would fly out of here," he said. "Mama said you were going to help her get rid of the magic I had put on her. I didn't want that. So I needed you to get out." He looked up then, his expression contrite. "I'm sorry."

"Everybody makes mistakes," I said. "But let's get this magic off right now. I don't like being a bird. I want to be human again as soon as possible."

LATER THAT NIGHT, long after the sun had set and we had spent our first comfortable meal together as a trio, Evangeline, Dominic, and I sat curled on the couch, watching an old movie. Every now and then, I saw out of the corner of my eye as Evangeline lifted the hem of her skirt to gaze at her smooth, unblemished calves. True to his word, Dominic had lifted the magic that had scarred Evangeline and me. I knew the magic had worked nearly instantly because the anxiety and trepidation that I had felt for the past several days immediately vanished. For the first time in a while, I felt peaceful. At rest.

When Dominic started yawning and it looked like he might fall asleep soon, my curiosity finally got the better of me, and I tapped the boy on the knee. "I was a little older than you when I came into my necromancy," I said. "I've never met my ancestors, though. What are yours like?"

The boy gave a huge yawn even as he shrugged his slender shoulders. "I don't know, there's lots of them. None of them look like Mama, though. They look more like Divina."

It took a second for that information to register, but then I realized that Dominic was only half Black. His other half was Creek. "They look like Divina? The ones who taught you how to do your magic?"

The boy nodded. "Yeah. There's usually lots of drumming and chanting and smoke and stuff. I'm getting sleepy," he complained, turning to face his mother. "Should I go say my prayers now?"

Evangeline nodded, a slow, sleepy smile spreading over her face. "I guess so. You had a long day. Don't forget to brush your teeth and wash your face!"

The silence that settled in Dominic's wake was like a warm blanket descending over our shoulders as we gazed at each other from across the room. "I guess that's why I didn't understand the message the bones sent me," I said after a while. "That morning when you and I did a reading to understand the curse. Remember? The bones said flowing water. I didn't know what that meant then."

Evangeline's brows raised. "And you think you know what it means now?"

I laughed then, mesmerized by my stupidity. "Remember I said sometimes the bones aren't literal? Well, sometimes they're literal but broad. They meant a specific kind of flowing water — they were telling me *a creek*. Creek people. The people of Dominic's tribe. But I had never been exposed to Native American magic before, so I couldn't read it in the bones."

Evangeline made a sound in the back of her throat like this information made sense. "I can't thank you enough for everything that you've done," she said. "It means a lot."

I laughed and shrugged, running a hand over my hair. "I didn't do anything. Not a single thing that I did the entire time I was here contributed to your curse being lifted. You could have done all of this yourself. You never needed me. Not once."

Evangeline shook her head, rolling her eyes. "You don't know what you're talking about. All I've ever wanted since I got into this work was to grow my family. I wanted to give Dominic more than just a mom. I wanted him to have a whole network of people who loved and cared for him. People who will take care of him and teach him as he grows. So if you think you've come this far with us but you're not part of our family? Then I guess you've got another think coming."

It was a lovely thought, but the compliment was wasted on me because I knew my relationship with Dominic was nascent and wouldn't have time to blossom. Even though I no longer felt the overwhelming urge to run, I had to go home. Big Ginny needed me, and I still had my jobs to think about. As much as I might've liked to, I couldn't just hide out at Evangeline's for the rest of my life. I had my own family to get back to. Such as it was.

"There's a flight leaving in a couple days," I said, "and I expect I'll be on it. I don't want to leave Big Ginny alone any longer. I just wanted to let you know. I really am grateful."

Evangeline's head listed to one side, her eyes narrowing in the dim light. "You ready to put what you've learned into practice?"

I stuttered then, unsure how to reply. A lot had happened over these past few weeks, but had I really learned anything to put into practice? I didn't want to say as much to Evangeline because I didn't want to hurt her feelings or imply that I wasn't grateful for the time she'd lent me, but I was no closer to eradicating my affliction now than when I arrived.

I guess I took too long to respond because Evangeline

chuckled then. "You don't know what you've been studying this whole time, do you?"

I sucked in a breath and held my hands out before me. "I didn't learn what I came here to learn, no," I admitted finally, hating the words even as they came out of my mouth.

But Evangeline didn't look offended. In fact, she was smirking. "What do you know about the others who have cured their afflictions?"

I gave a lame shrug. "Well, there aren't that many of them. There's that woman up in New England who's a director for the Girl Scouts if I'm not mistaken. Then there is that guy down in Florida who runs a bookstore. But I don't really know very much about either of them. Why do you ask?"

Evangeline shifted, folding her legs underneath her as she snuggled deeper into the couch. "It took me a while to find the link between all three of us, too," she began. "I made several trips up to Connecticut and down to Florida to try to understand the similarities between the three of us. On the surface, the only thing we have in common is that we're all necromancers. But after I started talking to the people who knew them, I came to understand what really linked us together. All three of us are *connectors*. We put people and healing projects together. That Girl Scout director? Her name is Heather Washington. In addition to running a Girl Scout organization, she runs a camp teaching young girls STEM projects. Computer science, math, engineering, things like that. Several of those girls have become mentors themselves. One is involved in her local robotics club, and another teaches classes to underprivileged kids who want to take the SAT. And the guy down in Florida? His name is Moses Benson. He runs a bookstore, but the bookstore also hosts classes: financial literacy, starting a business, things like that. The students from those classes work with each other to improve their community. They formed a non-profit to help low-income people earn degrees and start businesses. Those business owners go on to provide services for their neighbors. Do you see where I'm going with all of this?"

I felt like I should see a connection, but lots of people did charity, including necromancers, and most of us still had the affliction. "I'm not sure," I said, feeling stupid. "I think you might need to spell it out for me."

"Heather and Moses find work that needs to be done in the community and people to do the work. To cure your affliction, you have to actively work to heal your community. But what I've discovered is it's not enough to do the work alone. The healing you create has to be self-propagating. No person has enough energy or time in the day to heal all the ills that our people suffer: poverty, sickness, lack of education, lack of mentors. What we have to do is create an environment where the people we help, help others. We have to create opportunity to grow and flourish and spread on its own merits without our direct intervention. And once we set the wheels of that healing turning, that healing comes back to us. And it's that self-propagating machine of healing that wipes your affliction away."

Her eyes misted over as she leaned forward, gathering my hands in her own. "Did you think I sent you out to work with Rocky and Divina because I didn't want you hanging around the house? It was purposeful. I wanted you to get a taste for it. I wanted you see the results of what this family has created out in the world, and in turn, what those micro communities are doing to heal themselves. I could've told you, but hearing something and seeing it with your own two eyes, feeling it with your own heart are very different things. I want you to go home and cure your affliction, Kezia. You need to go home and create a self-propagating machine for healing. And that's how you're gonna get your baby back."

I stared at her a moment, processing what she was saying. But when the words finally sank in, all I could do was shake my head in disbelief. "But...there's no magic in that at all," I protested. "Don't I have to get my Godsend first? Don't I have to find my mother? I always thought —"

"Finding your mother is how you'll get your Godsend and flip the switch on your own personal magic, that's true," Evangeline said with a nod. "But healing is how you'll find your mother. These things go hand in hand, sweetheart. You heal yourself, and you heal the world. You heal the world, and you heal yourself. It's all connected. It's all about creating good here and now, in *this* world."

I blinked, holding out my hands, imploring. "But no one's ever said anything like that," I stammered, still unable to believe. "The focus in the literature is always on the magic, the gifts..."

Evangeline waited for me to quiet down before answering. "Necromancy has always been a complicated discipline," she said. "The soul is complicated. Death is complicated. *People* are complicated. Nobody really understands much about any of it, so they focus on the interesting parts. Godsends and gifts and genetic memory are *fun!* People are going to plumb those depths. But I'm telling you from experience. The most powerful thing we do isn't giving somebody Hacker or Sara Lee for three weeks, and it's not awakening their great-great-grandmother's recipe for nkwobi. It's giving people their true power back. Their ability to take part in civic government. To buy a house. To educate their children. We do this by building each other up, helping each other, and instilling a sense of pride and community. That's anyone's true power, Kezia. It's just that in our case, if we *don't* do it, we suffer, and those around us may die."

"If that's true," I said, the implications blooming inside me like spring flowers, "then necromancers need their community just as much as they need us."

"Probably more," Evangeline said. "It's a symbiotic relationship. We all need each other. Our successes depend on the success of everyone else. That's why I got so angry at Terrence and Devon for suggesting I try to put a stop to people visiting Conrad Tillison for their blessings. That scarcity mindset is what has our people turning on each other, cutting each other down for scraps. There are enough blessings in this world for all of us, Kezia. A rising tide floats all boats."

I swallowed, wringing my hands in my lap. It all sounded so beautiful. I could see the divine design of it all. Which just made what I had to say next all the more uncomfortable. "Evangeline. There's something I need to tell you about Terrence and Devon."

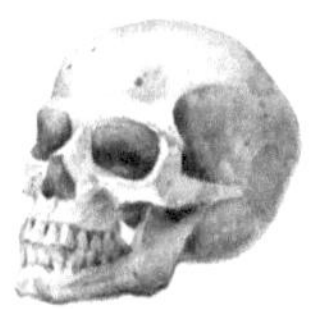

CHAPTER SEVENTEEN

OVER THE NEXT few days, things slowly returned to normal. With the curse lifted and no chance that Dominic would be removed from his home, it finally felt right to re-inter Delia Rae's bones. Evangeline, Rocky, Dominic and I gathered together in the cemetery, Delia Rae's bones carefully arranged over her burial site. I held the enchanted badger pelvis in my hands, letting the death current run through me. I smelled the familiar fragrances of palo santo, copal, and lemon as I gathered the magic around me, reciting the words David Pope had given me. I felt powerful once again, like I was finally in the right place.

My fingers clutching the pelvic bone, I recited the last line of the spell, and the earth began to shake, just as it did on the night I'd caught Devon and Terrence stealing Delia Rae's skull. My breath caught in my throat as I watched the bones sink into the earth before disappearing in a blink. The phenomenon lasted only moments, and then it was over.

Evangeline wiped at a tear, her voice shaking when she

said, "Y'all know these past few weeks have been some of the most difficult of my life. And I want each of you to know that your contribution to my mental health, the state of this household, and your contributions to our community have not gone unnoticed. Running a family is the most difficult and most rewarding thing I've ever done. So thank you all."

No one moved or said anything as Evangeline flipped open a small book she clutched in her hands. She opened it to a page marked by a ribbon. "This is an old journal of mine that I started writing after I adopted Dominic. I'd like to read a passage from it if y'all don't mind. It might not be significant to all of you, but I hope when I'm done, you'll know why I chose it." She cleared her throat and looked down at the yellowed pages. "To be a mother is the most fearsome predicament in which one can find herself. Not because your own heart forever beats outside your body or because the joyless Fates turn their eye most frequently toward those with much to lose. It is simply because it is impossible to look on your child's face and not see every way in which you failed them, for no matter how well you raised and loved them, they deserve the sun, the moon, and the stars, and all you can truly offer is the disappointment and heartbreak of life."

I swayed, lightheaded. The passage punched me squarely in the gut, damn near knocking the wind out of me. Evangeline caught my eye and offered me a small smile. "Rest in power, Mama Delia Rae," she said. Each of us echoed the sentiment.

To my surprise, even Divina showed up. I didn't think she'd have the balls to show her face for a while, not after admitting to trying to snatch our souls and our heritage all for a paltry bit of temporary magic. She wouldn't meet my eyes, even though my gaze followed her arrival, tracing her steps as she moved through our small assembly, making her way toward

Evangeline. I watched her with my heart in my throat, my nerves jangling. I hadn't known Evangeline long, but already I was very fond of her, and I'd be damned if I let Divina hurt her again. But the woman did nothing except collapse heartbroken into Evangeline's arms, shaking and crying as the other woman smoothed her hair, kissing her crown, whispering forgiveness and assurances I tried not to overhear.

Watching them, I felt a tide swell in my breast. I let out my breath in a whoosh, and not only because Evangeline's selflessness moved me, but because I knew at that moment that my Terminator gift had fled me. As I watched Divina for telltale signs of betrayal, I didn't feel a coil of strength and agility winding around my spine. I didn't feel my hypothalamus kicking my sympathetic nervous system into gear or my immune system shutting down to conserve energy. I was myself again. Just a woman searching to unleash her own power. For better or for worse.

After the funeral, we retreated into the house where Evangeline had provided an elaborate lunch to celebrate. I sat next to Dominic, who was chatty and energetic and showing me something more than disdain, which was a nice change. He dug something from his pocket, holding it out to me in offering. "This is for you," he said.

I reached out to accept the gift and found that he'd pressed a silver dollar into my palm. I turned the coin over, my expression quizzical. "What's this for?"

"It's for your daughter. Mama says everyone should always have a little money in their pocket. That's not for spending," he warned, his expression serious. "It's for keeping safe just in case. So the money ancestors know where to find you."

I couldn't help myself. I reached out and hugged Dominic hard, and to my delight, he let me.

"So when are you heading back to Los Angeles?" Angelo asked me around a mouthful of collard greens.

"Tomorrow. My flight leaves at 9 a.m."

The big man sighed. "I'll miss you, you know. You're welcome to come back and visit any time."

"You could come to Los Angeles, too," I chided, taking a bite of the macaroni and cheese. Evangeline had so many talents, and *damn* if her cooking wasn't one. "I can take you to Disneyland."

"Too many earthquakes," Angelo said with a frown. "I hear the beaches are nice, though."

The idea of Angelo in a swimsuit made me grin. I was sure he'd look great, but I couldn't imagine him in anything less than his customary jeans and t-shirt. "Well, the offer stands."

Later, when dishes were done and the others had gone home, I made two old fashioneds and Evangeline and I took our cocktails on the back porch. We hadn't sat out there since my first night, when Evangeline had shown me the vines on her legs. Roots, as they turned out to be. I smiled at the memory and how wrong we'd been about everything.

"You looking forward to going back to your own life?" Evangeline asked, savoring a sip of her old fashioned. "Change of pace is nice, but ain't no place like home."

I smiled, resting the glass against my chest. The cool glass felt good in the humid night air. "I'm looking forward to a bit of normal, I guess," I admitted, "though I don't know if I can really call it going back to my own life. I feel like my life was taken from me the day Lola got sick. I'm steady chasing it, trying to get it *back*."

Evangeline opened her mouth to reply when the back door burst open and Dominic appeared, a sheepish grin on his face. "I know I'm supposed to be in bed," he explained, pre-empting his mother's objections, "but I can't sleep because I have a question."

Evangeline pushed her hair away from her face and pinched her son's cheek. He was too old for that, but he didn't seem to mind. In fact, he blushed at the affection. "One question, then you best get to bed. It's late."

"Well," the boy drawled, "you know how I'm a necromancer now, right?"

Evangeline nodded. "Yep. We'll have to talk more about what that means later. It's a big responsibility."

"I know," he nodded. "But what I wanted to ask was...you know how necromancers can only give gifts to their own people, right? That's how it works?"

Again, Evangeline nodded. "So far as anybody knows. That's right."

"Well, I'm half Creek and half Black," he said, looking unsure. "And the ancestors that taught me the roots and wings magic were definitely Creek. They looked like Divina." He shifted his weight, his ear listing toward his shoulder as he thought about how to phrase his inquiry. "So what I want to know is, if I'm half Creek, does that mean I can give gifts to Divina now?"

In the darkness, Evangeline's eyes found mine, and we shared a silent wonderment. It was a profound question, really; there were no Native necromancers that I was aware of. But aside from the wider, societal implications of what it meant for Dominic to be a necromancer, I was acutely taken aback by the sensitivity of the question. He hadn't asked about how to get magic or if necromancy was going to make him rich or any of the questions I might have asked at his age.

No, he asked if he could give something to the very person

who had wanted a gift so badly, she had tried to steal a cultural identity to get it.

Dominic was Evangeline's son, all right. The boy was nothing but love.

"Well, you got to get your Godsend first," Evangeline explained once she found her voice. "And for most people, that doesn't happen till you're grown. So you got a while yet." The boy's face fell at this, but Evangeline was quick to press on. "But you got me to teach you, and I'll teach you everything I know, so we can get you that Godsend as quick as possible. And then, when you're ready, you can try to give a gift to Divina if that's what you want to do."

"It is," he breathed, the relief clear all over his face. "It'll make her feel so much better. Like she's part of our family."

Evangeline nodded and kissed the boy on the cheek. "Okay, I answered your question. You go on inside now. Don't forget to say your prayers!"

"I never forget," he said as he slipped back inside the house.

Evangeline took another deep sip from her glass. "Girl, you really know how to make a drink," she said with a chuckle. "It's too bad we didn't have many opportunities to put your talents to use while you were here."

"Well, we had other things to deal with," I said, smiling. "Besides. I would be very sad if this was it for us. I hope I'll have another opportunity to visit."

"Absolutely," she agreed. "I hope you'll come visit every chance you get."

We were quiet a moment, sipping our cocktails. But then my curiosity got the best of me. "What are you gonna do about Devon and Terrence?"

Evangeline sighed as she pinched the bridge of her nose.

"Already told them to destroy every single one of those binding jujus. That's a start, but we also got to make reparations. We owe those necromancers a *decade* of their lives and magic back. I'm not sure where to start or how, but the first thing to do is unbind them. Let them flourish. And then?" She shrugged, absently stroking a lavender lock. "I don't know."

I saw the heartbreak in her face. "But what about justice? Will you call the cops on Terrence and Devon? I'm not sure casting magic on a city is illegal, but surely you have dirt on their business, and —"

"Sounds like you're looking for revenge, not justice," she said, her gaze distant. "They can be easy to confuse. Taking down their business won't bring our people their gifts, and it won't return time lost to the necromancers. Justice I can do; revenge is a dish I have no taste for. Those sins are between them and God, and I trust that the Lord will make it right."

I wasn't so sure, but I saw no reason to argue faith with her. "Once Atlanta has its necromancers back, your following is gonna shrink," I said. "And people are gonna blame you no matter what. It could get bad here for a while, Evangeline, if you go public with what they did for you. You sure you want that?"

She chuckled then, a dry sound. "*Want* ain't got nothing to do with it. Nobody always gets what they want."

I left it at that. I'd made my point, and she was resolved to come clean with the whole story. I'd already suspected that, of course. Evangeline wasn't a person to go back on her morals just because it would inconvenience her. It was one of the things I admired about her.

As though suddenly remembering something, Evangeline set her glass down on the glass side table and hopped to her feet. "I'll just be a minute," she said, disappearing into the house.

When she returned, she pressed an envelope into my hands before settling back into her seat. I glanced down at it, then turned my gaze to Evangeline, my brow creased in confusion. "What is it?"

She shrugged, waving the question away. "Just a little seed money. If you're gonna get serious about curing your affliction, you might need to create something of your own. You *can* do it *without* help, but..." She shrugged again. "Well, I'm able to help, so I'm helping."

With my heart in my throat, I peeked inside the envelope. When I realized what Evangeline had given me, I balked, my mouth dropping open. "Evangeline. This is a check for $50,000."

"When I founded the church, I didn't have a child or an elderly grandparent to take care of. I was lucky that I could dedicate myself to my dream of giving back to my community without worrying about taking care of anyone but myself. I know you don't have that luxury," she said, "and I understand you're already working two jobs to make ends meet. So I just hope that little money can get you started. I want you to build something sustainable that you love."

I stared in disbelief, my hand going to my mouth as I searched for the right words. "Well, but this isn't just a little money! This is too generous; I couldn't possibly accept this."

"You'll accept it," she said, making no move to retrieve the envelope I held out to her. "I have everything I need and more. What kind of person would I be if I didn't share my good fortune with others who need it? That's what we're here to do, Kezia. Not just necromancers, though we're *explicitly* here to do that. But all of us. People. We're supposed to help each other. That's the whole damn point."

When it was clear Evangeline wouldn't take the money back, I set the check in my lap, tears stinging the back of my eyes. "I don't know what to say, Evangeline."

The woman grinned then, lifting her glass. "Well, you can start by calling me Angie." She moved closer to me then, lowering her voice. "Can I lay a gift on you?" she asked.

My throat was thick with emotion. "You've already given me so much," I said. "I don't —"

"Girl, you *got* to learn to accept love from folks. Okay? Work on that for me." Then, without waiting for me to agree, she placed her palms on the sides of my face. I smelled petrichor and cut grass, sandalwood and calendula.

I opened my mouth to say that I'd received Sara Lee, which granted likability and charm (*nobody doesn't like Sara Lee!*) — a gift I'd had many times before. But what came out of my mouth was, "E seun mo dúpé."

We stared at each other a moment in blatant confusion. But then, as though the universe thumped us both in the head simultaneously, we gasped with understanding. My hands shot to my mouth as my mind whirled, almost unable to believe what I knew in my bones to be true.

"Kezia," Evangeline whispered. "What language was that?"

I pressed my fingers into my cheeks as I chewed on my lip. "Yoruba," I whispered back. "I just said *I appreciate you* in Yoruba."

"Genetic memory," Evangeline breathed, smile lines deepening around her eyes. "I raised the dead in you. Did you know you had Nigerian heritage?"

I swallowed hard, tears welling in my eyes. I didn't even

bother trying to blink them back. "Never," I breathed. "My ex-husband — his family — they're Nigerian."

"*And* your daughter *and* you," Evangeline said, brushing a stray curl from my forehead. "Who knows what else is in store for you? Congratulations on your new knowledge. Enjoy it."

I threw my arms around Evangeline, my face buried in her neck, and sobbed with unspeakable joy.

DAYS LATER, I was sitting at the breakfast table with Big Ginny and Lamont, my hands wrapped around a steaming cup of coffee as I listened to my brother complain jokingly about the time he spent at our house. Big Ginny made a show of rolling her eyes, letting me know exactly what she thought of Lamont's account of how the last three weeks had gone. I could tell they'd grown closer in the time I'd been away, and I was grateful for that. Things had finally returned to normal, and while I missed the camaraderie I'd experienced in Georgia, it felt good to be home.

"Lamont," I said, drumming my fingers on the table, "there's something I need to talk to you about."

Lamont raised an eyebrow, settling back in his chair. "What's that?"

"Well, I told you what Evangeline taught me about how to cure my affliction. I need to figure out what kind of imprint I want to leave on the community. Whatever I do, it's going to eat up a lot of my time and energy. And I'm only one person, and I only have so much energy."

Lamont nodded and rubbed the bridge of his nose. "You asking me for my help? Because you know I'll do that, Kee. Whatever you need, I'm here for you."

My heart swelled at the kindness in his voice and the generosity of his offer. Lamont and I weren't close, but we were working on it, and I knew what a tremendous olive branch he had just extended me. Which made what I was about to say even more difficult. "Thank you. I really appreciate that, but what I need..." I cleared my throat, chewing the inside of my cheeks. "What I need to do is resign from the bar. I know I already don't work that many hours," I said, tripping over my words in an effort to get them out while I still had the courage, "but even so, I need to put that energy toward this new endeavor. This is everything I've been working toward," I said, smiling weakly. "So I hope you understand."

My brother said nothing as he readjusted in his seat and clasped his hands over his chest. "Let me get this straight," he said. "You expect me to let my best bartender quit without giving notice so she can take the $50,000 she got from a famous necromancer to start a community charity so she can cure her devil's breath and get her daughter back?"

I couldn't help the grin that spread across my face. "That's what I'm saying," I said.

"All right, sis, you got it," he said. "You're done at the bar. I love you, and I know you're gonna be successful. But if you need anything, you holler." He cut his eyes then, glancing quickly in Big Ginny's direction. "*Almost* anything. If you leave me alone for another three weeks with this old woman, I'mma hafta tell the cops where you live."

"Hush up now," Big Ginny warned, rising to her feet and hobbling over to the coffeemaker. "You ain't too big to go over my knee."

Lamont stood then and kissed Big Ginny noisily on the cheek. "A'ight, I'm 'bout to head out."

"Thanks for everything, Lamont," I said. My brother just grunted and let the front door slam shut behind him.

I HAD BEEN HOME in Los Angeles for several weeks when there was a knock at the front door.

"I'll get it," Big Ginny called from the kitchen.

I was sitting in the living room, surrounded by catalogs and piles of mail, my laptop propped on my knees as I sorted through the various documents. I'd opened a new business account with the money Evangeline had given me, and I was in the nerve-wracking process of figuring out how to start a 401c3 — a charity of my very own.

It hadn't taken me long to figure out what I wanted to do. Within days after arriving home, I'd visited both Papa Jinabbott and Mama Fat on the other side who had shown me the contents of my heart — and it was to pursue something that would let me serve my community and spend time with Big Ginny.

So we were getting into the urban gardening movement.

Big Ginny had called every one of her 900-year-old gardening friends when I'd told her, and they'd all brought over shoeboxes full of seeds and armloads of advice, suggestions, and love. And catalogs. I was drowning in catalogs.

As I was sorting through the documents I'd downloaded from the IRS website, I heard Big Ginny gasp. I looked up in time to see Big Ginny leading another woman into the living room.

My heart stopped when I saw her. It was Marcus's mother, Chioma Adeyemo.

Chioma was a striking woman, to put it mildly. Tall and

lithe with cheeks like the gods sculpted them from clay, she brought to mind a goddess or a warrior. I hadn't seen her in years, not since Marcus and I divorced, but the years had been more than kind to her. Her dark skin was unlined, long limbs still toned and slender even as swathes of silver colored her temples.

Though she was still stunning, standing in the living room wringing her hands and looking around like she hardly knew where she was, Chioma looked terrified. I scrambled to my feet, brushing my hands against my pants, trying to make myself presentable as I asked, "Chioma? What are you doing here? Are you all right?"

The woman swallowed as her eyes found mine, her hands fluttering to her throat. "Thank God you're here," she said, her voice trembling. Tears leaked from the corners of her eyes. "I should have called. I'm sorry. But I —"

"Is Lola okay?" I interrupted, fear making my heart a fist against my ribs. "Oh God, is something wrong with Lola?"

Chioma squeezed her eyes shut, shaking her head with vigor. "No, no, nothing's wrong with Lola. She's fine. It's Marcus."

Again, my heart skipped. "What's wrong with Marcus?"

Chioma's eyes flit between me and Big Ginny as my step-grandmother steered the much taller woman toward the sofa. Chioma looked grateful for the support, collapsing into the cushions as though her bones had turned to gelatin. Her gaze never wavered, and the agony in her face never lessened when she whispered, "I fear Marcus is losing his mind."

For a moment, I could do nothing but stare. The words made no sense. Marcus without his mind wasn't Marcus. I couldn't imagine such a person. "How...what do you mean?"

Tears streamed down Chioma's face, and Big Ginny hurried

out of the room, presumably to find tissues. As I saw her go from the corner of my eye, I recalled a time from before Lola got sick when we were a family, when Big Ginny and Chioma would canoodle over cocktails and tell stories about me and Marcus when we were young. A pang of heartache rang through my body as I focused on Chioma, her body quivering. "It started about a week ago. I heard him talking to someone, but when I went into his office, he was alone. I didn't think anything of it at first, but it got worse. He's begun ranting all the time, breaking into howls and..." Her voice trailed off as Big Ginny returned with a box of tissues. Chioma took one and wrinkled it in her fist. "He doesn't sleep. He doesn't eat. He talks to people who aren't there. He rants in a language none of us speaks. Sometimes he stands facing a wall for hours. Just...standing there."

A chill rolled down my spine as goosebumps prickled over my skin, causing all my hairs to stand on end. Chioma dug a phone from her purse and pulled up a video. She thrust the device into my hand, and I hit "Play" as she blew her nose and tearfully edged closer, watching the video over my shoulder.

It was Marcus, or at least, something that looked like Marcus. But even watching him on video, I knew something was wrong. The color of his skin was dull, the whites of his eyes slipping toward yellow. The corners of his mouth were wet with bubbling spittle as he snarled out phrases in a language I didn't recognize. Periodically, he'd ball his hands into fists and pound them against the side of his head.

I thrust the phone back at Chioma, my stomach churning. "Have you taken him to a doctor?" I asked. "It looks like he's having a fit, or a seizure, or —"

"He doesn't need a doctor," Chioma breathed. "The illness is not borne of his mind. It's borne of his soul. He needs an exorcist." She set her jaw then, her eyes turning to steel. "I know about the genie," she explained. "I know that you put that genie's vital spark inside my son."

Her assertion struck me like a slap, and I recoiled from the implication. "I didn't *put* it there," I objected. "Marcus was standing between us, and —"

"I'm not here to accuse you," Chioma said, a softness returning to her expression. "I'm here to beg for your help. I think the genie's vital spark is destroying my son's mind."

My breath caught as I thought over Chioma's words. I knew that displacing Marcus's vital spark with the genie's could have unforeseen consequences. But I'd expected that to mean he might live an unnaturally long life, possibly centuries. What I had not predicted was that it would push Marcus's brilliant mind to the edge of sanity. That it would *break* him.

"Chioma," Big Ginny whispered, "what can we do? Kezia's not an exorcist."

"And even if I were," I said, "that's not what he needs. He needs..."

What did he need, exactly? He wasn't possessed — his soul had been altered. He needed someone with an intimate understanding of soul, and not just human souls, either. He needed someone who knew how to transmute the soul, to turn the soul of a genie into a soul of a man.

An image of Dominic standing before me swam before my eyes. I heard his voice in my ears, distant, but clear: "She has a book called *Alchemy of Souls* in her car. I looked at it once when I was waiting for her to come out of the dry cleaners. It's all about dreaming down, and dreaming down is *definitely* magic."

I swallowed, balling my hands into fists. "He needs an alchemist. And I think I know just who to call."

Amber Fisher is the author of urban and contemporary fantasy books ranging from sweet and delightful to dark and morbid. She lives in Austin, Texas, in a near-empty house now that her two kids have flown the coop. She would enjoy the silence except her husband is noisy as hell.

Connect with me at: amberfishermedia.com

Facebook at: facebook.com/amberfisherauthor

Twitter: @amberla

Sign up for the newsletter: bit.ly/332eurl

www.ingramcontent.com/pod-product-compliance
Lightning Source LLC
Chambersburg PA
CBHW050145120726
47903CB00002B/505